Hilda McKenzie was born and brought up in Cardiff. She left school at fourteen to become an apprentice at a drapery store, left there to learn book binding at a local printers, was an assistant and a cashier for a grocery firm and later became a telephonist at a turf accountant's office. She was fifteen when her first short story was published and she has written four previous novels. She has a grown-up son and daughter, and still lives in Cardiff with her husband.

THE WAY THINGS WERE

The First World War has been over for six years when Becky Morgan and Laura Evans leave school at fourteen, promising to remain close friends. Laura goes into service, giving her mother one less mouth to feed. Becky, working in her widowed mother's grocery shop, longs to have a job like Laura's, particularly when Laura meets the cook's handsome nephew, Roy. Although Albert, the lad who helps out at the shop, can't compare to Roy, Becky accepts his offer of marriage. Then the Second World War breaks out, and the close-knit Cardiff community is torn apart by grief and loss . . .

Books by Hilda McKenzie
Published by The House of Ulverscroft:

ROSIE EDWARDS
THE SISTERS
A RAY OF SUNSHINE

HILDA McKENZIE

THE WAY THINGS WERE

Complete and Unabridged

ULVERSCROFT
Leicester

First published in Great Britain in 1998 by
Headline Book Publishing
London

First Large Print Edition
published 2000
by arrangement with
Headline Book Publishing
a division of Hodder Headline Plc
London

The moral right of the author has been asserted.

Jacket Illustration: Nigel Chamberlain

British Library CIP Data

McKenzie, Hilda
   The way things were.—Large print ed.—
   Ulverscroft large print series: general fiction
   1. Cardiff (Wales)—Fiction
   2. Large type books
   I. Title
   823.9'14 [F]

   ISBN 0–7089–4299–7

Published by
F. A. Thorpe (Publishing)
Anstey, Leicestershire

Set by Words & Graphics Ltd.
Anstey, Leicestershire
Printed and bound in Great Britain by
T. J. International Ltd., Padstow, Cornwall

This book is printed on acid-free paper

To my friend Carmel for her
great courage and sense of humour.

Acknowledgements

My grateful thanks to Dr Jonathan Bisson, Consultant Liaison Psychiatrist, for his invaluable advice on the symptoms of Post Traumatic Stress Disorder, particularly in regard to 'shell shock' experienced in the First World War. Any misinterpretation is mine.

To the ever helpful staff of Trowbridge and St Mellons Library and of Cardiff Central Library my grateful thanks.

1

'Becky! Becky! Wait for me.'

The tall slim girl turned at the school gates, her curling auburn hair copper-gold in the sunlight as she waited impatiently. 'I thought you were never coming, Laura,' she said as they hurried along the sun-dappled, tree-lined street. You know my mam's waiting for me to serve in the shop.'

'It was our last day at school, Becky. Miss Lloyd was asking where I was going to work,' Laura told her, adding when her friend didn't reply, 'I wish you were coming into service with me. You're lucky, being able to stay at home and work in your shop.'

'No, I'm not!' Becky answered with feeling. 'I'd love to be going out to work and meeting other girls.'

Sometimes these days the grocer's shop seemed like a prison to her, hurrying home from school each day and seldom being free to go out with Laura. How are we to stay best friends? she asked herself, her brown eyes sad, for Laura wasn't likely to have much time off and the shop only closed on a Wednesday afternoon. Not that that meant

1

you didn't serve anyone for whenever they were closed customers knocked on the side door and waited in the passage until Becky brought them what they wanted.

When her father had been alive he'd served people willingly and cheerfully at any hour of the day. In 1916 he'd volunteered for the army and had been away in France until the end of the war. At that time she'd been too young to work in the shop so Dada's sister Aunt Lizzie had come to live with them and work behind the counter, until her sweetheart was about to be demobbed and she'd gone home to the valleys to marry him. That had been nearly six years ago and her aunt couldn't help out now as she'd two small children to care for.

By this time they were approaching Wilfred Street and as Laura pulled the key on its string through the letter-box of her house, Becky turned away to brush the tears from her lashes — tears that were always quick to come whenever she thought of her beloved dada, though he'd been dead now for more than two years.

'See you before Monday, Laura,' she cried as the door swung open, then hurried along the narrow street to the corner shop which still bore the painted sign over the door: WILLIAM MORGAN, GROCER.

As she stepped on to the sawdusted floor one of the waiting customers cried, 'Here's Rebecca at last,' and all heads turned towards her. Skirting the corn-bin and avoiding the spreading brown patch where the tap of the vinegar barrel leaked into the sawdust, she saw there were three women waiting to be served and that Laura's mam was one of them. Her own mother looked up from a bill-book to give her a weary smile, then Becky was lifting the flap in the counter to go through to the house.

After washing her hands at the deep brown-stone sink in the scullery, she took a long white apron from its peg and, folding it twice at the waist, tied it tightly about her. In the kitchen-cum-living room her eyes went as they always did to the photo that stood to one side of the china clock on the high mantelpiece. Dada had been big and jolly, and in the picture was smiling, but the sepia photo did little to show off his warm colouring or the red-gold tint of his crisply curling hair, both of which she'd inherited.

When she reached the counter her mother whispered, 'Parched I am, love. I'll just go and put the kettle on the stove.'

A few minutes later it was Laura's mam's turn to be served, but as their eyes met Mrs Evans's thin face grew red with

3

embarrassment. She whispered, 'It was youer mam I wanted to see, Becky. I was wondering if I could have a few more things on the bill?'

As she went to ask her mother Becky wished with all her heart that she didn't have to know their neighbours' secrets, especially when one of them concerned her best friend. Only recently Laura had told her she'd been home from school with a cold, but her mother, unable to pay the bill at the corner shop, had confessed she'd no shoes to wear.

'Gone through in a hole they are, Dora,' Polly Evans had confided in a loud whisper that had easily reached Becky. 'Bert would have mended them in a jiffy if he'd been fit,' she'd added, sighing deeply, and Becky had thought of Laura's father, thin and pallid, hardly ever moving from his wooden armchair drawn up to the fire and then only to lie on the bed they'd brought down to the parlour, for the poor man had been chronically ill ever since he'd been discharged from an army hospital in 1919.

'The things people confide when they're desperate,' her mother had said. 'It's like being inside the confessional box, only they expect us to give more practical help.'

When Becky delivered the message from Laura's mother her mam looked grim.

'I hate to say no to her, poor soul,' she said.

4

'Your dad would have given her what she wanted like a shot. Too soft he was with people, love, which is why we have to tighten up now 'cos it's a struggle to settle our own bills these days . . . Oh, go on then! Polly was always a good payer in the old days. But only the basics, mind.'

Becky had put sugar, tea, margarine, lard and flour on to the counter and was cutting a piece of cheese, making sure before she drew the wire through it that it was a substantial one. When she'd added a pot of strawberry and apple jam, she weighed potatoes, carrots and onions and, putting them with the other things, looked at Mrs Evans enquiringly. Growing pink with embarrassment again, Laura's mam gave a nervous little laugh and said, 'They do say cleanliness is next to Godliness, *cariad*, so could I have a bar of soap?'

Chuckling at the feeble little joke, hoping to put her at her ease, Becky added a bar of white Windsor and one of carbolic to the groceries. Mrs Evans, still red in the face, murmured, 'And could you give me a few candles, love, to save on the gas?'

The cup of tea her mother brought when Laura's mam had gone tasted like nectar. There'd be no time for a meal until the shop closed at six. Going over to the biscuit cabinet and raising one of the glass lids, Becky took out two custard cream biscuits and ate them hungrily. Dada had always stayed open until seven, but with her mother on her own all day and no time to slip out and prepare food in advance, they'd decided to shut earlier nowadays.

Their evening routine was always the same. While her mother entered the day's accounts in the big leatherbound ledger, Becky would don one of her mam's wraparound overalls and go into the shop to cover the butter and cheese with clean muslin cloths. After sweeping up the sawdust, she'd scatter fresh over the worn, knotted boards. Then, making sure the sacks of rice, split peas, dried peas and lentils were covered up, she'd turn the gas low, knowing she'd need some light when she came to fetch things for late customers.

As she came back into the kitchen Fluff the cat, who'd been stretched out on the rug in front of the fire, rose slowly, arching his back, paws stretched out before him. He came across to rub his grey furry back against her legs, purring loudly and staring up at her with hopeful amber eyes. She fetched him his dish of lights and saucer of milk and watched him devour them rapidly, knowing that in the long, hungry night ahead he'd earn his keep by stalking mice, keeping them at bay.

Becky saw that her mother's blue eyes were sad as she looked up to say, 'Things are getting worse. It wasn't so bad when people settled up at the end of the week but with so many families losing their breadwinner in the war, and a lot of those that did come back either too ill to work or out of a job . . . ' Sighing deeply, she went on, 'Laura's mam never owed a halfpenny when Bert was working. God knows how she's going to pay for what she had today. Take something to the pawn-broker's, I wouldn't wonder. That's if the poor soul's anything left to take.'

'Laura's starting work Monday. That's bound to help,' Becky reminded her.

'She won't get much as a scullery maid. Run off her feet she'll be, poor child. Still, it'll save her keep. That's something, I suppose.'

A knock on the side door sent Becky hurrying to open it. When she'd fetched the quarter of tea and packet of Woodbines the customer wanted, she went along the passage to check on the store room, shivering a little as she always did now when passing the trap door of the cellar, remembering that awful summer's day when she'd been fetched from school. A Welsh lesson had been just about to begin and the class were intoning '*Bore da*', Miss Williams' when the door opened and their headmistress, looking very grave, had come in and spoken to the teacher.

Miss Williams had called Becky from the desk she shared with Laura, saying gently when the girl reached her side, 'Your father has had an accident, Rebecca, and you're needed at home. There's a lady waiting for you, dear.'

'What sort of accident was it, Mrs Evans?' she'd asked, anxiously going into Laura's mother's arms.

'Slipped and fell down the cellar steps he did, *cariad*. Waiting for an ambulance they are so we'd better be quick.'

'Perhaps he's only broken a leg or something?' Becky said hopefully as they left the school, but as they rushed along Stacey Road Polly Evans didn't seem to hear.

When they reached the street the ambulance was waiting outside the shop. Becky began to run, arriving fearful and breathless just in time to see the stretcher, with its still burden wrapped in red blankets, being lifted inside. She followed her mother up the steps and they were soon speeding away. At the Infirmary her mother's face was as white and anxious as her own as they waited for a door to open and someone to come and put their fears to rest. When presently a doctor in a starched white coat came towards them they rose as one, anxiously scanning his face.

'I'm so sorry, Mrs Morgan,' he said. 'There was nothing we could do.'

Tears streamed down her mother's face as they left the hospital and the hot tears that Becky had tried so hard to hold back gushed from her own eyes too.

She sighed now, remembering happier times and the shop ringing with laughter when her father had been there.

'You are a caution, Will,' one of the customers would say. 'Better 'n a tonic youer dada is, Becky.' And they'd be wiping tears of merriment away with a corner of their aprons as they left the shop.

Her mam had smiled a lot too in those days, with love in her eyes. Now most of the time her face wore a frozen expression, and Becky knew it had little to do with all the extra work that had fallen on her slim shoulders. Suddenly she felt very ashamed of her outburst to Laura on their way home from school.

2

When Laura said goodbye to Becky and went through to the kitchen there was no one there. Dada must be lying down, she thought, taking the heavy iron kettle from the hob and nestling it into the glowing coals before washing her hands at the sink and combing her long, silky, dark brown hair. The face reflected in the mirror was pale, with smooth dark brows and grey eyes wide with anxiety for where was Mama? Had she gone to the shop? Oh, no! Laura thought in despair, for Becky would be there by now and Mama, having spent all she had left on a bag of coal that morning, would be asking for credit. Her heart heavy at the thought of Becky's knowing their plight, Laura sat down in the wooden armchair and pressed her face into its cushions.

Presently she heard the key turning in the front door and raised her head, watching as her mother came into the kitchen and put the heavy basket on the table. Her voice shrill with anguish, Laura cried, 'Oh, Mam! Do you have to go to their shop? You know Becky's my friend.'

With a humourless little laugh her mother replied, 'Who else is going to give me strap, girl? We dealt with Will Morgan when youer dada was working and we could pay our way, and we'll be able to do that again one of these days, *cariad*, don't you worry.' But somehow her voice lacked conviction. Looking at her daughter's stricken face, and knowing how sensitive she was on the subject, tears came to Polly's eyes.

'Oh, Mam! I'm sorry.' Laura flung her arms about her mother, burying her face in her black woollen shawl. 'I know you've got to do it,' she went on, 'only surely not when Becky's in the shop?'

Suddenly Polly clapped a hand to her mouth, crying, 'Drat it! I've forgotten the corn for the chickens.' She looked at Laura, her eyes pleading. 'Will you go, love? I think there's enough in the pot on the mantelpiece for that.'

'Oh, Mam! I couldn't. Not after — '

'All right! All right! Where's our Tommy?'

'He was playing marbles in the street when I came home.'

'I'll give him marbles, the little devil! He was supposed to be keeping an eye on your dad.'

Laura's too sensitive for her own good, thought Polly, hurrying past the parlour on tip-toe to open the front door. Well, the girl would soon have that rubbed off her, going into service, and Polly ought to know, having been a servant herself until she'd married Bert.

She'd been born and brought up in a little village near Camarthen. Her father had moved his family to Barry in search of work when she was ten, and two years later she started as a scullery maid at a big house in the countryside nearby, so she knew just what Laura would be expected to endure: on her feet from morning until night, scouring endless pots and pans, up to her elbows in greasy water. Polly's heart ached for her.

Laura had been their first-born. She remembered Bert looking down at her in her cradle and saying, 'Our daughter will never be anyone's skivvy, Polly, not while I'm around.' And she wouldn't have been either, not if her father had come home from the war fit enough to go back to his job . . .

'Tommy! Tommy! I want you to go to the shop.'

'Aw! Do I 'ave to, our Mam?' The small fair-haired boy in the shabby green jersey straightened his back to look up pleadingly at his mother.

'Yes, you do, and look sharp about it. Better wash youer hands first, though, before

I give you the money and the note. It's only corn I want. Then you can come and feed the chickens.'

''Tisn't fair,' one of his tousle-headed companions moaned. 'It was my turn next.'

'We could mind yer marbles?' the other suggested hopefully.

Scorning the offer, Tommy picked them up, rubbing them one by one on his jersey as he followed his mother into the house.

'You promised to stay with youer dad while I was out,' Polly said sternly, putting the coins and a scribbled note into her son's hand.

''E was asleep, Mam, an' I stayed just outside the door until I saw our Laura coming down the street.'

'Where's Sal?' Laura asked when the door closed behind him. Her pretty, fair-haired sister was usually home by now.

'Gone to fetch the aprons Mrs Ridout's making you.'

Laura bit her lip anxiously, wondering what they'd turn out like, made as they would be from an old sheet that had gone thin in the middle.

'Not a brack in the sides,' her mother had said, packing them up with the new apron they'd sent as a pattern.

When presently they heard the door open and Sally's light footsteps in the passage,

Laura bit her lip hard again, praying the aprons would be all right.

'Can I try one on?' her sister begged.

Putting the rest of the sewing on to the table, she took an apron and tied it about her. Then, tossing back her fair curls, she set a mob-cap on her head. Laura gave a sigh of relief. No one, as her mother had said, would ever guess they were made out of an old sheet, and many boilings in the copper had ensured the cotton was snowy white. Mrs Ridout had also made the two rough aprons required from clean sacks provided by Becky's mother, and two plain blue cotton dresses had been donated by Jessie, their next-door neighbour, her daughter Winnie having just left service to get married. Only the caps and one apron were new. Looking at the things piled up on the table, Laura's feeling of apprehension at the thought of leaving home grew.

'Where's that boy?' her mother cried, glancing at the clock. 'He's been gone long enough to get a week's groceries.'

Hurrying to the door, Laura saw that Tommy was once more playing marbles, sending one spinning along the gutter as she cried, 'Tommy! Come here at once.'

He straightened up and looked warily towards her. The bag of corn he'd stuffed up

14

his jersey fell with a thud to the road, spreading a mound of golden grain over the grey surface.

'Oh, 'ell!' Tommy's look of consternation touched Laura's heart but sounding suitably shocked at his words, she cried, 'You'd better not let Mama hear you!'

'I was comin' in, honest,' he told her sheepishly. 'Warr'm I goin' to do now?'

Bringing a pan and brush from the house, she handed them to Tommy, and when he'd brushed up all the corn and tipped it back into the bag, said, 'You'd better take it in.'

'Aw! Thanks, Laura.' He breathed a sigh of relief.

A bloodcurdling yell coming from the direction of the parlour sent Laura rushing indoors. Her mam was already at the bedside talking soothingly to Dada who was huddled against the pillows, arms shielding his face from some imaginary peril. When at last Polly had calmed him enough to take his hands gently in hers, he looked wildly about him and would have covered his face again but she took him in her arms and cradled him gently, cwtching him close like a frightened child. At last Bert relaxed enough to be coaxed into lying down and they were able to cover him with sheet and blankets.

Closing the parlour door, they went to the

kitchen. Polly sank wearily into the armchair and said, 'God knows what horrors youer father sees in those nightmares, *cariad*.' It was obvious that in his mind he was back in the trenches in France, up to his thighs in mud, shells bursting about him. Sometimes he'd press his hands tightly to his ears as though to shut out some unbearable noise.

The nightmares were getting worse and Polly knew how much they were upsetting the children, particularly Tommy.

Laura and Sally were old enough to remember their dad before he'd volunteered. Bert had been a docker then and earning decent money. He'd loved his kids and on pay nights his pockets would be bulging with packets of lossins which the girls would be invited to search for, squealing with delight as they drew out the sweets. She could see him now, tall and broad-shouldered, a grin on his handsome face as he teased his daughters.

It had been a terrible shock when they'd brought him home on that stretcher, covered in red blankets; his face wan and pallid, eyes sunken into his skull. She'd wanted to cry at Tommy's look of stunned disbelief. Bert hadn't recognised any of them then, but that was over five years ago. Now he accepted them but still often withdrew into a world they couldn't share, the suffering he had endured there etched deeply on his face.

'He'll need plenty of good food and fresh air,' Dr Powell had told her when Bert first came home. 'We must get him to put on weight, that's our best hope.'

Easier said than done on the pittance they had to live on for there was no compensation for shell shock. But God knows she'd tried. It broke her heart to see Bert push away the meals she so carefully prepared. As for fresh air . . . where would he get that in this area of Cardiff?

Bert had put on a little weight over the years and thankfully the times when he'd shut himself away in some tortured world of his own were growing less frequent. But the nightmares, when he'd sweat and tremble and cry out as he had just now, terrified young Tommy. The boy had been brought up on fond tales of the father he'd never seen. Tommy had been born in 1915 just after Bert was drafted to France. He was now nine years old and ever since he could toddle had kept the photo of the handsome young soldier who was his dad on the rickety cane table by the side of his bed.

Poor little Tommy, Polly thought, feeling guilty at not preparing him better for Bert's homecoming.

'Youer dad will soon be coming home from

the hospital in England,' she'd told the children. 'We must take care of him and get him well again.' She'd known nothing at all about shell shock, had imagined Bert would only need rest and loving care to recover quickly. She'd been as horrified as the children when they'd removed the blankets and seen his thin twitching body in the rough hospital nightshirt as they lifted him on to the bed.

Now, as Polly caught sight of her son's white face when he came in from feeding the chickens, she put her arms tenderly about him and drew him to her. But he shrugged her off, muttering gruffly, 'I got to go upstairs for somethin'.'

Brushing the rough sleeve of his jersey across his eyes, Tommy rushed up to the little back bedroom and flung himself on his bed, pressing his face into the cool pillow. His friends had heard his dad yelling out again, hadn't they? Remembering how he used to boast to them about Dada when he was small, had even smuggled the picture out to show them before his father had come home, Tommy fought to hold back the tears. His dada was nothing like that photo and he felt cheated of all the wonderful things he'd been promised would happen when Bert Evans came home from the war.

Wriggling his hand deep into his trouser pocket, he drew out his marbles and fondled them lovingly, face blanching when he couldn't feel the cool glass of his favourite. Forgetful of his mother's warning to move quietly in case he upset his dad, Tommy clattered down the stairs and out into the street, the embarrassment of meeting his friends forgotten in the urgency of finding out which one of them had pinched his best taw.

3

On Sunday afternoon, when Laura lifted the bath from its nail in the yard, the weather was warm and sunny. Putting it in front of the kitchen fire, she drew several buckets of water from the boiler at one side of the range. It was much too hot for a fire but the water had to be heated. Then she waited impatiently for Dada to go to the parlour to lie down on his bed. Mama was next-door and Sally and Tommy out with friends.

On a chair by the table her rush holdall was packed ready, except for the change of underclothes she was about to take off and would have to wash and dry.

A lump came to Laura's throat as she looked around the shabby, familiar room: the deal table covered with a green chenille cloth in the middle of which stood a vase of yellow roses, cut from the bed in the garden; the scuffed brown leather couch with dark mahogany scrolling at its head where she'd lain whenever she'd felt poorly; her father's wooden armchair, pushed back now from the fire; the bookshelves he'd put up years ago in the recess to hold his beloved books, for although he hadn't had much schooling he'd taught himself from a book called *Jack's Self Educator* which had pride of place among his collection.

Laura's gaze lingered on the photographs of her parents to either side of the clock. One showed a pretty young woman with a frizzy fringe, the rest of her fair hair drawn back into a bun. The high neck of her blouse was edged with lace and she wore a long dark skirt that covered all but the toes of her boots. Like most of their neighbours Polly Evans still wore the long skirts that were in fashion before the war; Laura couldn't remember when she'd last had anything new.

In the other photo her dad stood proudly in his uniform. He looked so young and handsome, her heart filled with pity for the trembling haunted person he'd later become.

After tonight she wouldn't be sleeping in the familiar bedroom she'd always shared with her sister Sally. Instead she'd probably sleep in an attic room with another girl, as yet a stranger. Despite the stifling warmth in the kitchen, Laura shivered at the thought. I'll still be in Cardiff, she consoled herself. I'll be able to come home on my half-day. But the feeling of apprehension she'd woken with that morning persisted.

Laura had just emptied the bath and hung

it back on the wall when there was a knock on the door. Fearful the noise might wake her dad, she rushed to open it. Becky stepped in and was led immediately to the steamy kitchen which still smelled strongly of carbolic soap.

Pressing a bulging brown paper bag into Laura's hands, she said, 'We thought these might come in useful. I put in the hankies and the scented soap.'

Pink now with excitement and the heat of the kitchen, Laura drew out the first item which was wrapped in tissue paper: three lace-edged hankies embroidered with her initials. The second parcel contained two tablets of lavender soap; the third, a pretty tin with a hinged lid, was filled with sewing things: a small pair of scissors, spools of cotton, a measuring tape, a card of pearl buttons and needles and pins.

'Oh, Becky! You shouldn't have, but they'll be ever so useful,' Laura began gratefully.

'There's something else in the bottom,' Becky reminded her, but Laura had already guessed what it was. As she drew out the four candles Becky explained, 'Mama says the gas-light might not reach as far as the att — I mean, the upper floors. They'll probably give you a ration of candles but it's always handy to have more.'

Next Becky drew from her pocket a small bottle of Californian Poppy, saying, 'I want you to have this scent to remember me by.'

But Laura cried: 'I couldn't take that, Becky, not the scent! It's one of the presents your mother gave you for Christmas.'

When her friend insisted, she said, 'Well, thanks ever so much. And thank your mam too. But I'll never forget you, and anyway, I'll be coming home on my half-day.' If only she had something to give Becky in return!

'If it isn't a Wednesday, I'll be working, remember,' her friend said ruefully.

* * *

Next morning, getting up at dawn, Laura watched the clock on the mantelpiece anxiously. When the time came to leave she hugged her family with tears in her eyes. Glancing back many times, she stopped to wave at the end of the street. Shifting the heavy holdall to the other hand, she was about to turn the corner when her brother came hurtling around it, nearly knocking her off her feet. She grabbed him tightly and was going to upbraid him soundly when she caught sight of his tearful face and the reddening patch around his left eye.

'Tommy! What's happened?' she cried

accusingly. 'You've been fighting again, haven't you?'

He sniffed loudly. After blowing his nose on the clean hanky Laura felt compelled to offer him, he sniffed again, saying, 'Jackie wouldn't give me back my taw so I went round to get it an' 'e said our Dada's *Wedi-Twp*, Laura. An' Dicky says 'e's daft as a brush 'cos they heard 'im shouting out last night. So I punched 'im and now I'm going to tell our Mam.'

'No, don't, Tommy. Please! You'll only upset her,' Laura begged. 'Dry your eyes and stop snivelling. You know it isn't true about Dada. Just tell her you went to get your marble. She's been looking for you for the last half-hour.'

I ought to go back with him, she thought worriedly, but if I miss the next tram I'll be really late.

As Tommy ran homewards she saw her mother looking up the street, waving her on, and so Laura turned the corner with a heavy heart.

Poor Tommy. If only their father had come home from the war fit and well, how different things would have been for him. Her little brother spent a lot more time playing in the street than either Sally or herself ever had. They'd been company for each other and

Mama had always had time to spare for them then. Because of her father's illness and need for peace and quiet, Tommy had been encouraged to play outdoors, but he'd been in several fights lately and she knew her mam was worried about him.

As the tram took her towards town, Laura's thoughts were of home, but when she got off and was walking towards her new place of employment in a road at the top end of Dumfries Place, her nervousness returned and she took several deep breaths, hoping to calm herself. Heart beating fast, she went along the path that led to the side door and knocked timidly on it. When there was no answer she knocked louder and waited. Presently the door was opened by a flustered young girl, short and plump, her mob-cap askew and still wearing a greasy sacking apron on which she was trying to dry red chapped hands.

'You the new scullery maid?' she asked, eyeing Laura's holdall. When she nodded, the girl motioned her to come in, closing the door with a resounding bang that reverberated through the house, then led the way to the kitchen where a distraught-looking cook said snappily, 'You're late, girl. You'd better get youer apron on and start on that lot.' And she pointed to a stack of dirty pots and pans that stood on a wooden draining board by a deep stone sink.

Turning to the girl who'd let Laura in, she cried angrily, 'How many times have I got to tell you, Dottie, to remove that filthy apron before you answer the door?'

Shaking her head as though it was beyond her understanding, she turned to Laura once more, saying with a deep sigh, 'The kitchen maid left last week and the house maid went off in a huff this morning. Young girls don't know they're born these days. Why, when I started in service . . .

'Anyway, we don't know whether we're coming or going today. There's only the parlour maid besides us and she works upstairs, so the three of us will have to buckle down and do the lot. Get started on those pots, girl. Dottie will tell you what to do.'

Laura put on a cap and, after tying a sacking apron about her waist, was soon up to her elbows in grease, the generous portion of washing soda Dottie added to the scummy water stinging her hands.

When presently Cook went upstairs with a book and pencil, Dottie informed her, 'Gone to get the menu from the missus she is. Usually goes earlier than this she does. Only with Mary leavin', she's all at sixes and sevens.'

'Should I call her Mrs Coles?' Laura wanted to know.

'Yes. She isn't a real Mrs though. They always calls cooks that. She isn't a proper cook neither, not like in the big 'ouses. Cook general she is. That means she's got to do lots of other jobs, just like us.'

'What's the mistress like?'

'There's two of them. Miss Sophie is the eldest and a real tartar according to Sarah upstairs. Her sister, Mrs Pugh, is a lot younger. Lost 'er 'usband during the war she did, poor soul. Sarah says she's kind.'

When there were no more questions Dottie went on, 'Scullery maid for nearly a year I been, but I should get the kitchen maid's job now you've come.' She sounded eager. 'And we 'aven't got a house maid neither now so I should get one or the other.'

Cook's return silenced her abruptly but soon she was banging pots and pans around when Mrs Coles said to Laura, 'You'll have to take on the house maid's work for the time being, girl, as well as help out in the kitchen. I'll write out a list of your duties for you.' Then, catching sight of Dottie's sullen face, she said, 'And you can put youer face back while it's warm, miss. You can't even do your own job properly. And if I ever have to tell you again about answering the door in that filthy apron . . . '

'It was only the side door, our entrance.'

'And the tradesmen come to the side door, you stupid girl.'

' 'Tisn't fair! She's only just come.' Giving Laura a venomous look, Dottie stalked into the scullery and noisily began to scour the rest of the pots and pans. Laura's heart sank. She'd been prepared for hard work and long hours, but now, through no fault of her own, it seemed she'd made an enemy instead of a new friend.

'Go and help Dottie while I make out the list,' Cook told her, but when Laura entered the scullery and took up a cloth, Dottie kept her back to her and continued slamming things around.

'I've come to help you,' Laura told her, beginning to dry one of the pots that had been washed. But getting down from the low wooden box that enabled her to reach the sink, Dottie kicked it out of the way, saying, 'You can scour them, then.'

As Laura put her hands into the water the girl tipped in more soda, saying, 'Oops! I've put in too much but you can't change the water 'cause there's no more hot.'

When at last she'd finished, her apron as dirty and her hands now as red as Dottie's own, Laura asked: 'If there's only two of them to cook for, where did all this washing up come from?'

'They had people to dinner last night,' Dottie told her, in an aggrieved voice. 'Only Cook an' me there was, an' she said to put the pans to soak overnight. Then this morning Mary walks out and there was 'er job to do as well! Got a good mind I 'ave to go and see the mistress. I been 'ere the longest. I should be doing the house maid's job, not you.'

Laura didn't answer; she wouldn't have been heard in any case, the way the scullery maid was banging pots and pans about. Cook must be deaf to put up with this racket, she thought. When later she found out that Mrs Coles was indeed hard of hearing, she ceased to wonder that Dottie could be so noisy and insolent.

Just then Cook called to her to take the list of duties that had just been made out for her. 'You'll be sharing a bed with Dottie,' she told Laura. 'You'll be allowed two candles a week for personal use for there's no gas on the top floor. Youer half-day will be Thursdays; Dottie has Wednesday afternoons. You should get away by half-past two and must be back in by half-past nine. But there won't be a half-day for anyone until we've got someone to take Mary's place.'

Laura felt keen disappointment that her time off wasn't to be on a Wednesday when Becky's shop closed at one, but she was even more upset that she wouldn't be able to go home for a while, wondering for the umpteenth time if Tommy would have kept quiet as she'd begged, or if he'd upset their mam by blurting out the reason for the fight that had resulted in his black eye.

Laura looked down at the list of duties Cook had given her, trying to fathom how she was to get through it all in one day.

Rise at six-thirty, she read. Clean and blacklead grate in breakfast room. Brush carpet with hand-brush and pan. Once a week spread wet tea-leaves and brush up. Polish furniture. Do same in dining room and drawing room. Brush stair carpet, polish sides and banister.

At eight-fifteen breakfast in kitchen. Help with washing up. Lay up table for Cook.

At nine-fifteen bedrooms on first landing. Make beds, turning feather mattresses and pummelling until lump free. Clean bedroom grates and lay fires, fill coal scuttles, brush carpet and polish furniture.

After lunch, Laura thought ruefully, I revert to being kitchen maid. Prepare vegetables for dinner, clean silver, help Cook . . . This took her up to the servants' tea-time after which she must light the bedroom fires if needed, replenish coal scuttles, take up cans of hot water for the mistresses and their guests, if any, to prepare themselves for dinner. And turn down the beds.

'Do they have fires in the bedrooms this weather?' Laura asked in surprise.

'Fires are required upstairs and down unless it's very close,' Cook assured her. 'Anyway, make us a quick cup of tea before you start. There's some cherry cake in that tin on the dresser. Tell Dottie when you've made it. Might put her in a better mood,' the woman told her with a deep-throated chuckle.

Cook's all right, Laura thought, enjoying the hot tea and generous wedge of delicious cake. When Dottie came into the kitchen she munched sullenly. After draining her cup, she got up without a word to return to her tasks. While Mrs Coles busied herself preparing lunch, Laura washed the crockery and put it back on the dresser, plucking up the courage to ask, 'If I can't get all this in before lunch, where would it be best to start?'

'Mary did the breakfast room and dining room before the row blew up,' Cook told her. 'Do youer best, girl. Give it a good do tomorrow.'

That night, as Laura followed Dottie up

the creaking back stairs, she felt exhausted and filled with apprehension. The scullery maid had barely spoken a civil word to her since before lunch, and now, as the candle flared, throwing grotesque shadows on the distempered wall, the set of the girl's jaw was ominous.

Cook had told Laura to help herself to two candles from the cupboard outside their bedroom door, and as she did this she thought with pleasure that now she'd be able to give her mam the four Becky had brought her.

'The top drawer's youers,' Dottie informed her icily, pointing to a shabby chest of drawers. 'Cleared all my things out I have,' she added, stuffing the clothes she'd removed into the next drawer down.

Tired as she was, Laura emptied her holdall, putting the contents neatly away, candles and soap at one end, clothes at the other. When at last she got wearily into bed and blew out the candle, Dottie's back was towards her and she seemed to be asleep. Used to having the bedroom window open, especially in this weather, Laura tossed and turned on the lumpy mattress. The sash window remained firmly closed despite her efforts to raise it and in the hot stuffy room she soon became aware of the strong smell of stale sweat from the girl at her side. Presently Dottie turned on to her back and began to snore, the raucous noise slowly reaching a climax, when, with a snort, she would stop for a moment only to begin all over again.

Laura must have slept, for as dawn lightened the flimsy curtains she was startled into wakefulness by the shrill bell of the alarm clock, staring about her in dismay until she remembered where she was.

Dottie hadn't seemed to hear so Laura hurriedly poured cold water from the jug into the bowl on the wash-stand and washed to her waist, drying herself as quickly as she could on the worn towel she'd brought. She was buttoning her dress, wondering whether to wake Dottie for the hands of the clock stood at ten minutes past six, when the girl stirred. She got out of bed and dressed hurriedly without even washing hands or face. No wonder she smelled!

Going over to the chest, Dottie pulled open the top drawer. She had obviously forgotten it was Laura's now. She stared inside. Next minute she was rushing from the room, clattering noisily down the stairs, leaving an astonished Laura wondering what all the hurry was about. She didn't have to wait very long to find out.

Within minutes there were heavy footsteps

on the stairs and Cook, red in the face from the exertion, stepped in and went straight over to the chest. To Laura's amazement she pulled open the top drawer, pointing an accusing finger at the contents as she cried, 'Dottie's right. You are a thief! Thought I wouldn't know, didn't you? Five candles in this drawer there is besides the one you're using. Ought to dismiss you right away, I should . . . ' Then, as Laura tried to explain, she waved her away, saying, 'I don't want to hear any of youer excuses. You can work in the kitchen and scullery but Dottie will have to do the housework. *You* obviously can't be trusted with other people's things.'

As Cook swept from the room Laura saw the look of triumph on Dottie's plump face before she too left. Filled with despair, she wished the floor would open up and swallow her.

4

'You say youer friend will write and tell me she gave you the candles? But what proof is that, girl? Friends will say anything to get you out of trouble.'

'But it's true, Cook! She did give them to me,' Laura cried in desperation.

As Mrs Coles turned to leave the kitchen she gave Laura a pitying look, and, burning with the injustice of it all, eyes stinging with unshed tears, the girl tied a sacking apron about her waist and started on the kitchen range.

If only she'd insisted her mam have all the candles Becky had brought! Hearing footsteps behind her, she turned to meet Dottie's look of scorn and remembered Cook telling her: 'That girl's got lots of faults but she's as honest as the day is long.'

Over the next few days, whenever she saw the chance, Laura tried to convince Cook of her innocence but knew she'd failed when Mrs Coles told her, 'Perhaps calling you a thief because of a few candles was a bit strong, Laura, but I was surprised and upset. I thought you were a good reliable girl. We'd best forget it ever happened and start over again, 'cos I don't really think you'd take anything of real value.'

How could she ever forget it had happened, Laura thought gloomily, when Cook obviously still thought she was guilty? The unfairness of it all filled her with despair.

As she tossed and turned at night in the stuffy bedroom, forced to listen to Dottie's snores, or rushed from one job to the other during the busy days, she longed to go home to see her mam. But with half-days indefinitely postponed until someone was found to take Mary's place, she could only pray that release would be soon. If only she could confide in someone who'd believe her . . . but even when she did go home she couldn't burden Mama with her troubles. Her poor mam had enough worries of her own.

Laura had been working at the house for nearly a fortnight when Cook announced that she'd found a suitable new girl. As they were about to go back to their duties she called Dottie, telling her, voice sharp with disapproval: 'The dining-room grate looks as though it hasn't seen blacklead for days, and there's dust around the ornaments on the mantelpiece.'

'I'm doing my best,' Dottie told her sullenly.

'Well, it isn't good enough, girl,' Cook replied. 'You'll have to pull youer socks up, mind.'

As Dottie carried the blacklead and brushes to the dining room her colour was high, and Cook, the trouble over the candles obviously forgotten, turned to Laura confidingly. 'Poor Dottie's just not cut out for the job,' she said. 'An orphan she is, you know. Hasn't got a home to go back to, which is why I put up with her, hoping she'll get better. She's willing enough. Good in the scullery, she was — and she'll be back there before long if this new girl's up to scratch.'

When, on Monday morning, Laura opened the door to the new maid she saw a small girl, her black hat perched on top of long fair curls that reminded Laura of her sister Sally's. Ellen had plump rosy cheeks and a ready smile. Laura's spirits rose. Perhaps she'd find a friend in this household after all?

Loudly protesting, angry at losing the job she'd coveted for so long, Dottie went back to her old occupation. But when Cook told her that no one was better than her in the scullery she seemed mollified, obviously glad to be back in her good books. It wasn't long before Laura heard Dottie saying to Ellen in a voice

37

meant to carry, 'Stole them she did, cwtched them away in 'er drawer . . . ' Her heart sank for she'd wanted so much to be friends with Ellen and now she'd been branded a thief.

Ellen proved to be a quick learner and anxious to please, rapidly earning Cook's approval. With half-days restored, Laura eagerly looked forward to Thursday afternoon when she could at last go home. Then, to her delight, Cook told her to move her things for she was to share a room with Ellen. 'It's a bigger room, Laura. Got two single beds. I expect Dottie would like to have the room to herself again so she won't mind.'

Despite the cloud hanging over her, as Laura removed her things and carried them to the room further along the corridor, she could have jumped for joy. Ellen was already there, emptying her bag, putting things neatly away. Lace curtains stirred in the breeze from the open window; the beds were already made up, each covered with a clean but faded patchwork quilt, and on the little table in between stood an alarm clock and a pair of china candlesticks. A large oak wardrobe stood against one wall and a marble-topped wash-stand held a flowered bowl with matching ewer and soap dish. The oak chest of drawers in which Ellen was putting her things away completed the furnishings.

'I've left the top drawers for you,' Ellen told Laura. 'It's a lovely room, I'm glad we're going to share.'

Only one thing marred Laura's happiness: the memory of Dottie spitefully telling this girl about the candles Laura had supposedly stolen. Determined to clear the air she said, 'Whatever Dottie told you, Ellen, I didn't take anything.'

'I don't know what all the fuss is about,' she replied, with a friendly smile. Taking a small parcel tied with brown paper and string from under her clothes in the bottom drawer, she unwrapped it to reveal four candles.

'You brought some with you too?' Laura asked.

'No! I *took* some too. It's a perk, Laura. You shouldn't 'ave put yours where they could be seen.'

'I've just told you, Ellen, I *didn't* take them.' Why wouldn't anyone believe her?

'All right! All right! You didn't take them. But I wouldn't blame you if you had, the hours we're expected to work!'

That night, for the first time since she'd arrived at the house, Laura slept well. As the two girls washed and dressed she noted with approval how clean Ellen was, her underwear well darned but snowy white. Things looked so much better after a good night's sleep and never in her life before had she had a bed all to herself. Tomorrow when she woke it would be Thursday and her half-day — and it couldn't come quickly enough for Laura.

5

'Oh, dear! I've never laughed so much since youer dada's time, Becky.' Young Mrs John wiped her eyes with the edge of her apron and sighed.

There were three customers in the shop, all convulsed with laughter at Mrs Brown's mimicking of a middle-aged neighbour who was well known to be henpecked by his wife. When Dada had been alive it had been his jokes they'd laughed at, not other people, Becky thought.

'Said to me, 'e did,' Enid Brown went on, ' 'Tell youer Alfie I'll meet 'im at the allotment around seven.' Martha was coming full sail along the passage at the time and she towers over 'im — you know how big she is — and says, 'You won't be going nowhere tonight, Willie. Minding the kids you'll be while I go to see our Mam.' He didn't even argue, just muttered, 'Some other night then, Mrs Brown,' and follows her back into the house.'

'Poor bugger! I wouldn't get away with it with my Sam.' Lena John folded her arms and settled down to gossip. 'Still, Willie did get back from the war in one piece and that's more than some did. Must 'ave been a picnic over there for 'im after the way she treats the poor devil.'

Glancing at her mother, Becky noticed her lips set in a thin line of disapproval and remembered the advice she'd been given: 'Never discuss the customers one with the other. Even if you agree and want to take sides, stay neutral. Or it could be bad for business.'

She'd learned so much about the people in the streets around since working full-time behind the counter, and Becky marvelled to realise she'd been there less than three weeks for already school seemed a lifetime away. When she'd just helped out in the evenings and on Saturdays the customers would talk behind their hands, excluding her as a mere child. Now suddenly she was one of them, her friendly approach reminiscent of her dad's, and they automatically included her in their conversation.

Becky already knew a great deal more about the customers' affairs than any other girl in the neighbourhood, but as Mama was always reminding her it was none of their business: they were there to serve and be confided in. Now Mrs John and her friend had started on about Mavis Coleman.

'A trial to her poor mam she must be.' Enid Brown shook her head and tutted self-righteously for everyone knew what a good obedient girl her Sadie was. Becky had always been slightly envious of Mavis for she had a freedom Becky could only dream of, and her clothes were modern and very smart even though everyone said her skirts were far too short. Mavis worked as an usherette at the Empire and, with her bobbed hair and make-up, looked far more than her seventeen years. Her mam was a friendly, quiet little woman who wouldn't say boo to a goose.

As though Becky's thoughts had conjured her up, Mavis was stepping into the shop and at a nudge from her friend Enid stopped in mid-sentence to turn to the girl and say in a honeyed voice, 'Go on, love, if you don't want much you can 'ave my turn. You young ones are always in a hurry.' And as Mavis stepped forward to be served, Becky could only marvel at Enid Brown's duplicity.

When the girl left the shop, clutching a packet of tea, Mrs Brown turned to her friend, saying, 'Did you see that, Lena? Show 'er arse she would if she was to bend over.'

With her mother's expression more disapproving by the minute, Becky did her best to hurry up the gossiping pair. When a few minutes later Lena left the shop, her friend wasn't far behind.

'You don't want to encourage them, Becky,' her mother told her as soon as they'd gone.

'I wasn't encouraging them,' she protested. 'Just trying to serve them as quickly as I could.'

'I know you were and you can't tell them to shut up, but it gets my goat the pleasure they seem to take in other people's misfortunes. Ah, here's Albie! Are all the orders ready for him to deliver?'

Albert Lloyd was a lanky boy of nearly fourteen, his outgrown trousers well above his boots, the sleeves of his skimpy jacket nowhere near his wrists. His mother was a widow and often ailing, and when he left school at Christmas Albert, her only child, would be needing a full-time job. Dora Morgan was sorry that he'd have to seek it elsewhere for he was a willing worker, always ready to help, but with customers' debts rapidly accumulating the shop could barely support the two of them full-time.

'Leave it to me, miss,' Albert told her shyly when Becky went to load the carrier bike with orders. His thin face was flushed with warm colour and Becky remembered Laura saying teasingly, 'Got a soft spot for you he has, Becky. Blushes whenever he sees you he does.'

44

'Don't be daft, Laura.' She'd been embarrassed for she felt nothing but pity for Albert Lloyd — albeit pity tinged with respect for the way he looked after his invalid mam.

I wonder if Laura will have a half-day tomorrow? she thought. It would be lovely to see her and hear all about her job and the house where she works.

Mrs Evans had told her last week there'd be no time off for Laura until they'd replaced the servant who'd left. She hadn't been in this week and probably wouldn't come to the shop until she could pay one of the bills she owed; then she'd be forced to run up another. Poor Mrs Evans always looked so worried, and no wonder for Laura had said there was no knowing if her dad would ever get better.

Becky had just served the last customer and was about to close the door when Sally arrived breathlessly to tell her, 'Laura will be home tomorrow, Becky! She'll see you sometime in the afternoon.'

★　★　★

Excited at the prospect of going home at last, Laura woke early that Thursday morning. Refreshed by a good night's sleep, she flung back the covers and tip-toed to the window. She drew the curtain aside a little, enjoying

45

the cool breeze from the open window. Soon it would be dawn for apricot streaks were lightening a pewter-coloured sky and a blackbird was already in full-throated song.

Ellen was still asleep. Pouring water into the bowl as quietly as she could, Laura washed and dressed. Then, as she was about to wake Ellen, the brass bells of the alarm shattered the silence. As the girl put out a hand to search for and silence it, Laura hurried downstairs, anxious to start the morning's chores and get them done as quickly as she could.

It was mid-morning and she was humming a tune while she cleaned the kitchen window when she was surprised to see Ellen hurrying along the side path that led to the scullery door, looking anxiously about her.

'Posting a letter to my mam I was,' she told Laura, seeing her at the window as she came into the kitchen.

'Lucky for you Cook's gone to the butcher's.' It was a rule that servants mustn't leave the house unless given permission or instructed to do so. Still there seemed no harm in Ellen's going to the post-box which was only a few yards along the street.

By half-past two, dressed in the skirt and blouse she'd arrived in and wearing the same little black straw hat, Laura was ready to leave. It was a warm day and she was eagerly looking forward to getting out into the sunshine on her way home at last. Her oil-cloth shopping bag, containing only her purse, a hanky and a comb, looked almost empty, but she meant to buy sweets for Sally and Tommy and some small treat for her mam and dad.

Cook stood by the table as she entered the kitchen, high colour flushing her cheeks, obviously upset.

'Can I go now, Cook?' Laura asked anxiously, knowing something must be very wrong.

'I don't know how to put this, Laura,' Cook said, swallowing hard and seeming reluctant to go on. 'Now don't take this personally, girl, I'd have to do it to anyone leaving this house, but I — I must ask you to turn out that bag 'cos something's gone missing.'

As she emptied the bag of its few possessions Laura's heart plummeted. She didn't have whatever Mrs Coles was looking for but it was obvious she still wasn't trusted. Then an awful thought crossed her mind. Would Cook cancel their half-days until she'd found the culprit? Laura longed so much to go home; she needed to get away from this house where she seemed to be constantly under suspicion. Cook's face grew redder than ever as she stared down at the purse, hanky and comb.

'Well, I didn't really think you'd have it, Laura,' she was saying apologetically. 'But as you're the only one going out . . . Why else would anyone want to take a pie that size? Six of them there was in the pantry, best steak and kidney. Miss Sophie asked me especially to make them for when the family comes tonight. I'm sorry, Laura, but I had to do it. You must see that?'

Her heart heavy with the turn of events, Laura put her things back into the shopping bag, asking anxiously, 'Can I go now, Mrs Coles?' then waiting with bated breath for the answer.

'Of course you can, Laura.' Cook sighed wearily, adding, 'I only wish I hadn't had to do what I did, girl. Anyway you're in the clear now, but I'd be glad if you'd keep youer eyes open. Meat pies don't just disappear into thin air.'

It was a lovely day, the warmth of the sun tempered by a light breeze, but Laura's mood was sombre as she hurried towards the Indoor Market where there was a stall that sold boiled sweets. Business was brisk after Wednesday's half-day closing, and pushing her way through the crowds that thronged the Hayes entrance of the spacious ornate building, with its high glass roof and cool stone floor, she passed Ashton's the fishmonger's and poulterer's, breathing in the mingled smells of fish spread out on marble slabs and the poultry and game festooned about the stall.

The aisles were thronged with shoppers as Laura searched for the sweet-stall, fondly remembered from trips with her mam as a small child before the war. Here was the cockle-stall. She sniffed hungrily, remembering the savoury delicacy being served on tiny plates, the cockles soused in vinegar. In those days she'd been given the choice, shell-fish or roast chestnuts — very tempting as they popped and sizzled on a brazier on cold winter's days. She was still little more than a child but there was no choice for Laura today; the few coppers she had were for tram fares and sweets to take home. As she went down another aisle she was met by the strong smell of cheese, bacon, fruit and vegetables, then freshly baked bread, reminding her of Becky's mother's shop.

Choosing pear-drops, Sally's favourite, and for Tommy a couple of large round sweets that changed colour as you sucked, Laura carefully counted her coppers before deciding on liquorice allsorts for her mam and dad.

Sitting on the tram, staring out of the

window as it rattled along Queen Street and Newport Road, Laura's thoughts turned to the events of the morning and Cook's distress at finding there was a thief in the house. But who could it be? Sarah had been parlour maid for years and only joined them for meals. This morning they'd all been sitting at the table when she'd arrived and were still there when she left. Cook seemed certain Dottie was honest, for hadn't she said so? Anyway, poor Dottie was an orphan and didn't have a home to go to on her half-day, so what would she want with a large and very cold steak and kidney pie? That only left Ellen and she wouldn't have any time off until sometime next week.

Laura was still pondering the mystery as she turned the corner of her street and headed for home. Suddenly she was staring in disbelief and her heart missed a beat as she watched the policeman who'd been at their door mount his bike and ride away. She saw the front door close and neighbours, who'd been talking, arms folded, eyes fixed curiously on the house, slowly move away.

'It's youer Tommy, love. Run off, 'e has. No one's seen 'im since last night.'

Fear gripped Laura's heart as she turned to face Mrs John, but the question on her lips was never asked as Lena went on, 'It's youer

50

dad's the trouble, isn't it? Nerves they say 'e've got. Youer poor mam, I'm sorry for 'er. Time 'e bucked 'imself up if you asks me. There's men who 'ave lost limbs don't make half the fuss.'

Filled with anger, Laura couldn't trust herself to speak. But this must be what people were saying about him, she thought. If they couldn't see any injury, they wouldn't believe it existed. Then, remembering what Lena had said about Tommy, she took to her heels and ran.

6

Heart beating fast, Laura stepped into the kitchen. The day she'd looked forward to for so long had taken on a nightmarish quality. Dada, obviously in one of his trances, stared unseeingly before him. Their neighbour, Jessie Hughes, was comforting Mam who raised a tear-stained face to tell Laura, her voice filled with sorrow, 'Our Tommy's run away, *cariad*. We haven't seen him since tea-time yesterday. Oh, Laura! Where can the child be?'

As her voice broke, Jessie took up the tale.

'One of them new-fangled motor-vans backfired — sounded just like a gun going off. Upset youer dada something awful.'

'Our Tommy had the door wide open, talking to his friends,' her mam went on with the tale. 'Dada rushed out, yelling at the top of his voice. Nearly pushed the boys over he did. Scared them all stiff. Must have thought he was still over there . . . '

Looking nervously towards her dad, Laura hoped he wasn't listening. He seemed oblivious, lips moving convulsively, trapped in some dreadful world of his own.

'I expect you can do with a cup of tea, Laura?' Jessie took the black iron kettle from the hob to put it on the gas stove. Then, with the familiarity born of long friendship, she put three cups, saucers and spoons and the sugar basin on the table and brought the milk jug from the mesh-fronted safe in the yard.

Looking anxiously again at her father, Laura thought sadly, It's almost as though he doesn't exist. But from long experience she knew it was better he wasn't disturbed or they'd soon have proof of his tormented existence.

'I was hoping you'd know where Tommy's friends live, Laura?' Her mother's eyes were pleading.

'I know Alfie's address, he'll be able to tell us about the others. Where's Sally gone?'

'Walking to Castleton, she is, in case he's gone to youer Auntie Nell. Remember how he loved the animals when we took him to the farm before Dada came home?'

'How about Nana? He stayed with her once for a week?'

'But how would he get to Barry, *cariad*? He couldn't walk it and he hasn't any money.'

★ ★ ★

Tommy's friend Alfie grudgingly opened the door a few inches to tell Laura, 'Just run off, 'e did. We waited outside Band of Hope after tea but 'e didn't come.'

Worried and despondent she returned to the house. Seeing Jessie to the door, her mam looked at her hopefully but there was little to tell. Leaving the two women talking, she went through to the kitchen where her father still sat, tears streaming down his hollow cheeks now. As Laura's arms went about him, he clung to her, saying in a voice rough with emotion, 'It's all my fault, Laura. All my fault.'

There were tears in her eyes too as she held him close, telling him tenderly, 'It isn't your fault, Dada. You can't help being ill. You go and rest on the bed and I'll bring you a nice cup of tea, then I'll have another look for Tommy.'

Knowing there was little hope of finding him wandering around, she went along Broadway and into Clifton Street, her head turning this way and that. The sun beat down and the pavements felt warm beneath her feet as she crossed Splott Bridge, remembering that some time ago a friend of her brother's had moved to Railway Street. But what number? As Laura walked the length of the long street, stopping any boys she saw to enquire, 'Do you know Tommy Evans?' their blank looks told her it was a hopeless task. After turning into Beresford Road, then into Broadway once more, she returned home despondent.

She entered the kitchen shaking her head. Her mother said anxiously, 'I had to give the police youer nan's address, Laura. Worried out of her mind she'll be if they tell her Tommy's missing.'

Looking up at the clock on the mantelpiece and seeing that the hands were already at a quarter past seven, Laura sighed. Mama was looking at her hopefully but there was no way she could get to Barry dock and be back at the house by half-past nine.

'Sally should be home soon,' Mama was saying, 'and if he isn't with our Nell . . . '

Half an hour later there was the sound of footsteps in the passage, and hearing Sally's voice in conversation with another they both looked up expectantly. When the door opened and Nana stepped into the kitchen, her first words were, 'Come to put youer mind at rest, I have, Polly. Tommy's been with me since late last night. My neighbour's looking after him until I get back.'

'But why didn't you bring him home?' she cried.

'The poor boy was in a dreadful state.

Filthy he was, having got a lift on a coal cart. Agnes next-door offered to lend me some of her boy's clothes and I've put his to soak. Look, Poll, leave him with me until school starts again. 'E went with my neighbour's boy to the beach this afternoon, took a sandwich and a bottle of water . . . '

'Went to the beach?' Polly yelled incredulously. 'And us worrying ourselves sick about him!'

'Needs to take his mind off things, poor little soul,' Nana persisted, removing her coat and her rusty black silk hat and jamming the pearl-headed hat-pins back into place. 'It's all over Bert coming home like he did. And it's partly youer fault, our Polly, filling his head with all that talk about his dad being a hero.'

'Bert *was* a hero,' she protested angrily. 'They were all heroes, the men who fought that blasted war!'

'I'll talk to him, Poll. Help him come to terms. Leave him with me 'til September. Glad of the company I'd be. What Tommy needs . . . '

'What Tommy needs after all the trouble he's caused is a good smack on the backside,' his mother broke in angrily.

'The lad was upset.'

'Upset!' Polly's voice broke on a sob as

tears rolled slowly down her thin cheeks. They rushed to comfort her. Dabbing her eyes with the edge of her apron, she looked up at them piteously. 'Anything could have happened to him — anything,' she told them. 'I was up all night — '

'I didn't mean to upset you, *cariad*,' Nana said softly, smoothing the greying hair from her brow as though her daughter were still a child. 'Look, you both need a break. Leave Tommy with me like I said. Sally's gone next-door to tell Jessie he's safe, so you go and pack him a few things. Miss my train I will if I stay here much longer. Pass my coat, Laura, it's over by there.'

'I'll walk along with you when you go, I've got to be in by half-past nine,' Laura told her, helping her on with her coat which was as rusty with age as the hat Nana now settled on her bun, jamming the hat-pins firmly into place once more.

'Ask Sal to tell Becky why I couldn't see her,' Laura said, kissing her mam goodbye.

'She'll know already,' Polly told her sadly. 'And there's two round here who'll enjoy embellishing the tale.'

As they walked up the street, turning to wave at the corner, her nan said, 'Youer mama's at breaking point, Laura. I wish I lived nearer just now. If only youer dad would get better. But that doesn't seem likely, poor soul.'

Laura got off the tram at the beginning of Queen Street, leaving her grandmother to go on to the station. Her thoughts were sombre as she dwelt on the troubles at home, but when Dottie opened the door, cheeks red with excitement, eyes round as saucers, mob-cap askew, and told her importantly, 'That Ellen's had the sack, Laura, and Cook's got 'erself into a right tizzy!' she forgot her own troubles and listened with amazement to Dottie's account of what had happened.

'Caught thieving, she was,' the girl went on. 'An' she still had the nerve to ask Cook for a reference! Goin' at each other 'ammer and tongs they was, 'cos Mrs Coles wouldn't give 'er one.'

By this time they'd reached the kitchen where Cook sat at the table, her head in her hands.

Looking up at Laura, she took up the tale. 'There were two children down by the gate. Kept popping their heads up they did. I was just going to tell them to clear off when Ellen came around the side of the house carrying something wrapped in brown paper. When I saw she was about to give it to them, I dashed out, and the little one who'd taken the parcel dropped it in fright. It was the steak and kidney pie that went missing after lunch!'

'The crafty bitch,' Dottie breathed, obviously enjoying the drama of the situation.

'I'm pretty certain some of those Welsh cakes I made disappeared this morning, but I couldn't swear to it,' Cook went on. 'Noticed some were missing when I went to have one with a cup of tea after I got back from the butcher's . . . ' And Laura was remembering seeing Ellen on the path while she was cleaning the kitchen window, supposedly posting a letter to her mam.

'Think I'll take a Daisy powder,' Cook decided. 'Hand me one, Dottie, then make us a pot of tea. All this aggravation has left me parched.

'We'll have to rearrange the work again until we find someone suitable,' she told them. 'When I think that I left that girl alone in the rooms upstairs, it makes me shudder!' The tea had been poured and the three of them sat at the table eating Welsh cakes. 'If we all buckle in, and I'm willing to do my share,' she went on, 'I don't see that it need affect youer half-days.'

'Laura can be house maid if she wants to,' Dottie said magnanimously. Preening herself, she added proudly, 'You did say I was the best scullery maid you'd ever had.'

If Dottie's last remark was a bit of an

exaggeration no one bothered to disagree. Laura smiled to herself as she thanked Dottie for it wasn't very clear whether the girl was extending the olive branch, or just making sure she wasn't landed once more with the job that had caused so much aggravation between Cook and herself.

7

'I'm not really happy about you meeting up with a boy you haven't been properly introduced to, Becky.'

'But I'm *going* to be introduced to him, Mama. Derek is Laura's young man's best friend.'

'Oh, well, I suppose it's all right. But in my young days . . . ' Dora Morgan sighed.

She seems to sigh an awful lot now, Becky thought sadly. The business, precarious ever since the war, had been brought near to closure after the General Strike in the spring of 1926. Her mam wasn't yet forty but her fair hair was already well silvered, and her expression always anxious.

'What time have you to be at the dressmaker's?' her mother asked now.

'Half-past seven,' Becky replied.

The dress was her mother's present for her eighteenth birthday in a few days' time. The material had been purchased before Laura's invitation but Becky was very glad that she had ordered the dress and it would be ready in time for this occasion. Laura had apparently been going out with Roy for about two months. Laura had met Roy when he'd visited his aunt Mrs Coles who was cook at the house where she worked. Becky had never been introduced for her friend always called home first on her half-day then met him in town.

When Becky fetched the dress next day she was delighted with it. The material was a soft green crêpe-de-chine, chosen when the assistant said the colour went well with her hair; the bodice reached down to her hips, the skirt was fashionably just below the knee. Mama had thought it too short when she'd accompanied her to the final fitting but the dressmaker had assured them it was the height of fashion.

As Becky's birthday fell on Laura's half-day they were to meet outside the Queen's cinema at half-past five. 'We'll have tea at the Dutch cafe then go to the first house,' Laura had told her.

Becky was feeling more and more nervous at the thought of meeting Roy's friend. Working in the shop all day, she'd had little chance to meet anyone except the customers apart from Albert Lloyd who used to be their errand boy, for he was often outside when she opened the shop, his excuse the need for a box of matches or a few candles, his face turning red with embarrassment as he lingered after being served as though rooted to the spot.

'Why don't you put the lad out of his misery?' her mam would say with one of her rare smiles. 'It's plain to see he's smitten with you.'

But Becky still felt only pity for Albert and didn't want to encourage him into thinking she could feel anything else. Sometimes, despite all the people who came into the shop, she felt desperately lonely.

'Why don't you join the YWCA?' her mam once suggested. 'I believe they have lots of interesting activities. They play tennis for one thing. You'd enjoy that.'

At the thought of joining on her own, Becky shook her head. She'd never have time to learn to play tennis, and anyway she'd have needed a partner for that and the only real friend she'd ever made was Laura.

On her birthday, as she bent to gather the deckle-edged cards glowing with warm colour from the mat, Becky felt a tinge of excitement as she thought of the evening ahead. But when the time came and she stepped from the tram in her lovely new dress, she shivered a little despite the warm evening. Supposing we don't get on? she thought. Supposing we don't click? It was a phrase she'd heard in the shop. Her heart was beating fast with painful anticipation as she stood well back and surveyed the crowds milling about outside the cinema.

Laura had told her Roy's friend was tall with dark hair. There was a young man standing by the doors leading to the foyer who matched this description. As he turned to look in her direction Becky's heart missed a beat. Laura hadn't said he was handsome but this boy certainly was. His eyes were a warm brown, his cheeks smooth and lean, his chin firm, and his wavy dark hair shone with brilliantine in the early-evening sunshine.

Nervous of approaching him, Becky stood behind a pillar where she was able to observe him without being seen. Suppose he wasn't waiting for her? The thought of making a fool of herself kept her hidden, hoping fervently that Laura and her young man would arrive very soon. She was unable to take her eyes off the young fellow. Becky had never felt remotely like this before. Her hope that he was looking for her grew stronger as people paired off with new arrivals and disappeared arm in arm into the foyer. And still she gazed, unable to take her eyes from him.

A few minutes later she was relieved to see Laura arrive accompanied by a rather serious-looking young man. When the boy she'd been watching stepped forward to greet them, Becky could have jumped for joy. As she too stepped forward Laura cried, 'What were you hiding for, Becky? I sent Roy to fetch you ages ago because we thought we might go to the Empire instead and have tea that end of town.'

Trying to cope with her deep disappointment Becky's heart plummeted but she managed a tremulous smile as she was introduced to her serious partner. Then her heart seemed to turn a somersault and her fingers tingled as she shook Roy Bevan's hand. Laura was saying with a laugh, 'And I told Roy he couldn't miss you with your hair that colour! Anyway we've wasted enough time, might just as well have tea in the Dutch and go to the Queen's now we're here. Charlie Chaplin's always good for a laugh.'

When at last they were seated in the crowded cafe Becky bit into one of the delicious-looking cakes piled high on a plate and swallowed nervously, desperately trying to think of something to say. Laura and Roy, deep in conversation, seemed to have eyes only for each other and Becky felt a swift stab of longing, a feeling she'd never experienced before. The young man beside her seemed to be struck equally dumb, staring at his plate and fiddling with the cake he'd taken.

With a tremendous effort she managed to

ask at last, 'Do you work in town, Derek?' She didn't even hear his answer. Sensing Roy's eyes on her, warm colour flooded her cheeks, but when she turned eagerly towards him he was only offering her the plate of pastries and, embarrassed, she wished she'd listened to what Derek had to say.

The cinema was rapidly filling up as they were ushered to their seats, Derek moving along the row first, then Becky, Roy and Laura. Finding herself between the two strangers, she felt nervous. Roy sitting so close to her was having a disturbing effect on her heart. Then he took Laura's hand in his and stared up at the screen. Derek was shyly handing Becky a box of chocolates. She thanked him warmly and, after opening them, offered them around.

As the wrappings crackled loudly someone behind them whispered, 'Shush!' Up on the screen the funny, pathetic little man in his bowler hat and wrinkled trousers twirled his stick and twitched his moustache this way and that, shambling his way into their hearts. The captions were hardly necessary as every gesture he made spoke to them.

By the time the credits rolled there was hardly a dry eye in the house. When at last the lights went on and the strains of the national anthem filled the auditorium Becky heard Roy's voice above those around them. It was a good voice, strong and pure, and she stopped singing to listen. Then it was time for the slow shuffle to the foyer.

'Shall I walk you home, Becky, or would you rather we took the tram?' Derek offered.

Borne away by the crowd, she couldn't answer. Then, as they came out into the warm summer evening, Laura cried, 'Sorry, you two, we'll have to go. Roy is seeing me back to work.'

'We'll walk,' Becky decided, regretting it five minutes later when, their discussion of the picture well and truly exhausted, a long silence fell between them. Once more she racked her brains for something to say while Derek walked on, head bent, seemingly studying his boots. Taking a quick glance at his long, serious face she couldn't help comparing it with Roy's whose brown eyes always seemed to be smiling.

As they were passing the hospital in Newport Road, Derek asked, 'Have you enjoyed the evening, Becky?'

Bringing herself reluctantly back from a fantasy in which she was walking arm in arm with Roy, she said, 'Pardon?'

Then, realising what he'd asked, she admitted to enjoying the film, reflecting that if she'd really been walking with Roy the silences, if any, would have been companionable — not the embarrassing ordeal this walk home with Derek was becoming.

When at last they arrived outside the shop he asked, 'Shall I see you again, Becky?' Before she could answer he added, 'Is there someone else?' and foolishly she answered, 'In a way there is.'

From the blank look on his face she knew he was thinking: Then why on earth did you agree to meet me?

'Well, thanks for the evening,' he said stiffly, before striding away along the street. Watching him go, Becky called herself all sorts of fool. Derek seemed a nice boy. He was painfully shy but so was she with strangers. Would she have been satisfied with his company if she'd met him before she'd seen Roy? She hadn't been fair to him and felt badly about that. He'd bought her chocolates, had tried to make conversation, but she hadn't even met him halfway. Why had she said what she had? There was no one else, or only in her dreams.

Realising that she still had to face her mam who'd doubtless be waiting with a barrage of questions, she sighed as she turned the key in the side door.

8

'Why didn't you ask the young man to come in, Becky? I saw you talking outside.' The questions she had been dreading had begun.

'He was rather shy, Mam.' That was true anyway.

'When will you be meeting him again?'

'I'm not seeing him again.' And that was her own fault, Becky thought.

'Doesn't sound as though you made much effort,' her mother replied tartly.

Thankfully, late as it was, there was a knock on the side door. As Becky left to answer it Dora rose to put the kettle on, but as she went along the narrow passage Becky knew she hadn't heard the last on this subject.

When she returned her mother continued just as though there hadn't been a break in their conversation.

'I worry about you, Becky. You won't always have me, you know.'

'Are you ill, Mama?'

She looked at her mother in alarm, but Dora laughed, saying, 'No, thank goodness. Just tired out. Are you hungry, love? What would you like for supper?'

Several times over the next few days she broached the subject of Becky getting out and about more, then seeing there was nothing to be gained, she let it drop.

As the days went by Becky couldn't get Roy out of her mind. In vain she told herself he was Laura's young man and they were obviously made for each other. That she'd been a fool to act as she had that night for there was no future in hankering after someone else's sweetheart. Thinking back, Derek had seemed a nice boy; she might have grown fond of him if only she'd given him a chance. Laura and Roy must be thinking her most ungrateful after all the trouble they'd gone to on her behalf.

On one of her rare visits to town Becky couldn't resist standing in a doorway opposite Roy's office just to see him come out, telling herself as the minutes ticked by that it was a stupid way to behave, just like having a schoolgirl crush, but she couldn't seem to help it. Her heart beat faster when at last he appeared, deep in conversation with a colleague. As they crossed the road towards her she drew back into the doorway, getting a brief glimpse of his handsome face before he turned towards his friend and disappeared into the crowd, totally unaware of the havoc he'd caused in her heart.

A few weeks later Laura came into the shop glowing with the news that she and Roy were getting engaged at Christmas. Much to Becky's relief Derek's name wasn't mentioned. I'll buy them a nice engagement present, she promised herself, ashamed at the pang of envy she'd felt at the news. She was glad for Laura and Roy, she told herself, hugging her friend warmly.

The next time Becky saw Laura was the week before Christmas when her mam had given her a couple of hours off to do shopping. This time she was arm-in-arm with Roy. As they met he gripped her hand in greeting. Despite the bitter coldness of the day, the leaden sky threatening snow, her fingers tingled as though with an electric shock. She wanted to gaze into those warm brown eyes for ever but Laura was telling her excitedly, 'You know we're getting engaged at Christmas, Becky. We've come to town to choose the ring.'

Cold fingers seemed to clutch at her heart but Becky managed a smile as she hugged her friend and said, 'That's wonderful! Congratulations! I wish you both every happiness.'

'Derek's engaged to be married too,' Laura was telling her. 'Janet's ever so nice, we all go out together sometimes.'

It could have been me going out with them, she thought regretfully, though she had no real feelings for Derek whom she hardly knew. She seldom went out these days except for necessary shopping and an occasional visit to the last house at the cinema with her mam. Albert Lloyd was still finding excuses to come to the shop. He was obviously fond of her but she felt no pity for his predicament, which she saw as much the same as her own. If I don't give him any encouragement, she told herself, he'll get over it same as I have to with Roy. From now on she'd try to put Laura's fiancé right out of her mind; it was the only sensible thing to do.

Christmas came but with just the two of them and her mother obviously worried about the shop, Becky wasn't looking forward to closing time on Christmas Eve. Customers were jolly at this time of the year and sometimes the shop rang with laughter as it had in her father's day. She found herself craving for company but she could well understand her mother's gloom for the festive season meant customers going deeper into debt — an outgoing the shop could ill afford to carry. If only she'd been one of a large family . . . but not all large families were happy, were they? Look at Laura's.

She'd confided when Becky gave her an

embroidered table-cloth as an engagement present that she'd have loved a little celebration of her engagement, if it hadn't been for the fact that her dad still couldn't stand noise or strangers. As it was they were just going to have a drink at the house where she worked, with Mrs Coles, Dottie, and Roy's mam.

If only *I* was going to a party, Becky thought. The lovely green dress that she'd had last birthday had only ever been worn once.

Despite the paper trimmings they put up every year, the festive cards crowding mantelpiece and window sills, and the crystal-set that Albert had fixed for them, once Christmas dinner was over the time dragged and Becky found herself longing for a knock on the door, but none came. As Boxing Day drew to a close she looked forward to opening the shop in the morning and all the bustle of a working day.

★ ★ ★

One evening a few weeks into the New Year Dora was doing the books when suddenly she snapped the ledger shut and rested her head on her hands. Becky, coming into the kitchen after sawdusting the shop floor, gazed at her mother in alarm, crying, 'Are you all right, Mama?'

'Just a headache, Becky,' Dora told her, raising her head. 'Make a cup of tea, love, so's I can take a couple of aspirin.'

She seemed to have vague aches all over her body and it had come on quite suddenly: she'd been as right as rain a couple of hours ago, serving in the shop. As soon as Dora had taken the tablets and drunk the tea Becky brought she went up to bed, promising herself an early start on the ledger in the morning.

A worried Becky filled the stone hot water bottle and took it up, then went downstairs to wash the cups and damp the fire down for the night. Creeping into the front bedroom on her way to bed, she found her mother tossing and turning, her cheeks and forehead hot and dry to the touch even though the room was freezing. Tucking the bedclothes around her mam once more, Becky went down for coal scuttle, sticks and paper, wishing she'd thought to light a fire in the bedroom earlier; they never indulged themselves in this luxury unless one of them was really ill.

Watching orange flames lick around the shiny black coals she told herself she ought to send for Dr Powell even though she knew her mother wouldn't approve. But how could she leave the house to fetch him from his surgery in Newport Road? Glancing at the clock, she saw it was a quarter to twelve. Better wait 'til morning, Becky told herself, going downstairs to wash her hands. Upstairs once more she drew the basket chair to the side of the bed and began her long vigil.

Presently, remembering what had been done for her when her temperature was high, Becky went down to fetch a bowl of cold water and a flannel and bathed her mother's face. Dora briefly opened her eyes which now seemed bright with fever.

Becky must have dozed off. Waking stiff and cold, she went over to replenish the fire then to the window, willing the dawn to come, but it was still dark, only the gas-lamp spilling golden light over the damp pavements. Becky longed for it to be morning so that she could get someone to stay here while she ran for the doctor. Her mother began tossing and turning again, moaning in her sleep, her skin burning to the touch. Becky hurried downstairs for more cold water.

At last light filtered through the curtains and she rose thankfully. Seeing there was no change in the patient she wondered who she could approach to sit here while she went for the doctor. From the parlour window she could see Mrs Coleman scrubbing her step.

As Becky told her about her mam, Mavis came out to join them, hair still in curling pins.

'I'll go for him, Becky, won't be a tick,' she offered, rushing back into the house. Her mother said, 'You leave it to Mavis, love. She's a good girl, help anyone she will.'

Remembering Enid Brown's spiteful remarks about the girl all those years ago, Becky thought how wrong the woman had been. Mavis may be pert and pretty but she had a good heart — which was more than could be said of Enid Brown!

When Mavis came back and was mounting her bike to go to work, Becky thanked her gratefully. They'd find the money somehow, and anyway dear old Dr Powell always gave his patients plenty of time to pay.

He arrived about twenty minutes later and was upstairs a very long time. Becky had opened the shop and was serving a customer, straining her ears for his footsteps on the stairs. When Dr Powell did come down she rushed to meet him. He stood by the door leading to the shop and told her gravely: 'It's influenza, Becky. We must get her temperature down. Is there someone who will come to the surgery for the medicine?'

'Our Tommy will be home from school

when I get back, *cariad*, he'll go for you.'
Becky hadn't noticed Laura's mam waiting to
be served.

The days that followed were an endless
round of work and worry. The wild rose
colour soon faded from Becky's cheeks as she
coped with the shop and an invalid who,
though slowly getting better, was still too
weak to get up. The bitter cold weather
continued and a fire had to be kept going in
the bedroom night and day. Most of the
customers were patient and understanding as
they waited to be served. Then Mavis came to
offer help in any way she could and Becky
was grateful.

Willing and cheerful as she was, Mavis
didn't know the prices or where things were
kept, but she proved herself a quick learner
and soon Becky could see to her mam's needs
with an easy mind. With Albert also coming
in morning and evening to ask if there was
anything he could do, it should have been
easy but, not wanting to become too indebted
to him, Becky would say they were managing
even though it meant her getting up extra
early to sawdust the shop floor and do other
necessary jobs.

She had sat up with her mother each night
until the fever broke and Dora began to
perspire. Becky had to light the copper in the

wash-house in the middle of the night to wash the sweat-soaked nightdresses and sheets for there was little time during the day.

Why can't I be sensible and accept Albert's offer of help? she thought a few mornings later, knowing a sack of rice was needed from the cellar and also one of split peas. The side of bacon would have to be brought down from its hook in the ceiling too; she also needed it cut and boned. It had been a struggle even with two of them and she'd always left the boning to her mam.

Next morning, as soon as she'd unbolted the shop door ready for the baker to deliver, she went down the cellar to see if she could somehow drag the sacks up, grunting and groaning as she got the sack of rice as far as the first stair.

'Hang on, Becky!' Albert's worried voice came from somewhere above her and next moment he was by her side. Effortlessly lifting the sack, he took it up and put it under the counter with her panting along behind.

'Am I glad to see you, Albert!' she said gratefully.

'Why didn't you ask me to do it? You know I'll help out anytime. Anything else you want done?'

'There's a side of bacon we want down,' she told him, 'and a sack of split peas . . . '

'Shall I bone the bacon and get it ready for you?'

Becky's only answer was a grateful smile.

Now every morning Albert arrived, often before she'd even unlocked the door. He'd work tirelessly: filling fixtures, laying sawdust if she'd not had time to do it the night before, sometimes weighing sugar and fruit and packing it before he left for the Maypole grocery stores to start his own day's work. In the evenings he'd call in to see if anything else was needed from the cellar. By now, thankfully, her mam was on the mend and lay on the sofa downstairs. Mama always had got on well with Albert when he'd worked for them. Now they chatted easily over the tea Becky brought them.

A few evenings later she answered the door and, as Albert followed her along the passage, he told her excitedly that he'd just been made first hand on the provision counter at the Maypole.

'That's wonderful, Albert,' Becky told him. 'Your mam will be pleased.' But his look left her in no doubt that it was her approval he was looking for.

'Get a bottle of elderberry wine, Becky,'

her mother told her. 'This calls for a celebration.'

Albert was wearing a neat dark suit, white shirt and dark tie. He looks quite smart these days, she thought. His face became bright with colour at her scrutiny. Then, rubbing his hands together nervously, he said, 'I was wondering if you'd come to the pictures with me to celebrate, Becky? When your mam is well enough, of course.'

Before she could think up an excuse, Dora said, 'I'm feeling much better now. I'm sure Becky would enjoy a night out — she certainly deserves one.'

How could she refuse now? Becky asked herself. Especially after all he'd done for them.

'Next Wednesday be all right?' Albert asked hopefully, and when she nodded, 'I'll call for you about half-past five then.'

It's only to celebrate his promotion, Becky told herself as she saw him to the door. If he reads anything more into it that's his look out.

Next morning when Dr Powell called for the last time he said as Becky saw him out, 'Your mother will have to take a lot of care from now on, Rebecca. This illness has weakened her heart. She shouldn't be going back to work at all, really, and she must rest whenever she's tired. Can I rely on you to see that she takes things easy?'

Becky promised, knowing that without Albert's help there was no hope of being able to keep her word.

9

Much to Becky's surprise she really enjoyed the evening with Albert. Having known each other since they were toddlers they talked easily about the past and about Albert's future prospects, a subject dear to his heart. Since his time as errand boy many had come and gone, none having his tenacity or skill with the heavy shop bike and its unwieldy load. One of them, small and skinny, swore he could manage the bike but took so long delivering they were puzzled until they discovered 'managing' it meant pushing it along — and even then it had overbalanced twice, smashing two dozen eggs and several pots of jam.

When they were settled in their seats and watching the film, any fears Becky had had about their sitting close together in the darkness proved unfounded. There was no fumbling for her hand, no arm creeping about her shoulder. Their eyes on the screen, munching the liquorice allsorts Albert had bought, Becky at least was soon engrossed in the story of the poor unwanted children that pretty and lovable Mary Pickford was trying to rescue from awful Farmer Grimes. When, later in the film, the desperate children were forced to crawl along the rotten bough of a tree overhanging a stream, which seemed to be full of open-jawed reptiles, it was a nail-biting moment. As the tension mounted she was there with them, sharing their fear in an agony of suspense. As the poor little souls' fate hung in the balance, it was all Becky could do to stop herself from gripping Albert's arm. Instead she closed her eyes, opening them at last when an audible sigh of relief escaped from the audience. The pianist, who seemed to be able to mirror any mood, turned from tempestuous to gentler music as befitted the happy ending.

Glancing at Albert as the credits of *Sparrows* came up on the screen, Becky found herself thinking what a kind face he had — the nose a little too large, true, the mouth perhaps too wide. But, she told herself, it was definitely the face of a man one could rely on. Then she gave herself a little shake for what could it matter to her? She wasn't interested in Albert or any other man for that matter, except perhaps Roy — and she had no right to be interested in him. Surely when Laura and Roy married in a couple of months' time her heart would stop beating fast every time she thought of him?

She'd probably end up an old maid, she thought sadly. There'd be plenty of those in the future with so many sweethearts not returning from the war.

As soon as they'd reached the shop and Becky had turned the key in the side door, Albert said worriedly, 'I won't come in tonight, Becky. I've left Mam on her own too long as it is. See you both in the morning.' Then he was striding back along Paul Street, the steel tips on his boots ringing in the silence, turning to wave to her when he reached the pool of light shed by the lamp nearest his front door.

'I thought Albert would have come in with you, Becky.' Her mother was obviously disappointed to see he had not.

'Worried about his mam, he was,' Becky told her, and Dora nodded, saying, 'Not many sons as kind and thoughtful as he is.' Becky couldn't help feeling her mam was implying what a good, thoughtful husband he'd make for her.

Albert hadn't said anything about their going out again and although Becky was relieved about this, she was also a little piqued. But, the next morning, as soon as she'd opened the door to let him in, he said, 'Is it all right for you to come to the pictures again next Wednesday, Becky?'

Her mother called, 'Don't worry about me, love, I'll be fine on my own.'

So she nodded her head and, smiling at her, Albert said, 'Pick you up at half-past five, if that's all right with you?'

She couldn't have said no if she'd wanted to, though Becky was surprised to find that she didn't. He was already lifting the heavy side of bacon from its hook, preparing to bone it for them before he went to work. Anyway she had to be honest: she'd really enjoyed last night, especially after being shut up in the house and shop for so long.

Soon it was taken for granted that Albert would take Becky to the pictures on their mutual half-day, and nowadays he would tuck her arm in his and she wouldn't pull it away. She couldn't hurt his feelings after all he'd done for her and her mam. It was the same when, coming back to the street one Wednesday, he said, 'Mam asked me to bring you in for a cup of tea, Becky. She says she hasn't seen you since you were at school and used to walk down the street with Laura Evans.'

Becky followed him through the door with some trepidation. Had Mrs Lloyd too read more into their going out together than there was? Becky knew that some of the customers already considered them a couple.

Following Albert along a passage that smelled strongly of lavender polish, the gas-jet in its pretty shade casting a warm glow over the gleaming oil-cloth, soft rugs matching the strip of carpet that covered the centre of the stairs, Becky wondered who kept it like this. With Mrs Lloyd practically an invalid the answer, of course, was Albert. Was there anything he couldn't turn his hand to?

They were stepping down into the kitchen now and the first thing Becky noticed was a table covered by a white damask cloth laid with colourful china, a plate of daintily cut sandwiches and one of scones. Then, with a crackle of her starched apron, Mrs Lloyd rose from her chair, saying, 'So this is your young lady, Albie. I'm delighted to meet you again, Becky.'

Filled with consternation the girl swallowed hard. It was all she could do to keep the smile on her face. Albert's young lady! Wherever had Mrs Lloyd got that idea? Glancing at him, expecting him to demur, she found him worried only for his mother, admonishing her for all she'd done, saying, 'You should have left laying the table to me.'

Nellie Lloyd was a neat little woman, her brown hair streaked with grey and drawn back into a bun. Her blue eyes behind strong spectacles looked enormous; her face plump and unlined.

As Albert poured the tea and handed around sandwiches and scones, Becky fumed inwardly about his mother's remark. Becky wasn't anyone's young lady, not as yet. She'd have to put Albert straight on that point. His mother talked almost non-stop. First about how times had changed since she was a girl, and then about what a wonderful son she had.

He changed the subject to talk about the shop and Becky wondered how soon she could leave without seeming rude. Mama would be expecting her home by now. She'd eaten a sandwich and a scone and Albert was refilling her cup. When she refused another sandwich, Mrs Lloyd complained: 'But it'll all go to waste! Come on, girl, I'm sure you can manage another.'

Having eaten another, she appealed to Albert, saying, 'I'll have to go. Mama doesn't know where I am.'

Struggling into his jacket, he said, 'Leave those dishes, Mam. I'll be back in a second.'

As they said goodbye Mrs Lloyd hugged Becky possessively, and she was even more perturbed when, after seeing her to her door, Albert pecked her cheek. He'd given her no chance to say anything for, even as she turned the key in the lock, he was already halfway down the street again.

Dora's face wore a worried look as Becky went into the room, but when her daughter told her where she'd been, Dora seemed pleased, saying, 'Nellie Lloyd's lucky to have Albert, especially now her health isn't so good. A tower of strength that boy is. You're a very lucky girl, Becky.'

And she realised with dismay that her mother too thought they were courting. Dora's next remark further convinced her that she had marriage on her mind. 'Laura and Roy will be getting married soon, won't they, Becky? We must think what to get them for a present. Does Laura know you're going out with Albert, love?'

★　★　★

Polly Evans's face wore a deep frown as she washed the dishes and put them away, for she also had marriage on her mind. Laura hadn't said exactly when the wedding was to be and Polly hadn't asked for, much as she loved Laura and wanted to give her a good send off, how were they to do it with no money and two weeks' groceries owing at the shop? Roy was a nice boy but it was the bride's parents who were expected to pay for the little reception when they came back from the church. She couldn't ask Bert, it would only worry him further. Polly watched him, sitting in his armchair fiddling with an empty cigarette packet, until at last Tommy came in from tidying the garden.

'Get me ten Woodbines from Morgan's, will you, Tommy?' Bert held out the coins and the boy snatched them and made for the door without a word.

'Tommy!' Polly's voice was high with indignation. 'Come back here this minute and tell youer dada you're sorry.'

Turning sullenly in the doorway, he mumbled, 'Sorry,' and was gone.

As they so often did these days, Bert's eyes filled with tears. He longed desperately for the bond of friendship and understanding that should exist between father and son, but at thirteen Tommy was as distant from him as he'd been when Bert had first come home.

'He'll come round, love,' Polly told him, resting her cheek against his bristly one, but she knew that the assurance, uttered so many times over the past few years, now totally lacked conviction.

Bert is slowly getting better, she told herself. And yet now that he'd become more aware of the problems all around him and spent less time shut away with his own sombre thoughts, there seemed to be a new depth to his despair, a despondency easily triggered by Polly's endless struggle to make ends meet or Tommy's seeming indifference. The feeling of inadequacy, of helplessness to improve their lot, and guilt that he had survived, however precariously, while others had died, obviously weighed heavily on his mind.

'It's a lovely day, Bert,' his wife told him now. 'Why don't you sit in the garden? It would do you the world of good.'

'For God's sake, Polly, give it a rest.' He turned on her angrily. 'It's always 'Why don't you do this, Bert?' 'Why don't you do that?' Bloody sick of it I am!'

Used to these outbursts she put her arms affectionately about him once more, saying coaxingly, 'Loved the garden you did in the old days, Bert.'

Then she sighed, for despite young Tommy's occasional efforts, it was a wilderness now. Couch grass and weeds were everywhere. Before there had been neat rows of vegetables in the tilled black earth, and tender green runner beens and peas climbing to the tops of sticks, just waiting to be picked. There'd been flowers in the borders too, and she'd always kept vases of whatever was in bloom, one on the window sill and one on the table. She had long since given up such niceties.

Bert had been staring in front of him, thinking along much the same lines. He couldn't bear the sight of the garden that had once been his pride and joy, but hadn't the strength or interest any more to try to put it to rights.

Polly was still thinking nostalgically of those days before the war with Bert coming home to his meal, itching to get to work on the garden afterwards. Every now and then he'd rest on his spade to natter with Jessie's husband over the wall. Ted hadn't come back from France, leaving poor Jessie a widow at thirty-six with two children to bring up alone. They'd been wonderful neighbours — Jessie still was — and in those seemingly halcyon days before the war, Polly could never once remember Bert losing his temper, not as he did now.

'All part of his illness,' Dr Powell had told her. 'He feels frustrated, useless, blames himself for everything.' But his words hadn't made Bert's behaviour any easier to bear.

With Laura and Sally both out in service now there was always so much to do. Polly's knees ached from scrubbing the bedroom floors this morning, then all down the stairs and the passage. The oil-cloth in their bedroom was cracked and split where the castors of the bed had sunk into it. The strip that covered the centre of the stairs was badly cracked too and the brown varnish peeling at the sides. Bert had been so handy once: painting and decorating, putting up shelves, varnishing the doors and the sides of the stairs whenever they needed it. She'd been so houseproud then. But now, with him moping about all day, she had to wait her moment to beat the long strips of coconut matting on the line or scrub the kitchen tiles.

Tears of frustration filled Polly's eyes as she heaved the heavy basket of washing nearer the table on which an old grey blanket was laid ready for the ironing. She sighed as she picked up the holder with which to lift the hot flat-iron from the stove.

Thinking of Laura and Roy and the deep love they had for each other, she felt a glow of pleasure. And Roy was good for Bert, chatting easily with him, bringing him out of his shell. Polly prayed with all her heart there wouldn't be any more terrible wars to spoil their young lives, as the last one had hers and Bert's and countless others.

★　★　★

When five minutes later Tommy came back with the Woodbines, he murmured, eyes downcast, ''Ere's your fags, Dad, an' I'm sorry about just now.'

'Thank you, lad.' There were tears slowly coursing down his father's cheeks. Seeing them, Tommy turned abruptly and made for the door. He clattered up the stairs and, still wearing his boots, flung himself on to the bed. With his hands behind his head, he stared at the ceiling. He'd wanted to be friends with Dada; his nan had said they should be, last time they'd met. 'He needs you, Tommy,' she'd told him. 'Your dad's been through an awful lot. Make the effort, son.'

And he had. Then his father had cried, tears running down his face like a silly girl. Tommy had felt really embarrassed, and had to get away. *He* hadn't cried for ages. Grown men weren't supposed to cry, were they? Now, as his own bottom lip started to tremble, he clamped his teeth down determinedly and clattered back down the stairs and out into the street.

★　★　★

'Drat it!' Polly cried as she heard the door slam. She'd wanted him to do a few jobs

93

before it got too dark. Stringing some pieces of newspaper for the lavatory was one of them, and filling the two galvanised buckets that stood outside the WC, ready to flush the paper down. The girls had always done these jobs without being told. Oh, well! Dark or not, he'd have to do them when he came in. They needed a new candle in the brass holder that Bert had fixed to the lavatory wall before the war; the wax had run down and dripped over one side of the seat. Oh, and she needed some sticks chopped ready for the morning . . .

She could have asked Bert but his hands still trembled so she daren't let him do it. Looking out of the window at a pale half-moon set in a darkening sky, she hoped Tommy wasn't going to be long.

10

The kitchen was bathed in warm spring sunshine but Polly's face was sad as she scrubbed the tiles and put the mats down. Would Laura want to discuss her wedding plans when she came today? And how was her mother to tell her they wouldn't be able to afford much of a reception when Roy's mam and his auntie would be guests at the house? And that was another worry too, for everything in the place looked so shabby and worn . . .

Laura had saved for ages for her wedding outfit and bottom drawer, and that was as much as she could manage on a house maid's small wage. Polly would have loved to see her daughter walking down the aisle on her father's arm, wearing a long white wedding dress and orange blossom in her hair. But Laura had thought it better to buy a soft blue marocain dress trimmed with georgette, something she could wear afterwards. Oh, if only she could talk to Bert about her worries, Polly thought, but he was always so depressed and quick to blame himself for all their troubles.

It was Thursday afternoon and Laura should be here soon. Polly had made a cake on a plate in the oven at the side of the range. It cooked all right if you kept the coals glowing and turned the plate every now and then. Her mind went back to the worry that had haunted her ever since Laura had told her she was to be married in the spring.

How many would they invite back to the house? There'd be Roy's mam, who was a widow, his aunt, Mrs Coles, and of course Dottie. There was another new kitchen maid too . . . surely Laura wouldn't want to invite her? Then there was her own mam from Barry, and at least one of her sisters who lived near enough to come. And of course Becky Morgan — she and Laura had always been the best of friends, and Roy's friend Derek who was to be best man, and his fiancée. The list seemed to grow longer every time she counted. How was she going to manage? She'd have to ask Dora Morgan for yet more credit. Polly felt cold at the thought. And she couldn't get everything she'd need at the corner shop; there'd have to be a large piece of beef to cut up cold and the butcher would want ready cash for that.

Hearing her daughter calling as she let herself into the house, Polly hurried into the kitchen just as Laura was kissing her father's cheek, asking sympathetically, 'How are you feeling today, Dada?' Turning to her mother she said, 'Sorry I'm late, Mam. I had some shopping to do in Clifton Street. Just a few odds and ends for our room. I'll go and put them in there now.' And she took from her shopping bag several parcels containing towels and tea-towels and a pair of wooden picture frames.

It was the usual thing in the streets around for the first daughter to marry to live in rooms with her mam. Laura and Roy were to have the two middle rooms here until they could find a place of their own. The young couple had wanted their own furniture; they'd gone together to choose the dark oak bedroom and dining suites and had ordered oil-cloth and new rugs for the floor. Polly was looking forward to having Laura home with her again, but the girl was still going to help out part-time at the house until a new house maid was engaged.

Polly made them a pot of tea and put the freshly baked cake on to the table but Laura seemed ill at ease. As soon as the tea things were cleared she took the heavy tray to the wash-house, motioning her mam to follow.

Putting the tray down on the bench she said, 'Mrs Coles has offered to have the reception at the house, Mam. I mean — ' she lowered her voice but Bert wasn't deaf, was he, and the kitchen door was ajar ' — Dada can't stand any noise, can he? And Miss Sophie is quite willing for Cook to do it. Oh — I'll have to get used to calling her Auntie, like Roy.' She laughed nervously before going on, 'There's so many we have to ask besides the family. There's Becky and Albert, Derek and Janet, Enid the new kitchen maid — she'll be helping anyway.

'I'll have to go soon, Mam, I'm meeting Roy in town. You are pleased, aren't you? You and Dada will be able to relax and enjoy it all.'

Smiling at Laura, Polly sighed with relief, saying, 'I'm more than grateful, love. Been worrying for months I have about how I could give you the send off you deserve.' Then, as a thought came to her, the smile left her face and she asked anxiously, 'You didn't tell Mrs Coles we couldn't afford to have it here, did you?'

'Of course not, Mam. And even if you could, I don't think Dada could stand all the upheaval. He seems a lot better though, doesn't he?'

Polly nodded, too grateful to admit that with his growing awareness of what went on around him, Bert's temper hadn't improved. He was a worried man these days, his thoughts no longer solely of the past, knowing the problems they faced but acutely aware of his own inability to cope with them. He was so prickly and quick to blame himself, she hoped and prayed he hadn't overheard any of their conversation. Oh, if only they'd closed the kitchen door!

As soon as they entered the kitchen Polly knew that Bert had indeed overheard. His face wore that hurt expression it so often did these days. Apparently unaware of this, Laura was fondly kissing her father goodbye. Polly followed her to the door, watching her daughter in the spotted mirror of the hall-stand as she pulled the little felt hat over her bobbed hair, admiring the creamy skin and wide grey eyes under their silky brows. She kissed Laura and watched her walk up the street, knowing she must go back into the kitchen and face Bert's anger.

No sooner had the front door closed behind her than he said, in a voice filled with bitterness, 'It's always my fault, isn't it? Does she think I'll make a fool of myself or something?'

'You know it isn't that, Bert. Laura thinks it might be too much for you, with people tramping all over the house. Anyway, I think the real reason is because she knows we can't afford the expense.'

'That's my fault too, isn't it?' His voice was loud with anger now. 'My God, Polly, what's it coming to when our daughter can't leave for the church from her own home?'

'It was good of Roy's aunt to offer, and you'll still walk her down the aisle. Then, after the wedding, we'll all go back to the big house where she works. Wasn't it kind of that Miss Sophie to allow his auntie to do it?'

The slam of the kitchen door was her only answer, and she sighed, knowing Bert was deeply hurt. As she heard him stumping up the stairs, Polly went into the wash-house where she gripped the edge of the shallow brown-stone sink, closing her eyes against the burning unshed tears. Why couldn't Bert see the good in things and be thankful when someone tried to help? It hurt his pride, of course, when others offered to do the things he felt he should be doing himself. Well, her own pride had been battered to the ground long ago. No one knew how it hurt her every time she had to beg Dora Morgan for more credit, or tell the landlord she'd be late with the rent this week. No one knew what it cost her to go into a pawn-shop. But when those you loved depended on you, pride went out of the window.

Suddenly the colour drained from Polly's thin cheeks as a new thought came to mind:

what exactly were they going to wear? Thinking of the contents of her own scant wardrobe she rejected the two black skirts, rusty now with age, and the faded blouses washed to a frazzle. The hat she'd bought for Bert's homecoming was kept in a box on top of the wardrobe. It wasn't the sort you'd put on with a shawl, so that should be all right. Perhaps Jessie could loan her something else? Despite her worries, the thought made her smile. Her neighbour was short and plump while Polly was lean as a bean-pole. Anything of Jessie's would fit where it touched.

Bert's good suit from before the war hung on him like a scarecrow's, and the half-a-dozen moth balls she'd put in the pockets hadn't saved it either. At fourteen, much to his disgust, Tommy was still in short trousers. They grew shorter and shorter though once they'd come to his knees. Then Polly gave a sigh of relief. Laura and Roy would be paying her half-a-crown a week for the rooms; she had hoped to pay off her debt at the corner shop with that. Instead it could go towards a clothing club. There was nothing else for it, they couldn't let Laura down. Only last week Mrs Brown had asked her about taking one on. A shilling in the pound interest you had to pay, but when you'd paid that and the first week's money, you got the club right away.

The problem solved, Polly pushed any regrets she had about spending the money this way to the back of her mind and, deciding she'd take Bert up a cup of tea, put the heavy iron kettle over the glowing coals and set out the cups, wondering how she was to break the news that they would all need new clothes for the wedding and the way she intended to get them.

★　★　★

As she turned the corner of the street, Laura's heart was troubled. She'd seen her mother's anxious eyes, noticed with a sinking heart her father's hurt expression, had felt the stiffening of his face as she'd kissed him goodbye. He must have heard every word, and it was all her fault. Laura sighed. Planning your wedding should be such a happy time, not one fraught with worry and anxieties.

She was remembering how upset Roy had been when she wouldn't agree to a firm date. She'd had to tell him then her fears about the cost of the reception, and about her father's health.

'I thought you might be going off the idea,' he had told her, making a joke of it. She'd gone into his arms then and they'd kissed passionately, all the deep longing in their hearts laid bare. When at last they'd breathlessly drawn apart, they'd known the wedding would have to be soon.

11

The wedding was to be the first Monday in May. The banns were called for the second time on Sunday, and plans for the reception were going ahead. Laura had asked Sally, Becky and Dottie to be bridesmaids. Then Sally sent a tearful letter saying she couldn't get time off. 'Your wedding's on the same day as Mrs Hamilton's Golden Wedding do,' she wrote. 'No one can take time off that day.' With the banns being called it was too late to change the date and Laura was deeply disappointed. She saw so little of her sister these days, with their having different half-days.

Becky had asked if she could wear the pale green frock she'd had for her eighteenth birthday, saying she'd only ever worn it once. Remembering the lovely dress, Laura had readily agreed. Dottie too had insisted on choosing her own though both Laura and Cook had doubts about that.

'Wish it was a proper wedding,' Dottie grumbled. 'You know, with long satin dresses and us holding your train.'

'It will be a proper wedding,' Laura told

her indignantly, 'and you can still have a pretty dress so long as it's the right length.' But even as she said it her heart filled with misgiving. They're going to look like Mutt and Jeff, she told herself, especially if Dottie chooses something frilly. Becky was as slim and pretty as ever, and the pale green was a perfect choice with her wild rose colouring and curling auburn hair.

On her next half-day Dottie came back with her purchases, her face wearing a satisfied smile. But as she drew the pink chiffon creation from its tissue paper wrappings and held it against her ample form, Laura and Cook gasped with dismay. The top that ended in a dropped waistline was quite plain but the skirt was formed of several layers of chiffon 'petals' over a silk underskirt. Ignoring their reaction, and Laura's remark that it was really an evening gown, Dottie took off her blouse and skirt and slipped the dress over her head. For once she was spotlessly clean, Cook having insisted on a bath and a change of clothes before her shopping expedition.

'Lovely, innit?' Dottie's face was wreathed in smiles as she twirled around, sending the chiffon skirts flying.

'You can't wear that,' Cook objected.

'Why not?'

'It's an evening frock like Laura said, and a fussy one at that. Don't cry, Dottie, we can change it. I'll come with you after lunch.'

'Don't want to change it,' she said stubbornly. Then her eyes lit up as she added triumphantly, 'Can't change it anyway. I bought it in a sale.'

'You've got the receipt?' Cook searched the tissue paper. 'Here it is. We'll go as soon as lunch is over, if Laura will help Enid wash up and prepare the veg for dinner?'

'Of course I will,' Laura told her gratefully, giggling as she thought that in that dress Dottie would have made a very good pantomime fairy, if only she'd had wings and a wand too.

All this time Enid had been staring at Dottie open-mouthed. She was a sparrow of a girl, with long dark brown hair and bright brown eyes that at this moment were wide with surprise. Laura had shared a bedroom with her ever since she'd arrived. They worked well together, getting everything in the kitchen ready long before Cook and Dottie returned.

When they came in Dottie's face wore a sullen expression which deepened as her new dress was brought out for them to admire. It was straight cut and low-waisted, the skirt falling in pleats to below the knee. Again it was a deep pink. Dottie, it seemed, was fond of the colour. But this was at least a sensible dress. Laura gave a sigh of relief.

'Try it on, *cariad*,' Cook was telling the girl, and this time there was a general murmur of approval, for it flattered Dottie's lumpy figure. When she'd put on the new shoes Cook had also helped her choose, the heel giving her a little more height, everyone agreed she looked very nice.

'I'm going to treat her to a Marcel wave for the wedding,' Cook told them now, and Dottie's face, which had lost its sullen look at their obvious approval, now broke into a happy smile.

Roy's Auntie Vi had looked after Dottie ever since she'd arrived from the children's home. Roy had told Laura ages ago that his aunt had lost her fiancé in the war and vowed she'd never marry. 'My mam used to say it was a pity because Violet loved children and would have made a wonderful mam. Look how she's taken that girl under her wing. I suppose it's because she hasn't any family of her own.'

Laura knew she was going to miss Cook, Dottie and Enid when she finally left.

Preparations for the wedding seemed to be falling into place though Laura still had one worry. It had come to her as soon as she'd left home on her half-day. However was Mama to buy new clothes for them all? She'd been saved the anxiety of the reception but would surely be worried about what they would wear.

*   *   *

Polly stared down at the clothing club that Mrs Brown had put into her hands. Ever since she'd asked for it she'd been troubled over what she'd done, but vowed now that nothing was going to spoil the pleasure of spending it. When she'd told Bert of her plan, he'd sulked and hadn't spoken to her for hours, yet in the end he'd had to admit there was no other way. She'd taken money out of the rent to pay the poundage and first week. Next weekend, thank God, Laura and Roy would be paying in their half-a-crown.

If only our Tommy could stay in short pants for a while, she thought. Lots of boys wore them until they were fifteen, but Tommy was tall for his age and the ones he was wearing were ridiculously short. He was so envious of his friends who wore long ones, handed down from elder brothers. But short pants and a jacket were bound to be cheaper than long . . .

She'd measured Tommy carefully, and a

protesting Bert too who'd insisted there was nothing wrong with his suit upstairs. Feeling a flutter of excitement, Polly put on a freshly ironed blouse and donned the better of her two skirts, searching the wardrobe for a thick grey hip-length woollen jacket that had once been her pride and joy but was now a little moth-eaten, knowing she couldn't wear her best hat if she was to put on her shawl. Opening the door and seeing it was raining, she fetched the large black umbrella that was Bert's but served them all.

As she walked along Broadway under the shop awnings, avoiding the puddles for fear of splashing her skirt, a watery sun shone fitfully through the clouds and the rain began to ease. But the wind, as strong as ever, billowed her skirts, lifting the canvas overhead and tossing it up and down to shower passers by with the rain upon it.

Once in Clifton Street she made straight for the gents' outfitter's, and not seeing anything she wanted in the crowded window, stepped inside, setting the bell jangling. At once an elderly man came out from behind the counter, his own shiny suit hardly an advertisement for his wares. Rubbing his hands together, he enquired, 'How may I help you, Madam?'

Polly wanted to giggle but there was serious shopping to be done. She handed him Tommy's measurements and told him she required a suit.

'Was this what you wanted, Madam?' He laid a dark grey flannel jacket and long trousers on the counter and looked at her enquiringly. It was what Polly wanted, but what about the price?

'Eight shillings and sixpence,' she was told. The trousers were a little too long but Tommy was a growing boy; she could take them up and lengthen them when required. Soon a white shirt, blue tie and pair of grey socks lay on top of the suit. Perhaps Tommy could manage with the boots he had? She'd have to see if there was anything over when the shopping was done.

Despite her careful measuring the assistant was of the opinion that it would be much better for Bert to try things on approval, so Polly chose a navy blue pinstripe suit, adding a white shirt, a tie and pair of socks, and taking them with her.

As soon as she reached Goldberg's Emporium and gazed into the window, the pleasurable anticipation with which she'd waited for this moment disappeared for her petticoats would be far too long for her to try on any of the dresses on show. The last time

110

she'd bought anything for herself was in 1922 and then skirts had been longer. Anyway Polly couldn't see herself in any of the frocks on display, with their bodices to the hip and skirts to just below the knee. Perhaps these are just for young people? she thought hopefully.

As she entered the shop, walking slowly towards the steep wooden stairs, she looked about her with interest, at the narrow aisles between the departments, glass-fronted display cabinets beneath the dark wood counters, the assistants bustling about in their green shop dresses ... None of them was long, she noticed with dismay, and one of the women had been grey-haired. Several customers sat on bentwood chairs examining the merchandise, others waited their turn. But now, aware of a shop-walker coming towards her, she quickened her step towards the stairs, and seeing her intention he turned away.

Polly stopped when she reached the top to look over the banisters at the scene below, finding herself staring down on the lingerie counter at the displays of lace-trimmed celanese petticoats and scanty silk knickers, the like of which she'd never seen before. Even the corsets displayed on headless models seemed light and dainty; from the front anyway there wasn't a whalebone in sight.

One of the assistants caught her eye and smiled up at her as she screwed the little wooden cup containing money and bill into the overhead carrier and sent it whizzing along the wire to the cash-desk.

The lady in the fashion department gave Polly a long look when she asked if they had something a little more matronly than the frocks in the window.

'But Madam isn't old,' she answered with a smile. 'I'm sure the shorter length would suit beautifully.'

No, she wasn't old, Polly told herself. She'd be thirty-eight next birthday, but she'd never shown her legs and wouldn't feel comfortable about doing so now.

'Would Madam care to try something on?'

Polly looked at her hopefully, asking, 'Is there something a little longer than that?'

The assistant glanced down at the garment over her arm and shook her head, saying, 'We cleared all the old stock in a sale a few years ago.'

The dress she held out was a dark blue in fine wool with a neat collar and paler blue crêpe-de-chine bow. The bodice was belted at the hip, and the long sleeves meant Polly wouldn't need a coat.

'It's a bargain, been reduced because it's last year's model. Why not try it on?'

'I can't,' she admitted at last. 'My petticoat's too long.'

'Well, that's easily overcome!' And the assistant went over to a dummy covered by a dust sheet. Removing a silky petticoat, she handed it to Polly then led her towards a cubicle, telling her before she drew the curtains, 'I'll see what else we've got.'

A few minutes later, eyeing herself in the mirror, Polly thought the flimsy petticoat a poor substitute for her starched cambric one, and the dress, although it fitted perfectly, looked ridiculous worn with black lisle stockings and boots.

The assistant came back with a garment over her arm. 'I have found something,' she told Polly. 'It was in the matrons' department over there. I'd say you're too young to wear this, but a lot of the older people are slow to change their ways.'

As she held up the frock Polly's heart leaped with hope. If the price was right, please let it fit!

'It has its own underskirt,' the assistant went on, 'and shoes will make all the difference. Still, boots are best on a day like this,' she added kindly.

'How much is it?' Polly asked anxiously.

'Twelve and six. It's been in stock for a while.'

Slipping the soft, navy wool dress over her head, Polly watched anxiously as it slid down to below the calf, then gave a sigh of relief. It was loose-fitting with a crossover bodice trimmed with a lighter colour braid.

'I've just the hat to go with it,' the assistant persuaded her. 'You need something with a small brim. That hat you're wearing won't do at all.'

If I buy it, I'll have to have shoes as well, Polly thought. She'd never worn a pair in her life though she knew the boots she wore were well out of fashion.

In the shoe department she found a pair of lace-ups that were comfortable, and bought some beige lisle stockings too. Then worried all the way home that she'd spent far too much on herself.

12

'I wish I was free to ask you to get engaged, Becky,' Albert sighed when she told him of the wedding invitation. 'I can't leave my mam to fend for herself can I? And I know how much you're needed at the shop.'

Becky agreed, knowing that she still wasn't ready to commit herself. Changing the subject she asked, 'Will you be able to get time off for the wedding?'

'No, I can't, Becky. It has to be close family for the shop to agree time off. I hardly know Laura, and I've never even met Roy.'

Becky herself had mixed feelings about going. Laura was her best friend and she was flattered at being asked to be bridesmaid, but the sight of Roy still made her heart thump and turned her legs to jelly. In vain Becky told herself it was stupid to feel this way about someone who was about to marry; that Roy hardly knew she existed except as a friend of Laura's. Why couldn't she have fallen in love with somebody else? Why couldn't she love Albert? She was fond of him, but fondness wasn't love.

Nevertheless he had opened up a whole

new world to her, taking her to the cinema every week. Now Clara Bow, Mary Pickford, Gloria Swanson, Greta Garbo, Douglas Fairbanks, Charlie Chaplin and many other famous film stars were almost as familiar to her as the customers who came into their shop. Soon, too, the talkies would come to suburban cinemas. It was an exciting thought, something she was really looking forward to.

Remembering how bored she used to be, hardly ever getting away from the shop, Becky was grateful for their friendship. But what answer would she have given if Albert had asked her to get engaged? Mama got on well with him, always had. It would suit her if later on Becky were to marry him and they were to live here on the premises. There were several empty rooms over the shop. But he had said he couldn't leave his mother and for the time being anyway Becky was thankful for that.

The day of the wedding was warm and sunny and as she dressed for it, she felt a stirring of excitement. The ceremony was to be at half-past two at St Margaret's church, and afterwards they were all to go back to the big house where Laura worked. Years ago, when she'd become a maid there, she'd described the grand rooms there to Becky. But they wouldn't be seeing those rooms today for the reception was being held in the kitchen where Mrs Coles ruled.

Hearing her mother's footsteps on the stairs, Becky opened the door and twisted this way and that in front of the long mirror that stood on the landing.

'Lovely that dress looks, Becky,' Mama said, stopping to admire her. 'You look pretty enough to be the bride.'

Then as she perched the coronet of silk flowers on her auburn curls, her mother added with a proud little smile, 'Pity Albert can't see you now, but he's sure to be here when you get home.'

When Polly Evans opened the door to her, Becky smothered a gasp of surprise. The new dress, smart little hat and shoes made Laura's mother look years younger, and there was a hint of colour in the usually pale cheeks, no doubt caused by all the excitement. Then Mr Evans came downstairs and she hardly recognised him either: clean-shaven except for a neatly clipped moustache, wearing an obviously new pinstripe suit, a stiff collar and tie. Becky hadn't seen him for years; he was still very thin and seemed ill at ease as he loosened his collar with one finger. When Tommy came into the kitchen he gave her a nervous little grin, saying as he gazed proudly down at his trousers, 'They're my first long 'uns, Becky.'

Even as she congratulated Polly on the smart outfit, Becky was thinking, I won't tell Mama they've all had new. Laura's mother still owed them two weeks at the shop. But they'd have to buy clothes for the wedding, wouldn't they? They couldn't let Laura down.

When the car arrived Bert called his wife back to whisper, urgently, 'I feel all clammy, Poll, but I've got to get through it, for Laura's sake.'

'You will, Bert, you will. You look very handsome. Real proud of you she'll be.' Then, turning to Tommy, Polly said, 'Remember youer manners, son, look after youer dada if I'm not around — and don't you stuff youerself!'

As the car drew away from the kerb, its white satin ribbons shimmering in the warm sunshine, they waved to the neighbours gathered on the pavement then sat back to enjoy the novelty of the ride.

Becky watched Laura's father clasping and unclasping his hands nervously. There's poorly he looks, she thought. This must be quite an ordeal for the poor man.

They got out of the car in front of a tall house built of grey stone. It seemed to have lots of long sash windows. When a curtain twitched aside at one of the upper ones, Becky wondered if it was the mistress, interested enough to watch what was going on. She and her sister had been very generous to Laura and Roy; Laura had told Becky about the lovely china tea service she had been given as a wedding present.

A girl who fitted the description Laura had given her of Dottie dashed out to guide them to the servants' entrance, ushering them into a tiled hall then to a large kitchen where Laura waited to leave for church. Her grey eyes were bright with excitement; a crown of flowers with a short veil attached sat becomingly on her silky brown hair. The veil was flung back, and looking at her creamy skin, smooth dark brows and gentle eyes, Becky thought in wonder: She's lovely, beautiful . . . no wonder Roy loves her so much.

But by now they were being introduced to Roy's aunt, a stout lady in a navy blue dress with a dainty lace collar, who greeted them warmly before they went on to Dottie and Enid. Dottie's face was red with excitement; her plump arms wobbled as they shook hands.

At that moment a tall, smartly dressed lady came into the room and Laura's parents were drawn forward to meet Roy's mother Celia who'd made the long journey from the north where she now lived with another sister.

When the cars arrived to take the bridesmaids and guests, a bouquet of carnations was brought from the cool of the pantry. As they were handed to Laura their scent filled the room.

'You all right, Bert?' Polly asked in an anxious whisper before following the others outside. He nodded at her, too full of emotion to speak, unable to take his eyes from Laura as she stood there in the lovely blue dress and dainty little veiled coronet.

Waiting just inside the entrance to the church for the bride and her father to arrive, Becky stood by the door and let her gaze roam over the few relatives and many friends who had come to see Laura and Roy wed. There was Laura's nan and one of her aunts, who would be coming back to the house for the wedding breakfast. There were lots of neighbours and friends on this side of the aisle, far more than on the other side, but then Roy had lived in Chepstow before coming to Cardiff to work. The pews behind him held little groups of workmates and a few close friends. His mam sat with Mrs Coles in the pew just behind Roy, dressed in a lovely outfit in periwinkle blue. Everyone had admired it when she'd come downstairs as they were waiting for the cars.

Roy sat in the front with Derek and now

Becky allowed her gaze to linger on him. Even from the back he looks handsome, she thought, then found herself picturing his face: those warm brown eyes, that firm chin . . . She closed her eyes as the familiar feeling gripped her. Weak at the knees, lips moving in silent prayer, she drew back into the shadows. Just then the strains of the organ playing the wedding march broke into her thoughts.

* * *

Back at the house the long kitchen table, draped with a white damask cloth, was laid ready, gleaming with cutlery and sparkling with glass. At its centre stood a two-tier wedding cake made by Cook herself, with standing on its iced top a miniature bride and groom. As one delicious course followed another and the wine flowed, the talk never flagged.

Becky helped with the washing up to enable Enid, who'd been waiting at table, to enjoy her meal. Coming back for more dishes, she was worried to see Laura's father, who had seemed to be taking everything in his stride, looking grey with exhaustion and holding his head. Polly swiftly made their excuses, turning to Becky to tell her to stay if she wanted for Laura and Roy would be coming back to their rooms later on.

'No, I'll come with you,' Becky decided hurriedly.

About twenty minutes later, letting herself into her own house, she heard voices coming from the living room. She was not really surprised that one of them was Albert's. What she *was* surprised about on entering the room was his obvious excitement as he went to the table and poured wine into three glasses arranged on a tray. The wine wasn't her mother's home-made either so what were they celebrating? Looking enquiringly at him, she saw the admiration in his eyes as he stared at her in the outfit she'd worn to the wedding. Then, after handing her mother a glass, he put the other one into her hand and raised his own, saying with obvious emotion, 'To us, Becky, and our future.'

Seeing her puzzled expression, Dora hastened to explain. 'Albert says his aunt is coming to stay with his mam. It means that when you decide to get married, you can live here with me.'

Taking Becky's stupefied silence for approval, Albert said, 'There's nothing to keep us apart now, Becky. We can get engaged as soon as you like, then married. And like your mam's just said, we can live here over the shop.'

The colour had drained from Becky's face. 'B-but I thought your Aunt Ruth lived in Tenby with her other sister?'

'She does, but you seemed so upset when I told you why I couldn't ask you to get engaged . . . well, I just thought I'd write and tell her how things were, especially after you were decent enough to agree that I couldn't leave my mam. Isn't it wonderful she's decided to come? Come on, Becky, drink up. You too, Mrs Morgan — or Mam. I'll have to get used to calling you that now.'

If Becky was lost for words nobody seemed to notice.

'We can go to Newport Wednesday to choose the ring — most of the shops here will be closed half-day,' Albert went on. 'I'll call for you about two o'clock.'

How was she to get out of this? Becky was thinking frantically. It was all her own fault, she'd taken it for granted that he would never leave his mam. She'd just have to tell him when she saw him to the door. She took a deep breath and emptied her glass, but when twenty minutes later, alone in the gas-lit passage, he put his arms around her, pressed his lips to hers and kept them there, she knew just how much it meant to him. All she managed was, 'I don't remember saying I'd marry you, Albert.'

He laughed as though she had made a joke, hugging her to him and saying, 'Only because I wasn't free to ask you.' Then, holding her at arm's length, he said with mock seriousness, 'Will you marry me, Miss Morgan?'

A knock on the door saved her from answering, and when she opened it a gruff voice said, 'Can I 'ave 'alf an ounce of shag and some matches, Becky?'

'Come in, Mr Phillips. Shall I put them on the bill?'

'No, love, the missus don't like me bothering you at night. I'll pay for them then there's no need for her to know.' He winked at Becky and, smiling, she went into the shop. There'd been no smile on Albert's face; it was obvious he wished the customer would go. She could hear the murmur of voices as she lingered as long as she dared. Would Albert ask again when the customer had left? But when she returned with the purchases the door was still open and he had gone.

'Said 'e'd see you in the mornin',' Mr Phillips informed her, taking the tobacco and matches and handing over the coins.

After putting the money in the till and turning off the gas-light, Becky bolted the door and went back to the kitchen. Albert had obviously thought the proposal a bit of a laugh, her answer a foregone conclusion.

She'd tell her mam how she felt, Becky decided. Surely she'd understand? Mam would probably get annoyed and say Becky must have led Albert on, but she wouldn't want her to marry someone she didn't love.

But before Becky could even step into the room she heard her mother's voice, filled with happiness, saying, 'I know you must be tired, love, but there's so much to discuss . . . It's such a relief to know you and the shop will both be safe in Albert's hands.'

'But we're both safe in your hands, Mama,' Becky said, deliberately pretending to misunderstand.

'Oh, love! I might not always be here. Without Albert's help, I don't see how we could have carried on. Since my illness I haven't had the strength to lug things around. For you two to marry and live on the premises is the answer to all my prayers! Getting engaged is the first step, then there'll be plenty of time to furnish the rooms and get everything ready for the big day.'

The words she'd wanted to say died on Becky's lips. How could she tell her mother now? If she finished with Albert, he'd probably never come to the shop again. She was fond of him after all. But was fondness enough?

13

Their first argument was just after they'd chosen the engagement ring. It was a lovely warm spring day, a taste of summer to come, and Becky was still trying to push her doubts to the back of her mind.

Last night, staring at the pattern cast on the ceiling by the lamp outside, she'd gone over and over the situation. There seemed little alternative to marrying Albert now, especially as there was no one else in prospect. As the years went by Mama and the shop would depend more and more on his help. Becky knew she wouldn't have considered an engagement if it had meant living with Albert's mam. She felt so safe at home, had never felt the urge to stray very far. Things would continue much as before, except that once they were married Albert's home would be here at the shop. Becky's thoughts shied away from the intimate side of marriage, but she knew she wanted children and she wasn't going to get them by any immaculate conception, was she?

It was at this point that Albert disturbed her thoughts with, 'Pretty, isn't it?'

They'd been sitting at a table in a cafe and he'd just slipped the ring with its cluster of diamonds on to her finger.

'It's lovely, Albert,' she told him, but he went on eagerly, 'Now we're really engaged, love, we'll add the gold band just as soon as you like. No sense in waiting now that my auntie's coming to stay with Mam.'

Alarm bells rang in Becky's head. She'd anticipated an engagement of about twelve months at least. Anyway there was so much to do. Now she said, 'There's no rush, is there, Albert? We've got to plan the wedding and furnish the rooms — '

'It won't take that long to furnish them, Becky,' he broke in. 'We can choose what we want on our next half-day. I've never spent much on myself, I've quite a bit saved.'

'But how's your mam going to manage without your money?' Becky seized on the one thing that might delay the marriage.

'Oh! But Aunt Ruth's coming to share the house with her will make up for that. Mam's got a small pension, we used to have to live on that before I went to work.' He smiled at her reassuringly.

They'd been desperately poor when Albert had been an errand boy, Becky remembered, but now he was going on. 'We don't have to wait, Becky. My aunt said she could come the week after next. She's doing it for me, will be wondering why I asked her if we don't get married soon. Why don't we choose the wedding ring today? It would save coming in for it again.'

Feeling trapped, Becky said anxiously, 'I don't want to be rushed. Getting engaged is all right but there are lots of plans to make. Mama will want us to have a church wedding, I know. She still goes regularly on a Sunday evening.'

'Well, the banns will only take three weeks,' he told her stubbornly, and glancing at his face she saw he was upset.

They'd meant to look around at furniture, but after glancing into the window of the first shop they came to Albert turned away, saying in a voice heavy with disappointment, 'There's no point now, is there? Not if I've got to write to Aunt Ruth and tell her not to come. If I mess her about, Becky, she might change her mind and not come at all.'

He looked so forlorn her heart melted and she said with forced enthusiasm, 'Let's go and choose the wedding ring. But we've still got a lot to do, Albert. Besides getting the rooms ready, there's dresses to be made, bridesmaids to choose, the invites to go out. Everything.'

'All right, say a couple of months, but I'll have to have a firm date soon so that she'll know when to come, and I want to book us a few days' honeymoon. We only get married the once. Where would you like to go, Becky? How about Weston?'

Weston-super-Mare. She'd never been there, never been anywhere really, tied as they were to the shop. Becky felt a surge of excitement at the thought of a holiday.

'Weston would be lovely, Albert.'

The wedding band in its chamois case was soon safely buttoned into Albert's inside pocket. He looked so pleased she wished she felt that way too, but in fact Becky was a little frightened at the speed of events. Two months wasn't long, was it? It wasn't nearly long enough.

When she told her mother Dora gave a little groan, saying, 'Oh, Becky! I was depending on its being sometime next year.'

'It's because of his Aunt Ruth coming to live with his mam,' Becky put in quickly. 'She must have thought Albert wanted to get married right away.'

'Sounds as if he does too,' her mother said ruefully. 'Typical of men, that is. They've no idea of all the preparations involved.'

'It could be a quiet wedding,' Becky told her. 'Look, Mam, I know there's no money to spare. Why don't we have it in a register office?'

'Register office! My only daughter? Besides, whatever would they think at the church? The thing is, Becky, I thought there was plenty of time. I've got a small endowment policy that pays out next year, but if Albert is in that much of a hurry we'll have to see what we can do.'

'It isn't fair to worry you like this,' Becky told her. 'Look, Mam, I'll tell him. He'll have to understand.'

'I can see his point, Becky. His aunt's offer must have seemed too good to be true. He's probably afraid she'll change her mind. You don't want to have to live with Mrs Lloyd, do you?'

'Oh, Mam, I couldn't! Anyway, when her sister arrives they'll be company for each other. She'll miss Albert though, won't she? But then, as he says, he'll only be a stone's throw away.'

When, a week later, the man called for the insurance premium, Becky was surprised to see her mother lift the flap and take him through to the house for she usually handed book and money over the counter. When they returned to the shop her mam whispered with a sigh, 'Well, that's done. I've cashed in that policy early. It should be enough for the wedding dress and a bit over towards the other expenses.'

'Oh, Mama! You shouldn't have. You were looking forward to having some money every ten years. Now you won't get that any more.'

'No, but I won't have payments to make either.' Her mother hurried forward to serve a customer, leaving Becky fuming. She knew just how much her mam had been looking forward to having that twenty pounds next year from the policy. She'd been planning for ages just how she'd spend it, promising them both a new coat before the expense of the wedding had loomed, and in ten years' time she would have been looking forward to receiving the same amount again.

A few weeks later the money arrived and a trip to the Canton area of Cardiff was planned for their next half-day. They'd visited Mrs Ridout the evening before and Becky had chosen a dress pattern and been advised how much satin they'd need. On the Thursday afternoon, as she watched an assistant deftly unwinding satin from the block, Becky marvelled that so many yards were required for just one dress. The material parcelled up and the veil and orange blossom chosen, there were only the bridesmaids' dresses to be bought. Laura and her sister Sally were to wear shell pink.

It's all so final, Becky thought as she watched the assistant's scissors sliding through the silvery satin and Mama handing over some of the money she'd received from cashing in her insurance policy.

The days seemed to fly past. There were fittings for her dress with Mrs Ridout on her knees, mouth full of pins. Then on their next two half-days Albert and she went to choose furniture and carpets. Dora insisted on moving out of her room and going into a smaller one at the back so that Becky and Albert could have the two big rooms at the front. They would take their meals together, it was cheaper and much more convenient with the three of them working all day.

Becky dashed upstairs whenever she could to admire the rooms. She'd worked hard with Albert in the evenings, papering and painting, and when the new flowered carpet square was laid in the bedroom and a beige one in the parlour, Becky waited excitedly for the furniture to arrive. When it did and had all been put in place, she stood there admiring the bedroom with its walnut wardrobe, dressing table with bevelled triple mirrors, chest of drawers, and the bed with its lovely gold-coloured satin eiderdown. She could hardly believe it was all theirs. Very few girls around here started with everything new. But suddenly panic seized her at the thought that she'd be sharing the bed with Albert, and she moved hurriedly next-door.

The lounge looked restful and uncluttered with its deep-buttoned leather armchairs standing to either side of the fireplace, a matching sofa facing it. There was no dining-room suite as yet; Albert had said it was better to buy a good three-piece suite, and they could save for a dining set later, especially as they were to eat in the kitchen with her mam.

It had been exciting getting the rooms decorated and furnished, and when customers slipped little presents across the counter, but the banns were being called for the last time on Sunday, the lovely wedding dress hung in the wardrobe, the veil and orange blossom in tissue paper were on the shelf above, and Becky knew the real purpose of all this was not the new furniture or the new clothes but that Albert and she should become man and wife. She realised she didn't love him as she should, but she did like and respect him and had made up her mind to make him a good wife.

When Albert's Aunt Ruth arrived Becky took to her right away. She was a bright little woman with bobbed greying hair and a friendly smile. Even Mrs Lloyd perked up to see her and Albert's face seemed to wear a perpetual smile.

The wedding day dawned warm and sunny. After a restless night telling herself that in view of Dr Powell's warning about her mam's health she had no choice but to go ahead with the marriage, Becky pushed her qualms to the back of her mind and threw herself into the preparations. The service was to be at half-past two and Dora had decided to keep open the shop until eleven. A young man called Ernie who worked with Albert was to be best man, and her Aunt Lizzie's husband, whom Becky hardly knew, was to give her away.

'Lizzie can't come, Becky,' her mother had sighed when a few weeks ago they'd received her reply to their invitation. 'Says she's too near her time. How many is that? I'm beginning to lose count! But she says Bob will be proud to take you down the aisle.'

Albert had booked them into a small private hotel in Weston called the *Mon Repos* for three nights. Becky had never stayed in any kind of hotel, never been to Weston. It had been exciting getting her things ready to put in the case, but when he came across with his clothes and she'd packed them in with hers it had brought home once more the intimacy of being a married couple.

Mrs Evans arrived with Laura and Sally; she was to put the finishing touches to the

134

table while they were at the church. The girls made a pretty picture in their long pink dresses, Laura dark-haired and Sally, who still wore her hair in long curls, so fair.

'Albert's a very lucky man,' Bob told Becky when the two of them were left alone to wait for the wedding car. It was years since she'd last seen Lizzie's husband but he was a friendly soul and soon put her at her ease.

The church was almost full with customers, neighbours and friends. Albert, eyes shining with love and admiration, looked smart in a new grey suit. Although she smiled at him, thinking how nice he was, Becky still harboured some doubts and marvelled at the way she was able to make her responses, her voice sounding so firm and sure.

As they stepped outside the church a neighbour wanted to take a photograph of the wedding party, and they had to smile over and over again as Mr Thomson stepped further and further back in a vain attempt to include them all in the view-finder of his box Brownie.

Back at home the wedding breakfast was almost over, the best man on his feet, notes in hand, when there was a knock on the side door.

'People ought to have more sense than to bother you today,' Polly said indignantly as

Dora rose to answer it. When her mam came back holding a telegram, Becky thought it might be a greetings one — but who amongst their friends and neighbours would have the money to spare? Anyway Mama was going straight to Albert's auntie, explaining, 'The boy took it to the house, Ruth, but someone told him you were over here.'

Everyone's eyes were on Ruth as she fumbled nervously with the envelope and drew out the slip of paper, her face paling as she read. Turning to her sister, she said, 'It's our Phyllis, Nellie, she's got pneumonia! I shouldn't have left her on her own. I ought to have known she wouldn't take care . . .'

Albert had sprung to his feet. Turning to Becky, he said, 'I'm sorry, love, but I'll have to take Aunt Ruth home to pack her things, then I'll go to the phone box and find out the times of the trains.'

His mother was attempting to get up from her chair and he put a hand on her shoulder, telling her, 'You stay here, Mam, until I get back.' But Nellie was having none of it. Phyllis was her sister too. Why had Albert taken Ruth away from her? He and Becky could have lived with her as she'd suggested, it would have saved him a lot of money an' all.

The coats were brought, there were hurried

goodbyes. As Becky hugged Ruth in sympathy, Albert waited impatiently at the door. Then as it closed behind them the full import of what this would mean to them drew the colour from her cheeks too. Without Aunt Ruth to help out they'd have to live with his mam.

14

'I'm really sorry about everything, Becky. While I was at the phone box I cancelled the hotel at Weston. There's no chance of our going on honeymoon now.'

Albert looked so miserable she said gently, 'It doesn't matter about Weston, Albert. Perhaps we can go later on.' But she knew it did matter, very much, and that for the foreseeable future their chances of going anywhere were slim indeed.

They'd come upstairs to their rooms over the shop — rooms they wouldn't be using now, Becky thought bitterly — to talk things over. Sitting side by side on the new leather settee, he'd put his arms about her but it gave Becky little comfort. Her heart heavy with foreboding, throat aching with unshed tears, she knew the calamity that had befallen them couldn't be put right by words, but would just have to be endured. For want of something to say she told him, 'I expect you'll have to pay the hotel bill, cancelling at such short notice?'

And he answered, 'I expect I will, Becky. I'm going to make it up to you, love, just as soon as Aunt Ruth gets back.'

Did Albert really think his aunt would return after she'd blamed herself for leaving her sister? It was hardly likely she'd risk it again, was it? Especially now Albert was married anyway.

'Mam will be wondering where we are.' He got up and lifted the case Becky had packed for their honeymoon. 'I don't think we'll need anything else, do you? If we do, we can get it tomorrow. I thought I might just as well go into work, Becky. Save the time off in case we can get away later. I know they were going to be short-handed.'

'I will too,' she told him. 'There's no point in Mam managing on her own.'

When they went downstairs she saw that Dora looked pale and drawn. It had been a long and worrying day for her and Dr Powell had warned against any strain. If only I could stay here with her, Becky thought wistfully. But with the wedding ring on her finger there was no hope of that. Tonight she would sleep with Albert in the cramped single bed in his little back room. The very thought made her grow pale again. She had some idea what would happen — you couldn't work in the shop all these years, listening to some of the bawdier customers, without having an inkling — but with no brothers of her own, she knew very little about men.

★ ★ ★

They'd arrived at the Lloyds' house and prepared supper and now Becky was washing up in the unfamiliar scullery which was a white-washed lean-to, not a proper room like the one at the shop.

'I'll help Mam undress, Becky,' Albert told her, putting down a tea-towel.

But his mother called from the kitchen, 'Becky can help me to bed, Albert, as soon as she's finished out there.'

Becky's heart sank as she dried the enamel washing-up bowl and put it back on the wooden bench. Besides this there was only a gas cooker, built-in boiler and brown-stone sink in the scullery.

'Will you be long, love?' the voice came again, and as she went back into the kitchen, 'It's time Albert had a break.'

He carried hot water upstairs and poured it into the flowery jug standing in the bowl on the wash-stand. When the door shut behind him Becky helped her mother-in-law to take off her blouse and skirt, petticoats and vest. She poured hot water into the bowl and watched as Nellie soaped the flannel and washed and dried her face and neck then her sagging breasts.

'Do my back for me, Becky. It's the rheumatics — I can't raise my arms very high. Albert always stays outside until I'm ready to wash my back and I cover my front with a towel.'

Next Becky was requested to dip the big swansdown puff into the bowl of talcum powder, filling the air with white dust, then vest and nightgown were slipped over Nellie's head and she was settled for the night.

'Just like a daughter you're going to be, Becky,' her mother-in-law told her with a satisfied little smile. 'Always wanted a daughter, I did, but no daughter could have been kinder than my Albert.'

Having folded the clothes over a chair, Becky was thankful to get out of the room. She was tired and unhappy but in her way her mother-in-law had made her feel like one of the family, losing no time in letting her know what was expected of her as such.

How was Mama getting on? She'd looked exhausted when they'd left and would probably be in bed herself by now. Albert would go over first thing tomorrow to see if there were any heavy jobs to be done, and Becky would be over a little later to serve behind the counter as usual.

'Time we were getting upstairs ourselves,' Albert told her, yawning widely. Banking down the fire, he added, 'Perhaps we'd better give her time to nod off?'

Guessing what was on his mind, for the tiny bedroom they were to share was next-door to his mam's, Becky felt hot colour rush to her cheeks.

Fifteen minutes later, turning her back, she undressed on one side of the narrow bed while Albert did the same on the other. Then, after pulling the pretty nightdress that had been meant for her honeymoon over her head, Becky slipped between the starched white sheets and repressed a little shiver. If only I loved him more it would be different, she told herself, wishing the night was over and she was back behind the familiar counter at the shop.

When Albert had turned off the light and slipped into bed they lay stiffly side by side until he told her in a gentle voice, 'We needn't tonight if you don't want to, Becky?'

As she turned to kiss him gratefully on the cheek, he mistook the signal. He drew her closer to him, but it was soon clear that he knew as little as she did, until suddenly a sharp pain that came over and over made Becky bite hard on her bottom lip to stifle her cries, only too aware that her mother-in-law was just the other side of the wall. By now the bed-springs were creaking noisily yet Albert seemed oblivious as Becky lay rigid with embarrassment, determined not to utter a sound.

Presently, with her husband in a deep sleep, she let the tears flow. It was a nightmare. She hadn't realised how important love was in a marriage. Would this intimacy go on every night? 'Please God, no!' she whispered aloud. In the small space of the single bed there was no distancing oneself, no turning away. As Albert slept peacefully beside her, Becky's thoughts became sombre. She'd realised last night that his mother expected her to take the burden of caring for her off Albert's shoulders: she'd never minded hard work but hadn't bargained on looking after Nellie and being constantly at her beck and call.

When the alarm shrilled in the darkened room she couldn't remember having slept at all. Albert sprang up to put it off, explaining, 'I don't want to wake Mam yet.' He pulled on a woollen dressing gown, telling her, 'I'll go down and light the fire, love, then bring you up a cup of tea.'

'I'll come down,' Becky told him. 'I'll put the kettle on the gas while you do the fire.'

As she unbolted the back door and went

around the side of the wash-house to the WC, she thought wistfully of the shop and the rooms behind where the lavatory was indoors.

Despite all the disappointments, the home they'd furnished and couldn't use and the cancelled honeymoon, Albert seemed to be in good spirits as they sipped their tea at the kitchen table. It was barely half-past six but they still had to wash and dress themselves, and his mam must be got ready.

'I'll see to her this morning, Becky, she can do a fair bit for herself,' Albert told her. 'You get the breakfast, then I'll nip over the shop and see if anything needs doing.'

But Nellie Lloyd didn't agree. Becky must help her wash and dress; there were plenty of other chores Albert could do. And so the pattern was set and Becky could see day following day, doing whatever Nellie wanted, except when she was at the shop or in the cramped little bed with Albert.

He lay satisfied and sound asleep by her side while she stayed awake, tossing and turning, worrying in case her mam was taken ill again, for now there'd be no one there to see to her, no one to call the doctor. Becky felt like getting up and rushing across to the shop to make sure everything was all right, but she'd only frighten her mam stiff, wouldn't she? Not to mention what Albert and her mother-in-law, who now insisted Becky call her Nellie, would say.

Mama was paying her a small wage which Becky put into her post office account against a rainy day. Life seemed pretty dismal at present but she'd convinced her mam everything was all right and that she believed Ruth would come back when she could be spared, then Becky and Albert could live in their rooms over the shop as they'd intended.

Two months after the marriage, when there was still no word from Ruth about coming back, although her sister had long since recovered, Albert suggested they bring the new double bed across. He could get one of his mates at work to help shift it. 'We can soon take it back,' he hurried to assure Becky. With the lovely new walnut bed in place, it was at least more comfortable to lie there with her worries, not rolling into Albert all the time, and to Becky's relief the springs of the new bed didn't make a sound.

After Albert left to visit her mother the mornings were hectic for Becky, even though she got up at half-past six. Nellie found endless jobs for her to do. Could she slip around to the butcher's before she went to the shop? And if Becky peeled the potatoes and left them in water, Nellie could put the saucepan on the stove ready for their meal.

'It would be nice if you could come back home for a bit of lunch,' she told Becky as she was leaving for work. 'It's a very long day for me on my own and you're with youer mam most of the time.' The tone of voice was so sweet and pleading, Becky felt she had to agree, but she'd been looking forward to eating with her mam. But as more and more jobs were piled on her, and always when Albert was out of the house, Becky grew resentful that she couldn't spend more time at the shop she still thought of as home.

One day when she'd gone up to their rooms there to dust the lovely furniture they'd never used, she looked around her in despair. What was to happen to all of this? Would it just stay here, growing more old-fashioned with time? There were four deep indents in the new carpet square where the legs of the double bed had stood. Would it ever be returned? Opening the wardrobe, she took out her wedding dress, watching as the satin shimmered in the bright sunshine that streamed through the window. What a waste of money it seemed now. Money Mama could do with for a warm coat in a few months' time.

How different it might have been if only they could have lived here and enjoyed the comfort of these rooms. Her mother had never been demanding, even when she was ill. Whereas when she went back this evening, Nellie would be sure to have a list of things for Becky to do, but would be so sweetly long suffering about it that it would be impossible for her to refuse. Like the other evening when, with Albert home, she'd planned to go back to her mam's for an hour.

'I've been thinking, Becky love,' Nellie had said, her eyes behind the magnifying lenses of her spectacles fixed earnestly upon her daughter-in-law, 'it'll be light for ages yet and the windows could do with a clean again. It's awful not being able to lift my arms. Used to sit on the sill upstairs, I did, polishing them every week.'

'I'll do them, Mam,' Albert immediately offered.

'There's jobs for you in the garden, Albie,' she'd replied. 'And then you can chop some sticks.'

'I was just going over to Mam's for an hour,' Becky told her.

'Well, I'd be the last one to stop you,' Nellie had replied huffily, 'but you've already been there all day!'

15

'There's lovely it looks!' Polly cried gratefully, gazing enraptured at the newly painted and varnished passage and stairs and gleaming flower-patterned oil-cloth. She knew Laura had asked Roy to decorate in case his aunt called, and that was only natural, the state it had been in, but it raised her spirits to see the house look so nice and fresh again.

'Not good enough for them as it was, I suppose,' Bert had said when she'd told him what Laura and Roy proposed to do.

But for once Polly stood up to him, saying, 'Roy's auntie will be bringing his mam to see them when she visits Cardiff again. You can't blame them for wanting it to look nice.'

Despite his lack of enthusiasm for the decorating, Bert got on well with Roy who was trying to get him interested in the Labour Party of which he was a staunch supporter, thrilled that after the General Election last May, Ramsay MacDonald had been asked to form a government. But although Bert listened, glad of the company, his interest was slow to kindle. It was the government of the time that had led them into the horrors of the last war, wasn't it? Then sat on their backsides, letting the troops suffer and die. Although Roy protested that Labour hadn't been strong enough to be in power then Bert thought all governments were probably tarred with the same brush.

Laura had finished working part-time and was enjoying being a housewife, taking over the burden of scrubbing and polishing from Polly, glad to be home when Sally came on her half-day and the two girls could talk for hours.

Polly was feeling a lot happier too for she'd paid the last instalment on the clothing club a few weeks ago, though many times since the wedding she'd told herself the money could have been much better spent: a couple of warm nighties for the coming winter or a warm coat, perhaps? Her shawl, woollen though it was, gave little protection against a cold wind. Only that morning she'd taken Bert's suit and the dress from the wardrobe to make sure moths hadn't got at them, sighing with relief when they were both all right.

'We'll dress up one day and walk as far as the park,' she'd told Bert a few weeks ago, but he'd made it quite clear he didn't want the bother, and anyway her new dress and hat, beige stockings and shoes, wrought such a transformation in her she hadn't the courage to walk down the street in them. Besides, what would Dora Morgan think if she saw her all dressed up like that? Polly hadn't dared wear the dress at Becky's wedding, but as she was helping serve at table and with the washing up, it was perhaps just as well. Probably the next time the new clothes were worn would be at Sally's wedding and the girl wasn't even courting yet.

In contrast Tommy's grey suit had hardly been off his back. Polly was glad she'd been able to let the trousers down for he was growing at such a rate his ankles had soon been showing. He'd left school at the end of summer and was starting next week as a baker's boy on the local van. If only we could have afforded to apprentice him to a trade, she thought wistfully, but the money he would earn, small as it would be, was desperately needed. She'd have to take on another clothing club soon the way he was shooting up, growing rapidly out of clothes and shoes, and with no elder brother to pass him on outgrown things, most of his wages would be needed for these.

'Goodnight, Mam! Goodnight, Dad!' Laura was positively glowing with happiness these days. They're very much in love, Polly thought tenderly as the kitchen door closed behind her daughter and son-in-law. She could remember when she had glowed with love like that; when the only thing she'd longed for was to be in Bert's arms.

When he'd joined up she'd prayed for the day he'd come back to her, confident their feelings would stay the same. And when he did finally come home, a wreck in mind and body, not even knowing her or the children at first, she'd told herself: When Bert is fit again everything will be all right. It had been years before he'd been well enough for them even to bring the bed upstairs again. That first night, settled and more relaxed in their own bedroom, she'd put her arms about him and let him know she needed him. Bert had kissed her too and she'd waited, her heart beating fast, but after a few minutes he'd flung himself away from her, burying his face in his hands, dry sobs tearing from his throat.

'Bert, love, what's wrong?'

She'd tried to cradle him in her arms, to smooth his hair, but he'd pulled away, his voice a croak as he told her, 'It's no use, Polly. I've known for a long time — I'm finished. I'm no use to you any more. I might just as well have died out there with the others!'

She'd put her lips to his, smothering his words, and when he was quiet she told him, 'Don't ever talk like that again. We've still got each other, love. It would have broken my heart if you'd died.'

'I've nothing to offer you, Polly. Nothing. I can't even provide for you any more. I can't be a proper husband — I'm only half a man.'

Polly had held him close then and kissed him again and again, determined to show her love, murmuring, 'It'll be different when you're well, Bert. We'll have a wonderful life then, you'll see.' But how could she hope to convince him when she herself felt such despair?

The next time Roy's Aunt Vi came to tea she was carrying a big brown paper parcel. Turning to Polly, who'd come into the room to greet her, she said, 'I hope you won't be offended, Polly, but we are family now, aren't we? Miss Sophie was going through her wardrobe and she gave me this coat.' Vi chuckled, looking down at herself. 'Well, I ask you, look at me! And she's so tall and thin. Anyway, it's a pity to let it go to waste so I thought of you.'

Untying the parcel, she brought out a dark grey face-cloth coat with astrakhan collar and cuffs, the whole of it lined with silver-grey quilted satin. Polly's mouth opened in surprise but Vi was insisting, 'Come on, Polly, try it on!' and the next minute she was at the hall-stand, staring at herself in the mirror. Even reflected in the spotted glass she could see it must have been a very expensive coat and had had little wear.

'I must give you something for it, Violet,' Polly told her, wondering even as she said the words just what she could find to give.

But Vi was laughing, saying, 'Don't you dare! It's no use to me. I'm just glad it fits you so well.'

'It'll look lovely over the dress you had for the wedding, Mam,' Laura told her. 'And the hat you bought will go with it as well.'

Cheeks flushed with excitement, Polly bore the coat upstairs, but hanging it in the wardrobe she asked herself: Whenever will I have the chance to wear a coat like this? Anyway, although the dress she'd bought was the same length, the skirts she wore every day trailed well below it. Oh, but it had been nice of Vi to think of her and she was grateful. I'd best show it to Bert after Vi's gone, she thought. Roy's aunt had said they were family now. Surely even he couldn't object to that?

★　★　★

The day Tommy started work he went off whistling. 'Poke someone's eye out, you will, with that whistle if you're not careful,' Bert had told him and he'd laughed, but it hadn't stopped Polly wondering anxiously how he'd

153

get on. Tommy was making an effort these days to be friends with his dad, but sometimes even now it seemed there'd always be a barrier between them.

They were too much alike, Tommy and his dad, she reflected. Both could be generous and kind, but both were quick to flare up and take offence.

When Tommy came home from work Polly had made a pot of stew, begging bones from the butcher when she'd gone in for a bit of scrag-end. The boy would be hungry after being out in the fresh air all day, and he'd only taken sandwiches.

Having assured them in glowing terms that he liked the job, he slowly spooned the stew into his mouth, eating hardly any bread. Polly watched him anxiously. This was his favourite meal; he usually scoffed it hungrily, asking for more.

'What's wrong, son?'

Tommy was dawdling over the last few spoonfuls before saying, 'Sorry, Mam, I can't eat any more.'

Polly went to put a hand to his forehead, saying again, 'What's wrong? Have you got a pain?'

He laughed. 'No, Mam. When we got back to the bake-house, the baker was trimming the cakes. Told me to help myself, he did.

Lovely it was. Sponge and raspberry jam.'

The next evening he came home from work with a bag of the cuttings, telling Polly he'd asked if he could take them home as eating them would spoil his tea.

'Oh, Tommy, you didn't!' she felt bound to say. But he looked so proud and happy as he set the sponge pieces on a plate and put them on the table for everyone to have with a cup of tea. She soon found there were other little perks with him being a baker's boy. Stale buns were delicious toasted in front of the fire and spread with margarine, and he often brought home a loaf if one was left over and they weren't making bread pudding.

The way he was growing up and filling out, she'd have to take on that clothing club again very soon. Tommy was a different boy now that he was working, and seemed a lot happier and more content.

And there'd been more good news last time Sally had come home. She'd met a young man when he'd come to the house where she worked to demonstrate the usefulness of a vacuum cleaner, and now they were going out together. Sally had promised to bring Bill to meet them on her next half-day.

16

'There's a social at the Labour Club Tuesday, Mam. Roy wants me to go. I said I would if you'd come too?'

'Oh, Laura! It'll be all young people like yourselves.'

'No, it won't, Mam. Roy says it's mostly the workers. You know, those who canvass before an election or distribute the leaflets. He says there are new members joining all the time.'

'Oh, I don't know about coming, *cariad*. I'd feel like a fish out of water. What do they do at these socials?'

'There's someone plays the piano for dancing. Oh, but you haven't got to dance,' Laura hastened to add, seeing her mother grimace.

'I haven't been to a dance since before you were born. And that was only the church hop,' Polly told her. 'Went every week, we did, me and youer dad. But I wouldn't like to get up now.'

'Some of the people just sit and talk, Mam. There's tea and refreshments, and someone usually gets up on the stage and sings.' Laura looked at her mother hopefully.

I can't say I've nothing to wear, Polly told herself, feeling a stir of excitement at the thought of putting on the dress she'd bought for her daughter's wedding and the lovely coat Vi had given her. It was years since she'd been anywhere except the shops . . .

★   ★   ★

On Tuesday, her heart filled with pleasurable anticipation, Polly dressed in her best, even allowing Laura to dab some of her precious Attar of Roses behind her ears.

When Bert said, eyeing her appreciatively, 'You look a treat, Poll, and younger somehow,' she asked hopefully, 'Why don't you come with us, Bert? There's still time for you to change into youer suit.'

He shook his head, saying, 'I don't feel up to meeting a lot of strangers, Poll, but I'm glad you're going.'

As they opened the front door a blast of cold air made her lift the wide astrakhan collar about her ears. The roofs were white with frost, the narrow grey-stone houses looked dark except where they were illuminated by street-lamps which silvered frost-rimed hedges and everything in sight.

'I can't dance, mind,' Polly reminded

157

Laura, and the girl laughed, saying, 'Neither can I, Mam. Not really. Roy's been giving me lessons in our room but I'll only get up if it's a waltz. We'll keep each other company.'

There were few people in Broadway and those there were hurried past, heads bent, plumes of steamy breath heralding their approach. Crossing the road, there was neither horse nor vehicle to stop them. They turned into Cyril Crescent and soon reached Stacey Road where the lights of the Labour Hall streamed out, welcoming them and the small queue of people going in.

As they entered the hall the first thing Polly noticed was the strong smell from the tea-urns, taking her back to her youth and church socials when tea and biscuits had been the highlight of the evening. Handing in her coat and slipping the ticket into her purse, Polly gazed about her at the bunting looped around the walls against which shabby wooden chairs had been set and were rapidly being taken. Two young girls were shaking a fine white powder over the knotted floorboards in the centre of the room.

'It's to make it smoother for dancing, Mam,' Laura explained. Then Roy took her arm and steered her towards a row of pictures on a nearby wall, and, seeing his eyes go bright with enthusiasm, Polly bent closer to read the captions.

There was one of the Labour ministers at Buckingham Palace after their electoral victory in May. Roy pointed to the Prime Minister, Ramsay MacDonald, who was taller than the rest and smiling for the camera, as was Arthur Henderson whom she was told was Foreign Secretary. The other two wore more serious expressions. They were J. H. Thomas, the Lord Privy Seal, and J. R. Clynes who was Home Secretary. There was another picture of a man called Philip Snowden, the Chancellor of the Exchequer. In the picture he was leaning heavily on a stick; Roy told her that he'd had a serious bicycling accident many years before.

To Polly all these names were vaguely familiar, she'd heard them mentioned frequently on the wireless and in the *Echo* and had also heard Roy speak of them to Bert, but apart from Ramsay MacDonald she couldn't have said what post they held in the government.

A lady had taken her seat at the piano and was beginning to play. Now the haunting melody of *The Blue Danube* filled the hall and someone at the front of the stage urged, 'Take your partners for the waltz.' As Laura and Roy began to dance, Polly sat down to watch, one foot slowly tapping to the music.

She was quite near the refreshments table and the clatter of cups on saucers threatened to drown out the music.

When Laura and Roy came back he went for refreshments and was almost at the table when a man called his name. Polly rose and told him, 'You go and see what youer friend wants, Roy. I'll get the tea.'

She joined the queue at the table, marvelling at the intricate steps of the few dancers on the floor for the tango. The queue for refreshments was slow-moving as the one woman at the table, looking hot and flustered, explained, 'There's only me tonight. Carrie 'ad to go home, there was no one to look after the baby.'

Without stopping to think, Polly cried, 'I'll help, if you like? But I'll have to take my daughter a cup first, mind.'

Laura laughed when she was handed her tea, saying, 'In your element you'll be, Mam. Trust you to come out for a break and land up pouring cups of tea!'

And she was in her element. With Carrie's apron about her, Polly was enjoying the grateful chatter of the other lady, who introduced herself as Sarah, and the company of the customers, who all seemed to be in jovial mood. It was so long since she'd had real contact with people like this, so long since she'd had a good laugh, and when Roy brought over a form for her to sign, making her a member of the Labour Party, Polly's first thought was that she was looking forward to coming back.

The evening seemed to fly by. After a couple of hours the refreshments stall closed down and she went back to Laura and Roy. She hadn't been sitting down for more than a few minutes when a tall distinguished-looking man of about her own age approached to ask her for a dance. Taking her horrified silence for assent, he led her to the dance floor and Polly felt deeply thankful that the pianist was playing *The Blue Danube* once again. She hadn't danced since her courting days but he'd given her no chance to explain that.

It's only one-two-three, one-two-three, she told herself, remembering even now what Bert had told her the first time he'd taken her around the floor. 'Just follow me,' he'd said, and that's what she did now. This man seemed to be an excellent dancer, and despite his height and girth was very light on his feet, so she gave herself up to following her partner and the lovely haunting melody.

When the music stopped and she'd been escorted back to her seat, the pianist began to play *The Red Flag* and everyone rose to their feet, singing lustily. Well, practically everyone — Polly didn't know the words.

The moon was bright, turning frost-rimed roofs and pavements to silver as they left the hall and made their way home. Snuggling into her deep astrakhan collar, Polly felt happier than she had for many years. She couldn't remember when she'd enjoyed herself so much and now Roy had made her a member there could be many more nights like this.

But what would Bert have to say to that? she asked herself, feeling a little apprehensive now for Bert had voted Liberal before the war though he took little interest now. How would he have passed the time while she'd been gallivanting? she asked herself. Would he have sat all evening staring into the fire, or would Tommy, as she'd hoped, have stayed to talk to him after his meal? Feeling suddenly cold, the glow of the evening gone, she hurried for home.

'It's not a race, Mam,' Laura said breathlessly.

'A bit worried, I am, *cariad*, about leaving youer dada so long.'

'He's a grown man, Mam, and he likes his own company.'

But Polly wasn't so sure. Bert had become a loner since his illness but that didn't mean he liked being alone, and what would he say if he knew she'd been dancing with a stranger? The old Bert wouldn't have minded but you never knew what he was brooding about now.

A murmur of voices as she went into the kitchen soon stilled her fears. Tommy was keeping his father company after all. When Polly opened the door, Bert and he were sitting at the table playing dominoes. Bert looked up to smile at her, saying proudly, 'Our Tommy bought me these out of his bit of pocket money, Poll.'

Tommy, looking a little embarrassed, told her, 'It was nothing, Mam. I just thought we could have a game together, that's all.'

The kettle was singing on the hob and Polly's heart sang too as she took the brown tea-pot, spooned some tea into it and made them a good, strong cup.

* * *

When Laura and Roy had taken off their coats, he picked up the poker to stir the fire then turned to her to ask, 'Did you tell your mam, Laura?'

She laughed. 'I didn't have a chance, love, not with her helping with the teas, then dancing with that man as soon as she'd sat down for a rest. I'll tell them about the baby when we go out to say goodnight, but

163

couldn't the other wait for a bit?'

'If we're thinking of trying to rent a house, it's better we tell them now. I thought you wanted us to have a place of our own?'

'I do, Roy, of course I do, but I've been thinking . . . Mama relies on our half-a-crown rent and there's no rush, is there? Let's wait until after the baby's born. Remember Sally telling us that she and Bill are going to get engaged on her birthday? They haven't known each other very long but they do seem to be very much in love. Wouldn't it be wonderful if, when we've found a place of our own, they were to get married and take over these rooms?'

17

As Becky finally closed the shop door on Christmas Eve, she wished with all her heart she could stay a while to keep her mam company. It was 1931 and for the past two Christmases, except for coming to dinner on Christmas Day, and Becky popping over whenever she could, Dora had been alone.

It had been a long and tiring day, even longer than usual because they had halved the price of any item that wouldn't keep until the shop opened again, and news had spread from neighbour to neighbour. At closing time the shop had been full, and each time Becky had closed the door there'd been another knock. Now at last they'd all gone home to stuff the poultry, if they were lucky enough to have any, and to put the obligatory orange, apple, nut and new penny into the toe of each stocking before filling them with whatever small surprises they could afford.

After making sure the scuttle was full of coal and there were sticks ready for the morning, Becky kissed her mam and got as far as the front door before remembering the jumper her mother had knitted for Laura's little boy. Gareth was eighteen months old now and the image of Roy with his dark curling hair and ready smile.

Going back along the passage, she opened the door to find her mam gazing pensively into the fire. There was sadness in her eyes before she smiled, asking, 'Have you forgotten something, love?'

'The jersey you knitted for Gareth,' Becky told her, and Dora laughed, saying, 'Now where did I put it? I'd forget my head if it wasn't screwed on.'

Making for home once more, Becky's thoughts were troubled. It must be very lonely for her mam, sitting there night after night with only Fluff and the crystal-set for company.

'I'll have to take some presents to Laura's house,' Becky told Nellie when she'd made a pot of tea. 'I'll show you what Mam's made for the baby.' And she spread the tiny garment, knitted in soft, pale blue wool, on the table.

'I wish she was knitting for you,' Nellie remarked. Always one to speak her mind, she never failed to remind Becky that it was probably her fault there was no sign of a baby as yet. Becky longed as much as Albert and Nellie for a child of their own, but she sometimes wondered, if ever they were lucky enough, just how she would cope. With Nellie relying on her more and more, and her working at the shop all day, how would she find time to look after a child?

If only I had the chance I'd solve the problem somehow, Becky told herself, feeling that her own deep longing for a baby would overcome all obstacles. She could take it across to the shop during the day, she told herself, already seeing her mam drooling over the pram while she served any customers who could be prised away from making a fuss of it. And at home Nellie would be only too eager to watch over it while she did the work.

'I'll just go upstairs for the fluffy rabbit we've bought for Gareth. Won't be a jiffy,' Becky said, putting down her cup.

Their rooms, both upstairs and down, being about half the size of the ones they would have occupied at the shop, were crowded with the furniture they'd brought over. Besides which, Nellie had wanted to keep a number of items, so the lovely leather settee that had looked so well over there now rubbed sides with an ancient treadle sewing machine, and a battered dark wood organ was squeezed in between the two armchairs. The only table was a rickety cane one, covered with an embroidered cloth.

Reaching the equally cluttered bedroom

Becky sighed, for here too an old-fashioned oak wardrobe, its mirrored door spotted and dull, stood side by side with the lovely new walnut one, and Nellie had access any time she wanted something from its cavernous interior.

With the fat chicken that had been delivered from a farm in Rumney sitting on a plate on the marble shelf of the pantry, waiting to be stuffed, and mince pies still to be made, Becky put on her coat and hat again, gathered up several gaily wrapped parcels and made for the front door.

'Don't be too long,' Nellie warned. 'Albert should be home soon and there's still a lot to do.'

'All right, Nellie, I expect Laura will be busy too,' Becky told her before closing the kitchen door.

Roy answered her knock and soon she was sitting in front of a roaring fire with a cup of tea and a plate of biscuits by her side. She still admired Roy but marvelled that she could look at him these days without all the emotional upheaval she'd experienced for so long. If anything he was even more good-looking now, having put on a little weight, which suited him.

'Oh! This is lovely, Becky. I must go and thank your mam,' Laura was crying excitedly.

'And just wait 'til Gareth sees the bunny. Oh, it's beautiful!' And she pressed the soft white fur of the toy Becky had bought against her cheek before fetching a brightly wrapped parcel from the sideboard cupboard and putting it into her friend's hand.

'You shouldn't have bought anything for me,' Becky protested. 'I only bought something for the baby.'

'Well, when you have one of your own that's what we'll do,' Laura told her, bringing a lump to Becky's throat.

'I'll go back and finish that argument I was having with your dad, Laura,' Roy said with a grin. 'See you later, Becky.'

'They're always arguing over politics,' Laura told her, 'but it's only friendly and Mam says it does Dada good, gives him an interest.' She rose and said, 'Come up and see Gareth.' Becky followed her up the stairs, tip-toeing into the bedroom after her.

The baby lay in his cot, one chubby hand resting on the pillow. As Laura tucked it gently under the covers he stirred, yawned, then settled once more. Becky felt a strong desire to pick him up and hold him close, to feel those silky curls nestled beneath her chin.

'He's lovely,' she told Laura wistfully, picturing Albert's joy if they had a baby of their own. She knew how much he longed for one. If only she could give him a family.

Going downstairs, she heard voices from the kitchen.

'A traitor to the Labour Party, that's what Ramsay MacDonald is!' Roy's voice came to them.

'A coalition government's the best thing for the country.' Laura's dad was speaking now. 'Look at the number of unemployed, Roy. Over two and a half million last year. Something had to be done.'

The kitchen door opened and Polly came towards them smiling, her hands raised in mock despair. As the door closed again, she said, 'Oh, but it's good to see youer dada taking an interest, and we have Roy to thank for that.'

'He's genuinely upset about Ramsay MacDonald agreeing to a National Government,' Laura explained. 'But as Dada says, what else could they do?'

Mrs Evans looks so happy and so much younger these days, thought Becky as she sat by Laura's fire. Tommy's going to work and Laura and Roy's having rooms with them has made a big difference.

She had been able to clear her bill at the shop and Laura had said that her mother really enjoyed her nights out at the Labour Hall where she now served regularly on the refreshments table. Laura had persuaded her to have her hair bobbed and had confided to Becky that the smart clothes her mother wore were from Roy's Auntie Vi, all things given her by the mistress.

Regretfully, Becky rose to go. It was so cosy, sitting in front of the fire, but at home there was still much waiting to be done and Nellie would be getting into a flap. Out in the street she pulled her collar up against the easterly wind. Turning into Paul Street, she quickened her step.

★　★　★

The mince pies were in the oven, the chicken cleaned and stuffed, and still Becky kept looking at the clock. Surely Albert would be home soon? When it struck ten and she'd taken the pies from the oven, Nellie said worriedly, 'They close at nine. He should be home by now.'

'Shall I go to meet him?'

'No, love, he'd only worry about you being out so late and in this weather.'

Becky made another pot of tea and they sat by the fire, listening for Albert's key in the lock. Where was he? Albert was very conscientious about his work but he should have been home before ten.

A loud rat-a-tat at the door made them both jump, and Becky went rushing along the dimly lit passage. Opening the door, she blinked in surprise at the sight of a uniformed policeman, the steel tip of his helmet glinting in the lamp-light.

'Mrs Lloyd?'

Becky nodded, her heart beating fast. When he asked, 'Can I come in?' she led the way to the kitchen where at sight of the uniform Nellie, eyes wide with fear, cried, 'Oh my God! Something's happened!'

'It's Mr Lloyd, Ma'am. Set on and robbed he was, just as he was putting the takings in the night safe.'

'Where is he? Is he hurt badly?' Becky cried anxiously.

'He's in the Infirmary. Probably regained consciousness by now.' Becky was rushing to fetch her coat. When she came back to the kitchen, Nellie said, struggling to her feet, 'Get mine, Becky, I'm coming with you.'

'I don't think you'd make it as far as the hospital, Nellie, especially in this weather,' Becky told her gently.

'I'm coming, girl. He's my son, isn't he?' Nellie cried, hobbling towards the door.

'Look, Ma'am, the young lady's right. I'm going straight back to the station on my bike.

172

I can call a cab for you. It'll be here in ten minutes.'

Waiting for the cab to arrive, Becky prayed silently, Please God, let Albert be all right.

Cold with apprehension, she'd suddenly realised the depth of her feelings for him. She'd always been fond of him; now she discovered it went much deeper than that. There'd been no fireworks in her heart as there'd been the first time she'd seen Roy, just a gradually deepening love for a man who was generous, thoughtful and kind towards everyone.

In the front room, looking out for the cab, she pulled the curtains closed then fell to her knees, pressing her fingers together and whispering, 'Please, God! Please let Albert be all right!'

The honking of a horn sent her rushing into the passage where she found Nellie waiting.

She got her mother-in-law into the dimly lit cab and climbed in after her, settling them both on the cold leather seat while the driver cranked the engine. Becky bit her knuckles, wanting them to be off. She couldn't see her mother-in-law's face properly but, feeling the pressure of her fingers as they gripped her own hard, knew Nellie's fear was as great as her own.

At the Infirmary they were told to sit and wait. Looking around her, Becky was reminded of the day her father had had his accident and with Mama she'd sat, perhaps on this very seat, watching the long corridor for a doctor to come and put their minds at rest. She recalled him coming towards them then, his coat flapping, and remembering the dreadful news he'd brought, she felt the colour drain from her cheeks.

There was a white-coated figure coming along the corridor towards them now. When he saw them sitting on the bench, he came across, enquiring, 'Mrs Lloyd?'

They both answered, 'Yes,' but it was Becky, fingernails digging into the palms of her hands, heart beating fast, who sprang to her feet.

'Mr Lloyd has just regained consciousness,' he told her gravely. 'There is some concussion and a lot of bruising. We'll need to keep him under observation for a few days at least. You can see him now, but only for a few minutes. Follow me.'

She sighed with relief, and linking her arm with Nellie's, vainly attempted to keep up with the doctor's long stride.

18

He stopped at a ward called Mametz and beckoned them in. Becky looked nervously along the rows of neat beds; most of the patients seemed to be asleep though some were stirring restlessly, raising their heads to see who had come in. Then she saw Albert propped against pillows in a bed on the left-hand side. Taking Nellie's arm, she urged her forward. They were almost at his bed when a nurse hurried past them carrying a tray of dressings. She put them on a locker near his bed and turned to draw the curtains, but not before a horrified Becky had seen his face. One eye was closed and badly discoloured, there was a swelling the size of an egg on his forehead and his upper lip was swollen to twice its normal size.

It was some ten minutes before the curtains were drawn back again, minutes in which she vainly tried to reassure a frightened Nellie who'd also caught a glimpse of her son's face, whispering so as not to disturb the sleeping patients. But with all the grunting and groaning and a man at the far end snoring loudly, it could hardly be called quiet.

Nellie, voice rough with emotion, whispered, 'Killed at Mametz my Evan was on the day the British captured it in the Battle of the Somme. First of July 1916 it was an' I thought my world had come to an end. Thank God I had Albert to fend for!'

Becky had known Nellie's husband was killed in the war, but not where. Torn between sympathy for her mother-in-law and the feeling of inadequacy she often experienced these days over not being able to provide Albert with a child, she gazed about her at the ward. It was dimly lit at this hour of the morning except for the part where he lay, his bed almost opposite the night sister's table where she sat in a pool of light from a lamp, head bent over a book. Becky was thankful when the curtains were drawn back from Albert's bed and the little nurse whispered, 'You can see him now. No more than five minutes, mind.'

His head and one eye were now swathed in bandages. He seemed dazed but must have recognised them for when Becky gently took his hand in hers, he smiled, the pain of his swollen lip making it a brief one. When Nellie bent to kiss him she saw his wince of pain. Becky sat holding her husband's hand, her fears rekindled at the dazed look in his good eye. She'd said no more than, 'Albert, love, we've been so worried . . . ' when the nurse appeared again, saying in an urgent voice, 'Doctor's coming. Could you visit him tomorrow? He should be feeling a little better by then.'

As they walked the long corridor once more, Nellie, looking pale and exhausted, asked worriedly, 'How are we going to get home?'

Becky had been wondering the same thing, but as they stepped outside a cab drew up and a middle-aged man got out and hurried into the hospital. Becky sprang forward before the driver could leave. As they turned into Newport Road, street-lights moving intermittently across the dim interior, they were both lost in their own thoughts. A lamp momentarily lightened the darkness and Becky glanced at her watch. Ten minutes to three and it was Christmas morning. What a strange and worrying one this had turned out to be!

Back home the fire had gone out. Chilled to the bone, Becky took the heavy iron kettle from the range, thankful it was still warm. She put it on the gas stove, and brought Nellie's hot water bottle down to be filled. The priority now was to get her a hot drink and into a warm bed.

'Best keep your coat on, Nellie,' she told

her mother-in-law, pausing on her way upstairs with the bottle clasped tightly to her breast.

'Will he be all right, Becky?' Nellie asked plaintively.

'He's in the right place, Mam.' Becky rarely called Nellie 'Mam', but at that moment her mother-in-law looked so frail and pathetic. Really she didn't know any more about Albert than Nellie. All they could do was to hope and pray there wouldn't be any lasting damage.

Seeing Nellie's anxious eyes still on her, Becky added, 'Albert's strong, he'll get over it. Must be all the good food you gave him when he was a child.'

She herself was still worried sick but the remark brought a smile to Nellie's face as she said, 'You're right, Becky. Albert's got a strong constitution. He's much stronger than he looks, you know.'

A few minutes later they went up to bed but as far as Becky was concerned not to sleep. She tossed and turned, worried that she might not be up in time to make an early start on the dinner so as she could visit Albert in the afternoon. She'd let Mama know what had happened as soon as she'd lit the fire, seen to Nellie's breakfast and got the chicken into the oven.

The next morning Becky was just about to do this when there was a knock on the door.

'Mam! I was coming over to see you,' she cried when she'd rushed down the passage to open it.

Dora's eyes were anxious as she said, 'Whatever's happened, Becky? Mrs James saw a policeman here last night, and you and Nellie going off in a taxi.' By this time she was seated at the kitchen table.

'Albert was robbed and beaten up,' Becky told her. 'He's in the Infirmary, Mam. I was coming over to you as soon as I got the dinner started. We'll have to have it early so's I can get to the hospital at visiting time.'

'What an awful thing to happen! I may as well stay now I'm here, Becky. I'll pop over later for the few things I wanted to bring. How was he when you saw him?'

When Nellie at last came downstairs she looked pale and exhausted, her rheumatism obviously playing her up. Dora sat talking to her over a cup of tea before asking Becky if she could help.

'Shall I come with you to the hospital?'

'No, Mam. But I'd be grateful if you'd keep Nellie company until I get back. It's cold meat, tinned fruit and Christmas cake for tea. It won't take much getting.'

When Becky told her mother-in-law she

was going to the hospital on her own, Nellie was upset. 'No, I'm coming with you, Becky,' she insisted.

'But you can't walk all that way and there are no trams today. Even if we could afford it, you wouldn't get a cab for love nor money on Christmas Day.'

Looking sorry for herself, Nellie grudgingly agreed.

After dinner Becky packed chicken sandwiches, a slice of Christmas cake and some fruit into a basket, and taking a small case she'd packed with Albert's pyjamas and toilet things, set off for the hospital. The case, small as it was, grew heavier with each step as she battled against the cold easterly wind.

As she entered Mametz ward she saw Albert lying propped against his pillows, watching the door. His face broke into a smile at sight of her — a smile that quickly turned into a grimace of pain.

'How do you feel, love?'

'Not too bad. My head aches but that's just from the blow.' He took her hand, squeezing it reassuringly. 'Don't worry, Becky, I'll be right as rain.'

The bandage had been removed from his eye which was still almost closed and had seemingly gained a few more shades of purple and blue.

180

'Do you know if they caught the man who attacked you?'

'Yes, and thank God the money's all right! I held on to it as long as I could.'

'You must have to take a beating like that. Oh, Albert! You should have let go. You could have been killed.' When he didn't answer she went on, 'Your mam sends her love. She's very disappointed she couldn't come in but there's no trams today.'

'You shouldn't have walked it, Becky, especially with that case. But don't think I'm ungrateful. I'll be really glad to get into my own things.'

Biting into a chicken sandwich, he grimaced with pain but quickly assured her it was worth it as the sandwich was delicious.

He still looked a little drowsy and when he seemed to have fallen asleep, after waiting some time Becky crept away, intending to ask the staff nurse, who was in the little office at the end of the ward, about his progress. But she was talking to a doctor and there was no sign of any of the other nurses. After hanging about for some time Becky went back to the bedside but Albert was still asleep and somewhere a bell was clanging, heralding the end of visiting time. In the long corridor once more Becky made slow progress as visitors from other wards swelled the crowd. As she turned into Newport Road, the biting wind stung her cheeks. She tightened the scarf about her throat and hurried for home.

It was lovely to see her mother's welcoming smile when she opened the door. In the kitchen a bright fire burned in the grate and the table was laid for tea.

'Nellie's dozing in the parlour,' Dora told her. 'It seems a pity to wake her, Becky. Shall we have ours?'

A fire was only lit in this Holy of Holies at Christmas and on special occasions. Quietly Becky opened the door and peeped in, smiling when she saw Nellie, mouth open, gently snoring against the cushions of one of the big old-fashioned armchairs. The furniture here was of heavy dark oak, Victorian at its most ornate, and there was hardly any space to walk around. Yet last week Nellie had insisted Becky and Albert must take up the floral carpet square and beat it over the clothes line in the garden. Usually she was content with cold tea-leaves scattered over its surface and swept up with a brush and pan, but with Becky's mother coming for Christmas Day she'd insisted they give the room a full spring clean.

There was little to say about Albert except that he seemed much brighter and Becky was disappointed that she hadn't found out more about his condition. Pouring a second cup of tea, Mama said, 'Why don't you go to Laura's for an hour this evening, Becky? It would be a break for you, love.'

'Oh, Mam! I couldn't leave you here again. You've been on your own most of the afternoon. And I took the presents last night.'

'Nellie will be awake soon and there's no need for you to rush back, I'll help her get to bed. I saw the hot water bottle when I was washing up, and I'll see she's nice and warm.'

Hugging her mother gratefully, Becky said, 'I'd love to see Laura, Mam, but it doesn't seem fair. You haven't had much of a Christmas Day with me going to the hospital and Nellie upset.'

'Nonsense, love. I want you to go. Forget your troubles for a while.'

Dora had thought of it that afternoon. Today had been an eye opener for her. She hadn't realised how demanding Nellie Lloyd could be. It had been 'Fetch me this or that, Becky', or 'The fire needs some coal, better fill the scuttle you had'. The place was gleaming and there were no prizes for guessing who kept it like that. It certainly wasn't Nellie's doing! And the poor girl worked so hard at the shop too.

Staring into the fire while Becky was upstairs getting ready, Dora felt a twinge of guilt for it was she who'd encouraged this match. Things would have been so different if they'd been able to live in the rooms they'd furnished over the shop. Becky and Albert would have had a life of their own then and not been constantly at Nellie's beck and call. Becky was still only twenty-one and even in her schooldays she'd had to work hard, coming home each day to serve behind the counter. That was Dora's fault too but how could she have managed without her daughter's help? If she hadn't had to rely on Albert so much, would Becky even have married him? No, she loves him, Dora consoled herself. Look how upset she was about what happened to him.

As Becky came downstairs, wearing the new blue cardigan her mam had given her for Christmas, Nellie was just closing the parlour door.

'Went off to sleep I did,' she said, following her daughter-in-law to the kitchen, adding as she saw Dora, 'I'm sorry, love, but I was that whacked. Now, Becky, how did you find Albert? When are they going to let him come home?'

'He seemed much brighter today, Nellie. I couldn't find anyone to ask about him coming home, but you'll see him yourself tomorrow.'

'Well, I'd 'ave hung about until I *did* see someone. Still, if he's feeling better . . . ' Her voice trailed off when she saw Becky putting on her hat before the mirror. 'Where you going, girl?' she cried. 'Not back to the hospital, surely?'

'Your tea's ready, Nellie,' Dora put in. 'Becky's going to see her friend for an hour or so. You and me can keep each other company.'

'Wouldn't 'ave thought she'd feel much like gaddin' about, seeing what's happened,' Nellie said tartly. 'Still, who am I to say? I'm only his mam.'

19

Roy opened the door wearing a purple paper hat and a wide grin. As Becky followed him into the parlour where all the family were gathered with glasses in their hands, it was obvious as they welcomed her warmly that they knew nothing of what had happened to Albert.

Handing her a brimming glassful of port, Sally, whom Becky hadn't seen for ages, came to sit beside her.

'Bill's gone home to see his family,' she told Becky. 'I could have gone to the Rhondda with him but I'd promised Mam I'd be here for Christmas dinner and he'll be back tomorrow anyway.' She twisted the engagement ring she'd worn for more than two years, adding wistfully, 'We're getting married just as soon as we've saved enough.'

Sally was as fair and as pretty as ever. Her lovely long blonde hair had been cut and now curled becomingly about her face.

When Becky told them what had happened to Albert they were all concern and she felt sorry to be casting such gloom over their evening. They all drank to Albert's speedy recovery and Laura rummaged in the sideboard and brought out a packet of digestive biscuits, telling her, 'It isn't much, Becky, but take these in to Albert tomorrow.'

When Polly was about to go to the kitchen for her contribution, Becky, embarrassed by their kindness, stopped her with, 'I expect he'll be out in a few days, Mrs Evans, and he's got far more in his locker than he's going to use now. But thanks for the thought.'

The unaccustomed glass of port was going to her head and when Laura filled her glass for the second time Becky wished she'd sipped the first one more slowly. Jessie had just come in from next-door, her plump face beaming and already flushed, and by this time Bert and Roy had retired to the kitchen for a game of crib and Tommy to his bedroom to fiddle with the crystal-set kit he'd had for Christmas.

Jessie was now filling everyone's glass from the bottle of rhubarb wine she'd brought with her and, seeing Becky hadn't yet finished the one she was drinking, filled a fresh glass and put it beside the port. Becky, eating a second piece of Laura's Christmas cake and feeling rather muzzy by now, looked at it in dismay.

A few minutes later Roy came back to fill two tumblers from the flagon of beer on the sideboard. Seeing him at the door with his hands full, Becky rose unsteadily to cross the room and open it. She was about halfway across when, setting down the glasses, he came towards her. He put his arms about her and kissed her full on the lips. Her feelings heightened by the heat and the wine, heart thumping and the kiss acting like an electric shock, she kissed him back. It was Roy who put her away from him, saying with a laugh, 'Don't tell Albert, Becky. It was only under the mistletoe!'

Looking up, she saw the branch of mistletoe suspended from the ceiling above her head and, feeling very foolish, abruptly sat down.

They were all laughing now and Sally cried, 'It's my turn next, Roy!'

She was hurrying towards him when Bert yelled from the kitchen, 'How much longer have I got to wait for that bloody beer?' As Roy, still laughing, went out with the full tumblers, Becky closed her eyes against tears of mortification. She'd thought all those feelings she'd had for him were in the past. Why, oh why, had she kissed him like that? He'd treated it as a joke, something brought on by her drinking too much wine, but she'd known the moment his lips had touched hers that nothing had really changed, that he still had the power to send her heart racing.

'You all right, Becky love?' Polly Evans's voice broke into her thoughts. When she didn't immediately open her eyes, Polly cried, 'Put the kettle on, Laura. Make us some coffee. There's a bottle of Camp on the pantry shelf.'

'I'm — I'm fine, Mrs Evans.' Becky looked up at her. 'I'm sorry.'

'Nothing to be sorry about, cariad. Made us laugh you did, and it's obvious you're not used to Jessie's rhubarb wine. Make some sandwiches I will to go with the coffee.'

Perhaps nobody noticed? Becky told herself hopefully. But Roy knew, didn't he? How was she to face him after this? She knew he'd only done it for fun but that kiss had awakened all the old feelings she'd tried so hard to suppress.

When presently he and Bert came back to the parlour, Laura's father brought along his concertina.

'How about a sing-song?' he asked hopefully, and Becky was surprised by how much he'd changed since Roy had come to live there. 'Mind you,' he was warning them, 'only know the old tunes I do. Never got round to learning any new ones.'

As they stood around waiting for him to start playing, Roy put his arm round Becky's shoulders and smiled down at her. 'Coffee

189

done the trick?' he asked. 'Jessie's rhubarb wine ought to be labelled 'Drink this at your peril'.'

'Cheeky beggar!' Jessie gave him a playful clip. 'Watch out, Roy, or I won't give you any next time.'

They were all laughing again. Sighing with relief, Becky joined in. Then Bert began to play *She's Only A Bird In A Gilded Cage*, and when they'd sung that he played *Daddy's On The Engine*, then *If You Were The Only Girl In The World*. As the final notes faded away Becky glanced at the marble clock on the mantelpiece, and was horrified to see it was almost ten o'clock.

'I'll have to go,' she whispered to Laura. 'Don't disturb anyone, I'll let myself out.'

'Roy will see you home, Becky.'

'No, really. It's only round the corner.' To be alone with him was the last thing she wanted.

As she closed the front door behind her, Becky heard Mrs Evans's voice. 'You shouldn't have let her go like that, Roy would have seen her home . . .'

Becky rushed up the narrow street, stopping for a moment at their shop on the corner to look up at the windows of the rooms she and Albert had planned to live in, one facing Wilfred Street, the other the street she now lived in.

'Windows on the world,' she told herself with a smile. 'Well, on our little world anyway.' My, that wine was having a strange effect on her! But Mama would be waiting, and wondering why she was so long. Her mam hadn't had much of a Christmas, had she, looking after Nellie all day? Quickening her step, she was soon turning the key in the lock. Opening the door, she found the house in darkness.

In the kitchen her mother was asleep in the armchair by the fire. Becky's heart filled with remorse at leaving her for so long.

Dora opened her eyes, blinked, then smiled up at her. 'You had a nice time then?'

'I didn't mean to be so late, Mam.'

'Don't worry, love. I let my fire go out anyway. Shall we have a cup of tea? Then when I go over I can get straight to bed.'

'How was Nellie? Was she upset I wasn't here to help her get undressed?'

'No. We had a good long chat about old times. People always seem to look back at the past when they're getting old.'

'You're not getting old, Mam,' Becky told her with a smile, but looking at the fair hair, now greying rapidly, the tired blue eyes and thin face, she felt a surge of contrition.

Dora didn't tell her that Nellie had

grumbled most of the evening about Becky's going out.

'Surprised she was in the mood to enjoy herself! I know I'm not with all this worry about Albert.'

'She went over to tell them what happened, Nellie,' Dora had protested. 'Laura would have thought it funny if Becky hadn't let her know.'

'Well, it didn't take all this time to say that, did it? Pity there's no sign of a baba as yet. Big disappointment to me it is, Dora. But as you know, I'm never one to interfere . . . '

★ ★ ★

When Albert came home a few days later he seemed a lot better and said he intended to return to work the following Monday. Becky had taken the morning off to fetch him home and when she left for the shop about two o'clock, Albert and Nellie were comfortably settled in armchairs to either side of a roaring fire. The dishes were washed and put away, potatoes peeled and in the saucepan ready for their evening meal. Nothing needed to be done except perhaps to make themselves a cup of tea.

Returning earlier than usual, Becky was greeted by the appetising smell of dinner cooking as she opened the door. The table was laid ready and Nellie was dozing by the fire. Hearing Albert moving about in the scullery, she found him stirring gravy at the stove.

'They told you to rest, love. You shouldn't be doing that,' she protested.

'I can't sit down and do nothing all day. Fed up I am with all her fussing.' He nodded towards the kitchen. 'Anyway, I'm going back to work tomorrow.'

'But the hospital said to see how you felt next week.'

'I know they did, but apart from the bruising I'm fine. And when Evan brought that little parcel from the staff, he said they were short-handed.'

Becky was just about to protest when Nellie's voice came from the kitchen. 'Stubborn you are, Albie. Just like youer father — '

'Oh, come on, Mam.' He stood in the doorway, basting spoon in hand. 'If I sit around here all week doing nothing, I'll become a nut case, that's for sure!'

20

Polly's kitchen was once more decorated for Christmas. It was early in December 1935 and the family, except for Tommy and Roy who were at work, were sitting around the table drinking tea, their expressions anything but festive as they listened to Sally's tearful tale.

'When will Bill be going to London?' asked Polly, bringing a fresh gush of tears from her younger daughter's eyes.

'Oh, Mam! I won't see him for ages.' Sally's voice ended on a sob and it was some seconds before she could continue. 'Going up to London next week he is, to find somewhere to stay.'

'Has he got to take the job?' Laura asked gently.

'No, but he wants to. It's a promotion really. You know he's on commission and we haven't been able to save enough to get married and buy furniture and things? Well, it's because the people in his area can't afford luxuries like vacuum cleaners. They ask for demonstrations out of curiosity but he doesn't get any money for that. He says in

London he could do much better. A good salesman Bill is, mind.'

'Look on the bright side, cariad,' Polly told her. 'If he can save more money, you'll get things all the quicker.'

'Yes, and we'll have to live in London, Mam, an' all,' Sally told her.

Now Polly's face fell too as she murmured thoughtfully, 'Well, I hadn't thought . . . '

'It could be exciting, Sal, living in London,' Laura said, hoping to cheer things up. 'And who knows? In the future, if Bill does well, you might even be able to save for a house of your own.'

'But I won't see any of you or my friends.' Sally seemed determined not to be comforted.

''Course you will,' Polly told her. 'You'll come home on visits. Perhaps when you've got a place, we'll be able to come up there?'

'What does Bill want to do?' It was the first time Bert had spoken.

'He thinks it's a good chance to get on. Says he'll be sending for me in no time.' Taking another cake, Sally gave them a watery smile.

'Sensible lad,' her father remarked. 'After all, when we came to Cardiff all those years ago, we didn't know a soul.'

'Wants us to get married before he goes he

does. Says we can have a quiet wedding 'cos it'll have to be soon.'

'Well, I don't know why you're crying, our Sally,' Polly told her sternly. 'A very lucky girl you are, having a man like Bill who's determined to get on.'

'It'll be a register office wedding, Mam. There won't be time — '

'You mean, it'll have to be almost right away?' She looked at her daughter keenly, her face wearing a worried frown. 'There's no need for all this rush, is there? You haven't *got* to get married?'

Sally blushed. 'Of course not, Mam. It's just he'd like us to be married 'fore he goes.'

Plans for the wedding were soon going ahead. Sally bought a neat suit in the now fashionable tan colour, something she could wear in the years ahead for she was determined not to fritter away the hard-earned money they'd been saving for a home of their own.

* * *

With just over a week to Christmas, Sally and Bill were married. Bill's parents arrived early for the wedding; the families had met many times before and got on well. Peggy, his mam, was plump and jovial with rosy cheeks and brown eyes. Mr Thomas, named Will, was equally plump and jovial and had obviously formed a deep attachment to his cap which, at a nudge from his wife, he'd taken off but still twisted round and round in his hands.

'For God's sake, Will, hang that blooming thing up!' she protested with a laugh, taking it from him and hanging it on the hall-stand.

After tea and biscuits they waited impatiently for the taxis that would take them to the register office. They all went, except for Jessie who stayed to lay the table and finish preparing the meal, and Bert, cheated this time of walking his daughter down the aisle though he'd readily given permission for the marriage, stayed home too, looking forward to the time when Bill's dad returned so that they could enjoy a couple of pints of Dark together.

The witnesses, friends of the bride and groom, were waiting outside when they arrived and they all trooped into the waiting room to talk in low whispers until the marriage in progress came to an end. At last the door opened and a slim young girl came out, smiling and holding on tightly to the arm of a tall young man. Followed by their guests, they left the building noisily. The next wedding party all rose but the inner door remained closed for several minutes before

Sally's and Bill's names were called and they could all go in. Once Bill's mam had managed to part her husband from his cap the ceremony began.

Back home, one of Polly's Christmas cakes held pride of place, iced and decorated with the little china bride and groom from Laura's cake, then circled with a white satin ribbon tied into a wide bow. There were large plates of ham and chicken, bowls of various tinned fruits, little iced fairy cakes and fruit cakes set out on doilies, potted meat sandwiches for those who didn't have a sweet tooth and a tray of hot sausage rolls keeping warm in the oven at the side of the range.

When the party came hurrying in, Sally holding out her left hand for the ring to be admired, Mrs Thomas took off the wide-brimmed hat and smart coat she'd bought for the wedding and also took charge of her husband's cap, hanging them on the hall-stand. They all sat around the table. 'Where's youer friends?' Polly asked, looking at the two empty places.

'Oh, they both had to get back to work, Mam.' Sally was glowing with happiness. She and Bill had a few days together before he went to London and they were going back with his parents to their home in Tre-Mynydd for a short honeymoon.

Soon it was time to go to the station and Laura and Roy accompanied them. They all trooped up the steps to the platform, Peggy and Will panting with the effort. The train was coming to a standstill in a great hiss of steam, and as Laura and Sally hugged each other the guard raised his flag. Bill, standing by the open door, urged Sally to get in. As he lowered the window to talk there was a shrill blast on the whistle. The flag waved and the train began to move noisily away, drowning their goodbyes. They continued to wave to each other until a drifting plume of smoke was all Laura and Roy could see.

★ ★ ★

The train was full of Christmas shoppers returning home laden with parcels and boxes. Though they could have done as well if not better at Pontypridd market, a trip to Cardiff was special, especially when the kiddies wanted to see Father Christmas in his grotto and have a trip to Lapland at Howell's or David Morgan's Bazaar. Two elderly women who had got in behind Sally were clinging to overhead straps, swaying precariously to the rhythm of the train, and Bill and his dad quickly got to their feet and guided the pair to their seats.

It seemed that Peggy was acquainted with half the occupants of the compartment as she chatted with one or the other. Snatches of conversation drifted across.

'*Duw!* And there was me thinking the little beggar was at school, an' all the time 'e was up the tump with 'is friends. 'E 'ad the length of my tongue, I can tell you!'

'Awful one ouer Bron is for cockles. 'Ad a plate in the market, she did, just before we left.'

''Aven't been able to get out much, pooer dab. Under the doctor 'e is, with the dust on 'is chest.'

They were shouting to each other now above the noise made by a crying baby and a fractious little boy who stared up at Sally from a tear-stained face and howled. Seeing that his mam was nursing a baby Welsh fashion, Sally patted her lap invitingly and tried to pick him up. He wriggled free and the howl became a shriek so she gave in and let him go.

As they left the station they were met by drizzling rain and umbrellas were instantly raised. Half the people in their compartment accompanied then up the steep street. Finally the last one left them with the by now familiar, ''Ave a nice time, gul. An' you, Will. An' you, young 'uns.'

'Ouer Mostyn must be out,' Peggy said when there was no answer to her knock. 'You got a key, Will? Save me searching in my bag.'

Wet coats were shaken and hung up then they all trooped into the kitchen where they were greeted by a roaring fire. 'Can't 'ave been gone long then,' Peggy remarked. 'Choir practice, I expect. Back soon he'll be to go on his shift.'

Mostyn's pit clothes hung over a wooden clothes-horse in the wash-house that led off the kitchen. Sally was suddenly glad Bill sold vacuum cleaners.

She didn't see her brother-in-law that night for after their meal Bill wanted to take her to the Working Men's Club where there was some entertainment. When they arrived there was much back slapping and offers of free drinks as one of his mates cried, 'Lucky bugger you are, Bill. Any more like 'er in Cardiff, mun?'

Sally watched anxiously as Bill downed several pints, the glasses replaced as soon as they were emptied. She was relieved when he pushed the fourth one away, saying with a grin, 'Got to keep sober, mun. Some other time, OK?'

She herself had only sipped at a port and lemon, refusing all further offers by pointing to her almost full glass. Back home after supper they sat around the fire, but even Peggy was yawning widely and was soon telling them, 'You two can go up whenever you want, but I'm going to bed.'

Knocking out his pipe on the bars of the grate, Sally's father-in-law said, 'Don't forget to bank the fire down and put the guard in front, ouer Billy.'

When the door had closed behind them Bill yawned and stretched, saying, 'Time we went up too, *cariad*.' He gathered her into his arms, pressing his lips to hers in a long kiss. Sally, who'd been feeling nervous, relaxed immediately, feeling only pleasurable anticipation now about the night to come. She loved Bill with all her heart and soon he'd be many miles away; they must make the most of their short time together.

'Shall we let your mam and dad settle down before we go up?' she asked nervously, twisting her lace-edged hanky round and round.

He smiled down at her, saying, 'Don't worry, love. We've got their bedroom at the front, they've gone into mine at the back, and there's our Mostyn in between — and he's on nights.'

The fire was banked down with small coal, the guard put in place and the lights turned off. Then they crept up the stairs, hand in hand, undressed quickly and fell into each other's arms.

★ ★ ★

Although over the years Sally had been a frequent visitor, she'd never stayed overnight before and so wasn't familiar with the house's morning routine. Waking early, watching Bill lovingly as he slept on, she decided to creep downstairs and make them a cup of tea. She'd put the kettle on the stove then go around the side of the wash-house to the *Ty-bach*. She'd felt much too shy to use the flowered pot that she knew was under the bed.

As she opened the wash-house door she could hear splashing and blushed scarlet when she realised it was Mostyn, taking his bath in the tin tub. The surface of the water, which was up to his waist, glinted like tiny black diamonds in the artificial light where he'd soaped the coal dust away.

He was grinning at her, saying, 'Scrub my back for me, there's a good gul.'

Cheeks burning with embarrassment, Sally did as she was asked, glad she didn't need to answer as Mostyn kept up his banter. When he rose from the bath, quickly flicking a towel about his waist, she averted her eyes, too embarrassed to speak. But chuckling to himself, he muttered, 'No miners in youer family then, *cariad*?' and went into the kitchen, closing the door behind him. Sally hurried around the corner of the wash-house to the *Ty-bach*, cheeks still burning in the chill morning air.

★ ★ ★

As Laura and Roy left the station the smile had faded from her face. In a voice heavy with disappointment she said, 'Well, that's that. We'll never be able to move to a place of our own now.'

'Oh, come on, love,' Roy humoured her. 'They mightn't like it in London, and Sally hasn't even gone there yet.'

'Yes, but we could put our names on the list for a council house now we're expecting another baby. There's lovely ones at Pengam and Tremorfa, and there's Ely as well. We're going to be awful crowded when we've got to put a cot in the bedroom.'

'Wouldn't your mam consider letting to someone else now Sally's going away?'

'Dad wouldn't want strangers about. Since his illness he's been funny that way. And with our Tommy getting engaged on Josie's birthday, Mam'll soon be losing his money anyway. It was decided ages ago that they're going to have rooms with Josie's parents.'

Tucking her arm in his, Roy sighed. 'Come on, love. Something'll turn up. Let's find a cafe and have a cup of tea.'

21

Thinking Bert was asleep, Polly crept into the kitchen in search of a tea-towel that was drying over the brass rail above the range. But seeing him slumped in his armchair, head in hands, she crept away again, her mind troubled.

It was now sixteen years since he'd been discharged from the army, so ill they hadn't expected him to live. Many a time she'd thanked God for his return, and by now should be used to Bert's black moods, the times when he'd avoid all company and become irritable and lose his temper over nothing at all.

The trouble was, Polly told herself, before the war he had been such a proud man, a good provider, good husband and father, and, although she could never have brought herself to tell him, a good lover too. But since that awful night when he'd wept at his inability to make love to her, the physical side of their marriage was over, doing even more harm to his fragile self-esteem.

A knock on the door sent her scurrying through the kitchen, then hearing discordant young voices singing *Away in a Manger*, she went back for her purse. They'd started on *God Rest Ye Merry, Gentlemen* before she'd opened the door. It was Enid Brown's youngest, a girl of about nine or ten, and a small girl of about Gareth's age whom Polly didn't recognise. As she slipped some coppers into the two outstretched hands, Daisy Brown said, 'Ta! Ta very much, Mrs Evans.' And in the same sing-song voice the small girl echoed her words. 'Ta, Mrs Evans!'

Polly was smiling as she closed the door, remembering the time when she wouldn't have answered it to carol singers for then she hadn't had a copper to give them.

Looking around the kitchen at the brightly coloured paper chains that Laura and Roy had hung to Gareth's delight, Polly thanked God the young couple were living with them for if anyone could bring a smile to Bert's face it was his young grandson. Laura was expecting another child in the summer. Would that mean they'd want to move?

Hearing the front door open and Gareth's voice high with excitement, she went to meet them. The child came running towards her, crying, 'Look, Nana! Look what Daddy Christmas gived me.' And held up a little metal van.

'Father Christmas was in the toy bazaar at Goldberg's,' Laura explained.

'You spoil him, Laura,' Polly told her, but her eyes wore an indulgent expression as she said, 'Go and show youer granddad, *cariad*. Perhaps it'll cheer him up.'

The kitchen door was open and a moment later he was on Bert's knee and she heard her husband asking, 'What's this then, young man?' and the child replying, 'It's a motor-van, Granddad. Not one with horses like Uncle Tommy drives.'

Hearing them laughing, Polly followed Laura into the middle room where a cheerful fire burned behind the guard and the dark oak dining suite, new when Laura and Roy got married, shone with polish and elbow grease. There was a Christmas tree in the corner, glowing with coloured glass baubles and silver glitter, and the two leather armchairs drawn up to either side of the fire invited you to sink on to their velvet cushions.

'Sit down, Mam. I'll put the kettle on,' Laura told her, laying her coat, hat and scarf over a chair.

She looks well these days, Polly thought contentedly as she waited for her daughter to return with the tea. The baby wasn't expected until the end of June, and apart from a mild bout of morning sickness Laura was blooming with health. Oh, if only there was some way they could stay here, she thought. Tommy and Josie were planning to get married sometime next year and when they'd set up home with her mother there'd be his bedroom going spare. Josie was a nice girl, plump, pretty and very good-natured. She'd make Tommy a good wife. Yes, she'd a lot to be thankful for, Polly told herself.

★ ★ ★

On Christmas Day Polly, Laura and Sally were sitting by the fire in the middle room waiting to hear the King's Speech. Bert and Roy were in the kitchen playing with the train set Gareth had had for Christmas, laying the track and putting tunnel and station in place as eagerly as any child.

'Let me wind it, Dada, let me!' Gareth danced with impatience, hands outstretched, but Roy was already turning the key.

'You've got to be very careful. You might break it, son.'

'I won't! I won't!' Gareth pulled at his father's sleeve, tears of frustration glittering on his lashes, for they'd taken over as soon as he'd opened the box.

'Let him have it, Roy. It is his, mind,' Bert said gently. And the cream and brown train in his hands at last, Gareth carefully set it on the track.

In the middle room Laura was turning the knobs of the new radio they'd bought. She was very proud of the polished oak cabinet with its fretted front behind which gilt mesh gleamed. You only had to turn a knob to bring in a number of stations, the reception clear as a bell, the volume easily controllable.

It was two minutes to three and they'd drawn their chairs around it, waiting expectantly, when there was a knock on the door. Tutting with annoyance at being disturbed, Polly rose to answer it. As she hurried back to the room, an apologetic Jessie following her, the latter said, 'Winnie and Bobby are there with the kids. Talking nineteen to the dozen they are, an' I'd promised myself I'd hear 'im speak, especially after we listened when it was their Jubilee. God! That was a day to remember, wasn't it, Poll?'

And Polly was seeing again the street decked with bunting on that day early in May, tables covered with red, white and blue paper cloths, children wearing paper hats and waiting with eager expectant faces as jelly was doled out and sandwiches and cakes handed round. Then the races when Gareth fell and grazed his knee. And afterwards the adults had had their own tea, and a sing-song with beer and home-made wine flowing. But King George V actually speaking to them on the wireless, his voice filled with emotion, that had been the highlight of the day. The realisation that he was a human being, touched by all the loyalty he'd been shown, his voice vibrant with feeling as he'd promised to dedicate himself anew to serving his people for all the years that might still be given him, had been a revelation.

The clock struck three and His Majesty was announced. As the kindly voice filled the room Polly thought it sounded tired. It's probably the wireless, she told herself, for although Laura had twiddled the knobs the reception wasn't as clear as usual.

When they'd discussed this, coming to the conclusion that it could be the set, Jessie turned to Sally to ask, 'When you going to London to live then?' and Sally replied, 'Next week. Bill's got us furnished rooms in Lambeth.'

She sounded a little uncertain for, after the initial excitement of receiving his letter, and especially now in the familiar surroundings of home with all her family about her, London seemed a world away and the thought of living in furnished rooms in a stranger's house in a strange city more than intimidating.

Seeing her younger daughter's expression, Polly said quickly, 'London isn't the end of the earth, Jessie. She'll be able to come home sometimes, and we'll be able to visit.'

'Oh, Mam! That's just it. We've only got two furnished rooms. There'll be nowhere to put anyone up until we get a place of our own,' Sally wailed.

'Well, we started like that,' Polly comforted her. 'But youer dada soon got us a place of our own. Bill's a good lad, he'll do his best for you, but he'll need you there to encourage him.'

★　★　★

It was damp and very cold when, the following week, Sally set off for the station accompanied by Laura, carrying all her possessions in a large cardboard case. Boarding the tram at Clifton Street, Laura tried to keep the conversation going but soon realised her sister had something on her mind. And it's only natural, she told herself, with Sally going so far away and heading for rooms she hasn't even seen yet.

As the train hissed slowly to a stop in a great cloud of steam Sally was remembering the last time Laura had seen her off at the station, on the day they'd got married and were going back to Bill's home in the valleys. Was it less than a month ago?

'Best get a seat, Sal,' Laura told her as they hugged each other. Sally stepped into a carriage and stood in the doorway.

'Write to us often,' Laura said. 'You know Mam will worry until she hears. Better close the door, Sally, he's going to wave his flag.'

'And you write to me,' she answered, her voice drowned as the train moved noisily away from the platform.

Suddenly her eyes filled with tears and she gazed mistily out of the window, hoping the other passengers hadn't noticed.

At Newport the carriage filled up as people tramped the corridor, looking for seats. There was a white frost on fields and hedges as they flew past, and when they were nearing Bristol and entering the Severn tunnel her heart lurched with fear. Someone hurriedly closed the window and those talking raised their voices to be heard. Apart from that no one seemed to take any notice, but with the darkness streaking past and the roar of the tunnel, Sally stared as though mesmerised at her reflection in the glass, thankful when at last they emerged into the light of the murky afternoon.

When they'd left Bristol behind and towns and villages were rushing past as the train gathered speed, Sally brought out the thermos flask and sandwiches her mam had packed, sure everyone was watching her until one or two of the other passengers brought out theirs too. She was shaking the crumbs from her skirt when the lady opposite smiled at her and she smiled too then went back to staring out of the window at the frost-rimed hedges and leaden sky. The scene matched her troubled mood for she had something else to worry about besides going to live in a strange city. Sally was pretty certain she was pregnant. She'd always been so regular before; now with each passing day her hopes were fading fast. It wasn't that she didn't want a child, but Bill had said he must be careful for they had to save if they were ever to have a home and furniture of their own. What would he say when she told him her fears?

As the train neared Paddington her heart sank. All the buildings looked drab and dirty, and the vastness of the station as they drew into it, the way people were pushing each other in order to get off, filled her with dismay. Steam, noise, porters trundling luggage . . . these were her first impressions as she was jostled on to the platform then carried along by the crowd making its way to the barriers, her eyes anxiously probing beyond to where Bill would be waiting. Then she was in his arms, her fears receding. He picked up her case and steered her towards the underground.

The journey home was a kaleidoscope of impressions: her fear of putting her foot on an escalator that seemed to disappear into the bowels of the earth; underground platforms where trains roared through; constant noise and bustle. It was dark by the time they reached Lambeth, her head ached, and Sally wished with all her heart they were back in Cardiff or the friendly valleys where they could have lived with Bill's mam and dad.

'Here it is, love,' he told her, stopping outside a drab-looking place in a long street of dingy houses that opened straight on to the pavement. As he turned the key and they stepped inside a strong smell of cabbage water wafted towards them.

'We got the two front rooms, like I told you,' he said proudly.

'Shut that bleedin' door!' a voice yelled from somewhere beyond the stairs.

When Bill pushed her gently before him into the front room Sally's worst fears were confirmed. A three-piece suite covered in stained green velvet took up most of the space. A bright fire burned in the grate, which she noticed thankfully had an oven at the side, but the whole thing was red with rust as was the metal fender. As she looked around her at the peeling walls, Bill said hurriedly, 'We'll soon get it put right, love. I've only been here a few days. A lick of paint will make all the difference.'

He looked so upset at her reaction that Sally flung her arms about him and held him close. They were young and strong and they had each other. Together they'd scrimp and save and soon be able to rent a house of their own.

Then she remembered the baby she was pretty certain was on the way and the dream of a place of their own receded into the distant future.

22

'Terrible, isn't it? And only last summer we had a party for their Jubilee.'

Dressing the side window in purple crêpe paper, Becky lifted the photograph of King George V and began to pleat wide black satin ribbon around the frame as her mother replied, 'The end of an era it is, Jessie. Nothing will ever be the same again.'

Every time a customer had entered the shop they'd commented dolefully on the death of King George for people felt a genuine affection for him. Many had hardly left their wireless sets since the sombre message had been broadcast: 'The king's life is moving peacefully towards its close.'

Now the Prince of Wales would be King Edward VIII. Becky had seen photos of him in the *Echo*: a slight young man with a worried look on his face. Tying the bow at the bottom of the portrait, she closed the door to the window and joined her mam behind the counter. At least the king and queen had a family to carry on the line; after nearly seven years of marriage she'd almost given up hope and knew Nellie would never stop blaming

217

her for their childless state.

'You've heard about the king then?' Polly Evans had just come in and was nodding towards the window.

'Yes. Becky's done her best but we've been too busy to send out for any more crêpe. Have you heard from Sally?'

'Had a couple of letters, we have. She says the rooms are quite comfortable.' It was what Sally hadn't said that was worrying her mother. No description of their accommodation at all, and she knew Sally well enough to expect a glowing and detailed account if she'd been pleased with what she'd found. Laura had said that Sally mightn't have had time to write much but Polly thought that excuse didn't really hold water, for since the rooms were furnished Sally wouldn't have had much to organise. She just had to put her clothes in the wardrobe and food in the cupboard . . . and that's what Polly had come to Dora Morgan's for, food, so she'd better get on with ordering it and keep her worries to herself!

'The Prince of Wales will be King Edward now,' Becky said, going back to their earlier conversation. 'I read somewhere he's promised to help the miners.'

'That's what I was telling Bert, but he's got no faith in kings nor governments these days.

Says their promises are like pie-crusts, made to be broken.' What he'd also said was, 'What the hell can a bloke brought up in luxury know about the miners' suffering?' only he'd put it much stronger than that. They'll be at it again tonight when Roy comes home, she thought. Never known anyone argue like those two and still be good friends.

'It's Queen Mary I'm sorry for,' Dora said, remembering her own agony when Will had died.

When it was time for the shop to close Becky hung about filling the fixtures with blue bags of sugar she'd weighed earlier, then fetching the muslin wraps to cover the butter and cheese. When she took the brush to sweep up the sawdust, Dora said, 'I can do that, love, you'd better get off home.' Becky relinquished the brush grudgingly, knowing in her heart she didn't want to go.

Over the years Nellie's rheumatics had grown steadily worse and now she hobbled around the house and garden only with the aid of a stick. A few weeks ago they'd brought her bed down to the parlour, Nellie protesting to the last. But, unable as she was to climb the stairs, they'd had no choice. Her own increasing inability to do any work hadn't altered her expectations of how the house should look.

Now, as she let herself in, Becky realised she could never really bring herself to think of this house as home. She sighed, for even as she'd turned the key in the lock, Nellie's plaintive voice reached her. 'Where've you been, girl? Thought you'd 'ave been home ages ago, I did. We want some coal brought in before it's too dark, and you know Albert said he'd be late . . . '

'I'll make you a cup of tea before I put the dinner on,' Becky told her soothingly. 'Then I'll get the coal.'

Slightly mollified by her daughter-in-law's tone, Nellie said, 'I've been thinking, Becky. When the washing up's done, why don't we cut out those cushion covers? Then you could sew them on the machine. It'll be a good job when the evenings are light enough to clean some windows. God knows they need it with all that rain . . . '

She was still nattering away about all the things she'd like done when Becky went to the coal-house, taking a torch so she could see to shovel it into the scuttle. As she set it down by the side of the range and took off the cover to begin building up the fire, Nellie said, 'Time the fender and scuttle had a bit of Brasso on them.'

'I did them the beginning of last week,' Becky protested. 'Then you wanted the parlour turned out and you know how long that took to do.'

'Yes, well, it's you going out to work, isn't it? Most young married women stay at home doing the cooking and looking after the house. With all day to do them in the jobs would soon be done. If only you had a baby to look after, you'd *have* to stay at home.'

'You know I've got to help my mam,' Becky told her, tears of frustration stinging her eyes.

'Yes, well, I can't help noticing things that need doing, stuck here on my own all day. The front step hasn't been scrubbed for nearly a week . . . '

'That's enough, Mother.' Neither of them had noticed Albert come into the house and stand in the kitchen doorway. 'Becky's nobody's slave,' he went on. 'She works hard all day at the shop.' Then turning to his wife he said, 'No need for you to bother with cooking tonight, love. Just lay the table while I fetch some fish and chips.'

It was an uncomfortable meal as Nellie sulked and the two of them tried to keep up a conversation. In their room afterwards Becky said, 'I'm sorry about all the fuss. I was a bit late coming home, and it must be lonely spending all day on her own.'

'You come home in the middle of the day especially to get her a meal. She should be grateful. And it's me who should be apologising, love, for bringing you here when I'd promised we'd live over the shop.'

'It wasn't your fault, Albert. You weren't to know your aunt would have to go home. You'll be miserable now, having words with your mam. I know how much you love her.'

He took her hands in his and, eyes shining with devotion, said, 'Oh, Becky, there's one person I love even more than my mam and that's you. It really upsets me to see you slaving away every evening when I'd hoped to do so much for you.'

Looking into his earnest face a great wave of tenderness towards him swept over her, prompting her to say gently, 'You'd best go and make it up otherwise you'll both be unhappy. Anyway she's right about one thing: if we'd had a child I could have stayed at home all day, and I'd have been very houseproud too. I'm sorry about us not having a baby, Albert. I know how much it means to you.'

'If you can't have a child, love, well — we've just got to accept it. The main thing is we have each other. I couldn't live without you,' he told her. 'And as for the house, it looks fine to me. God knows, you and I work hard enough on it.'

'Yes, but go out and make it up with her,

Albert. And tell her I'll be out in a few minutes to cut out those cushion covers. I suppose I could have stitched them before . . .'

As Albert went to make peace with his mam, Becky's eyes filled with tears for it was plain even he thought she alone was to blame for their not having a child.

'Why?' she asked aloud. 'Why me?' She was healthy and strong and kept telling herself it might happen one day, but Albert seemed to have given up hope. He'd said they must accept it and that he was thankful they had each other. Fond as she was of Albert, for her it wasn't enough. Would she just go on, year after year, serving in her mother's shop and looking after Nellie and the house, with no hope of a child of her own to make it all worthwhile?

★ ★ ★

Just after Whitsun Albert came home from work to tell Becky excitedly, 'One of our customers has got an invalid chair to sell. When I told her Mam was housebound, she said we could try it out and see how she got on.'

'You'll have to ask her, Albert,' Becky warned him. 'Nellie's got a mind of her own.'

'Well, she's always saying how much she misses going out. With the chair we could take her to the park at weekends or on our half-day.'

At first Nellie flatly refused, saying, 'I'm not a baba to be pushed around in a pram.'

In the end it was the promise of Gareth's accompanying them that persuaded her. For months now Becky had been bringing him to the house whenever she could to give Laura a break and, contrary to expectations, Nellie and the boy had become firm friends, Gareth making a beeline for the kitchen as soon as they entered the house. All Nellie's crabbiness would disappear as he sat at the table munching biscuits or cakes or some other treat she'd kept for him. So when he asked, 'Are you comin' with us to the park on Sunday, Auntie Nellie?' she readily agreed.

Albert got the shop's van to deliver the chair. As he jumped out and wheeled it in Nellie had mixed feelings, telling herself she didn't want anyone's pity. Still, now he'd brought it she'd have to try it out, she'd promised young Gareth, and it did seem to be just a chair on wheels, not at all like the bath-chairs they'd had in her youth.

When Sunday came and Gareth arrived she was glad she was going out too and laughed when he said, 'You're going in your push-chair, Auntie Nellie.'

It was a lovely sunny day and a treat to be out in the fresh air. She took great gulps of it as she was wheeled into the park, and Gareth brought golden buttercups to hold under her chin: 'To see if you like butter,' he explained. A little while later he brought a bunch of daisies, already wilting in his hot little hands, for Nellie to mind for his mam.

As they returned to their street neighbours stopped them to talk, saying how nice it was to see her out again, and for the first time in many a day Nellie, feeling pleasantly tired, was looking forward to her tea.

23

On a warm Monday morning early in June Polly had just got home after taking Gareth to school when Laura told her she thought the baby was on its way. 'It's only a dull pain in my back at the moment, Mam, so I could be mistaken,' she explained. 'But I'll get things ready just in case.'

Laura hummed a tune as she took the little garments from the drawer and fetched towels and soap ready for the midwife. She couldn't wait to hold the new baby in her arms, she loved babies and had adored Gareth from the moment he was born. But at six years old, though he still enjoyed bedtime stories so long as they were adventurous ones, he didn't like too much cuddling and kissing especially if anyone else was around. If she lifted him on to her knee he'd quickly clamber down to play with his toys.

Half an hour later Polly brought in a tray of tea and they sat by the fireplace.

'Made up youer mind yet about a name?' Polly asked with a smile. Laura had been dithering for weeks between Dilys or Mary if it was a girl. If they had another boy it would be Peter after Roy's dad.

About an hour later Polly watched anxiously as her daughter grimaced in pain, saying, 'Do you think we should send for the midwife, *cariad*? The contractions seem more regular now.'

Laura just nodded.

'Shall I ask Jessie to come in with you while I go? I won't be more than a few minutes, nurse is only in the next street.'

'I'll be all right, Mam. Dad's in the garden and I could knock on the wall for Jessie if I had to. Won't Roy be surprised if the baby's here when he comes home tonight?' Laura said happily. 'I'm glad it's not going to drag out 'til the end of the month. Before the pains come again, I think I'll get upstairs and into bed. Everything's ready and there's plenty of hot water on the stove.'

Carrying the little garments upstairs she felt a deep contentment. She had longed for this baby as much as she had for Gareth and was looking forward so much to holding it in her arms. Another bout of pain interrupted her thoughts and she lay on the bed, gripping the bedclothes, until it passed. Gareth had been a long time coming. Perhaps this one would be in a hurry? She pictured herself when Roy came home, sitting up in bed in her best nightie, the new baby in her arms.

Perhaps he would come home early. Someone could go to the post office and phone him with the news as soon as the child was born.

Polly came in with the midwife, a plump cheerful little woman with big brown eyes and a high colouring.

''Ullo, love. How we doing then?' She smiled at Laura before rolling up her sleeves and washing vigorously in the bowl. 'Let's have a look then. Oh, it'll be a while yet. I've got another mam just around the corner — I won't be more than half an hour.' And she rolled down her sleeves again and went on her way.

By the time she got back Polly was looking anxiously out of the window for the contractions were coming much faster now. Making sure the midwife had everything she needed, she went downstairs, worried that it would soon be twelve o'clock and time to pick Gareth up from school. She would have asked Jessie to have him but knew she was meeting their Winnie in town.

'I'll fetch him,' Bert offered when she voiced her worry.

'But you've never met him from school,' Polly said before she could stop herself.

'Only because I've never been asked,' he told her. 'I know where it is, though.'

Bert was so much better now, more

Balance

£0.01 plus

We pay intere

earn, please c

AER stands for

added each ye

For details of int

phone our Custo

g Society

s Park

o.uk

confident, and though he still had his grey days, much happier too. She watched him going down the street with a deep feeling of contentment.

'Where's Mama?' were Gareth's first words when he came in.

'Gone to fetch youer new baby,' Polly told him, putting his dinner on the table.

'Will it be here when I get home from school tonight?' he asked excitedly.

'I don't know, love — '

A knock on the door cut the conversation short. It was Becky, saying, 'One of the customers said they'd seen the midwife. Is everything all right, Mrs Evans?'

'Yes, she's still here,' Polly told her. 'Gareth thinks his mam's gone to fetch the baby,' she explained hurriedly as they went towards the kitchen. 'I'll just slip upstairs, see if anything is needed before I get him ready to go back to school.'

'I'll take him,' Becky offered, 'and fetch him tea-time if you like? Mam won't mind, we're not very busy today anyway. He can stay to tea, Nellie loves having him.'

'Thanks, Becky,' Polly said gratefully.

It was late in the afternoon and seemed to be getting hotter as the day progressed. Bert was working in the shady part of the garden, smoking his pipe. She could tell he was anxious about Laura by the way he was puffing at it. She'd been in labour a long time. Should they send for Dr Powell?

Suddenly a baby's cry broke the silence and Polly dashed through the house and up the stairs. She was almost halfway when the midwife rushed from the bedroom, white as chalk, crying: 'The doctor! Fetch the doctor . . . I can't stop the bleeding.'

Polly hurried back downstairs and opened the front door. Luckily a neighbour's boy was gliding past on roller skates. Scribbling a message, she gave it to him and he was off like the wind.

Upstairs the midwife was bending over Laura. 'I can't stop the haemorrhage,' she told Polly in a frightened voice. 'I just wish he'd come.'

Laura's eyes were closed, her face like alabaster, the silky brown hair damp with perspiration. By contrast the midwife's apron was splattered with blood and the bedclothes soaked in it, the red stain still spreading as Polly watched in horror. Wrapped in towels, the baby whimpered in its cot and Polly glanced over at it.

'A little girl, Mrs Evans.' The midwife sounded distraught.

The front door had been left open and Polly had just gone back to the kitchen when she heard the doctor come in and bound up the stairs. When she went up the bedroom door was closed and, filled with foreboding, she went slowly downstairs again. She'd better send for Roy . . . Glancing at the clock, she saw it was a quarter to five. Jessie was calling to her over the wall. Polly's legs felt like jelly as she went outside. Bert looked up anxiously from the kitchen chair he'd put under the apple tree, asking, 'Any news yet, love?' At his words she burst into tears.

Jessie was over the wall in a second and Bert cried, 'My God! Polly, what's wrong?'

Jessie's daughter Winnie, who'd just got back from shopping with her mam, dashed to the phone with a message for Roy and the three of them waited in the kitchen, anxiously listening for sounds from above.

Ten minutes later the doctor came down. Looking into his grey face, Polly's heart lurched with fear.

'It's a girl,' he said, but his eyes didn't meet hers and as Polly's hand went to her mouth he went on, 'I'm sorry, we did our best. It was the haemorrhaging. Laura just slipped away.'

Polly's cry of anguish brought Bert's arms about her but there was no comfort to be found there. Laura had been so happy this morning, looking forward to the baby coming. Now she would never hold the little

231

mite in her arms or suckle it. And Roy would be here soon, he must be told, and Gareth — poor little soul.

Bert sat in his chair, head in hands. Polly, sick with grief, watched as Dr Powell signed the death certificate. She couldn't believe it. She would wake up soon. Jessie had come into the kitchen and was making tea, sweet and strong, but when a cup was put into her hands, Polly found she couldn't swallow.

There were footsteps rushing along the passage. Roy flung open the kitchen door, crying breathlessly, 'How is she, Mam? Can I go up?' His anxious expression soon turned to one of incredulity, then of horror when Polly, rising slowly to put a comforting arm around him, said, her voice breaking, 'I'm so sorry, son, so very sorry. Laura's passed away . . . '

Roy's face blanched. Clutching the doorpost for support, he stared at Polly, taking no notice when she told him gently, 'You've got a daughter, Roy.' Turning on his heel, he bounded up the stairs.

★ ★ ★

Becky, fetching Gareth from school, was greeted by eager questions.

'Has my mama brought the new baby back yet?'

'Not yet, love,' she told him, wondering how Laura was getting on. She may have had the baby by now but Polly would have plenty to do. It was best to keep Gareth out of the way for the time being.

'After we've seen Auntie Nellie, can I come to your shop and weigh up some things?'

'Yes, of course you can, but we'll have a cup of tea first. I've got some of those iced biscuits you like and you can have a glass of milk.'

Nellie greeted him with open arms and when the tea things were washed and put away Becky took him to the shop where, with an apron tucked up and tied about his waist, Gareth stood on a low box and played at weighing dried peas.

It was just after she'd gone behind the counter that Jessie came in, looking distraught, her face white and eyes filled with tears. Becky closed the stock room door on Gareth as she listened to the awful news.

'Oh my God! Jessie, how are we going to tell him?' Becky nodded towards the closed door.

'Best leave it to Polly, *cariad*,' Jessie told her sadly. 'I can't believe it, I really can't. Our Winnie's just phoned for Tommy to come home but he's still out on the van.'

Becky couldn't concentrate on anything as memories of Laura flooded her mind. The tears kept rolling down her cheeks, to be hastily wiped away in case Gareth tired of his play.

She was dreading taking him home. Poor Roy, poor Polly and Bert, and poor Sally when she heard. She was expecting a baby in three months' time. Besides the tragedy of losing her sister, it was bound to worry her.

When Becky took Gareth home Roy came to the door, his face pale and drawn. Putting his arms about his son, he drew him close.

'I'm so very sorry, Roy. If there's anything I can do?' Becky said, her eyes filling with tears. 'I could keep Gareth?'

'No. Thanks all the same, Becky, but he'll have to know sometime. Come in.'

'Where's my mama?' Gareth looked around him. Then, seeing the baby in Polly's arms, 'Did she bring it home?'

There were tears in his grandmother's eyes as she laid the baby in the Moses basket and lifted Gareth on to her lap. 'Mama couldn't come home, *cariad*. God wanted her in heaven, she's staying there with Him, but we've got a little sister for you. Look!' And

Polly pointed across to the basket resting on the table.

But after one glance at the baby Gareth began to scream: 'I don't want her, take her away! I don't want a sister — I want my mama back!'

24

The funeral was over, the house filled with mourners. Sandwiches, tea and beer were handed around while family and friends reminisced. Polly, her face haggard from grief and lack of sleep, went to the kitchen to give baby Dilys her feed, grateful that early that morning Becky had taken Gareth, leaving him with Nellie Lloyd while she'd attended the service in the front room.

Almost as though she knew the heartbreak surrounding her birth little Dilys was fractious and Polly had walked her up and down for most of the night, rocking her to and fro. She was thankful to be kept busy, dreading the time when they'd have to discuss the future, for Celia Bevan had said she wanted to help and was in the front room now discussing her plans with her son.

Despite all the extra work, Polly didn't want to part with this precious babe who already had a look of Laura about her, and was determined Dilys would suffer as little as possible from the tragedy of losing her mam. Gareth had been fractious too, refusing to have anything to do with the new baby and asking awkward questions.

'Why do God want my mama?' he'd asked, his face blotched with tears, and when Polly had tried to answer, he'd asked bluntly, 'Won't she never come back, Nana?'

Polly had hugged him tightly, wiping her own tears away before they dropped on his dark curly head. Then Tommy came to take him by the hand and, as they joined Josie waiting in the doorway, Polly sighed.

She had just laid the baby in her Moses basket when the kitchen door opened and Roy and his mother came in.

'This is a sad time for us all, Polly,' Celia Bevan began. 'It's a pity I live so far away but I've suggested to Roy that I take Gareth back with me. It's a long time since I had Roy and I don't think I could manage a young baby but I'm sure I could cope with my grandson.'

Polly's face blanched even further and she felt relieved when Roy said, 'I told you, Mam, I don't want the children split up. But it's you who will be doing all the work, Polly, and I haven't the right to ask — '

'I can cope, Roy,' she told him, giving a great sigh of relief. 'I know Laura would want the children brought up together. But it's good of you to offer, Celia.'

That evening when she was getting Gareth to bed he asked in a worried voice, 'Will God want me as well, Nana?'

'No! I'm sure He won't, *cariad*. We need you here to help with youer little sister.'

'I wish she hadn't come,' he said in a sad voice. 'I wish Mama hadn't gone to fetch her. Then she wouldn't have had to stay, would she?'

Polly was feeling out of her depth and worried as to where the conversation might lead. She'd ask Gareth's Sunday school teacher, she decided, then remembered the girl was little more than a child herself.

Sally had travelled from London for the funeral and didn't look well. Nearly seven months pregnant, she shouldn't have made the journey, Polly thought. She'd tried to reassure her that what had happened to Laura rarely occurred, but knew Sally would be concerned about it herself now until the baby was born.

Reading between the lines, she'd gathered the young couple weren't much better off than they would have been if Bill had stayed at his job in Cardiff. He earned a little more but everything was so much more expensive in London and Polly wished, with Sally nearing her time, that they were living here or with Bill's parents at Tre-Mynydd.

With the funeral over they settled into some sort of routine. Bert took Gareth to and from school and Polly was glad because it got him out of the house. When Roy came home he saw to his son and got him to bed, but as soon as the boy was settled he'd sit in the middle room, head in hands, and Bert would sit in his armchair in the kitchen doing the same. Very soon she wished the two of them would argue as they used to, anything to bring them alive again.

Now every Wednesday and Sunday afternoon Becky and Albert took the children to the park if it was fine, or back to their house if it wasn't. If they were going out Albert would push his mother in the invalid chair and Becky would wheel Dilys in her pram with Gareth walking by her side. When they returned she'd bring the baby back home but Gareth would stay with them until it was time for bed, allowing Polly to do some much-needed housework.

Watching Albert playing with Gareth in the park, Becky couldn't help thinking what a wonderful father he'd have made. Then she remembered his words when he'd held her in his arms last night.

'For the very first time, Becky, I'm really glad we can't have a child,' he'd said. 'I'd be worried sick if we could, after what happened to Laura.'

'But that doesn't happen very often,' she'd

told him. 'Anyway, I'd be willing to take the risk.'

'Well, I wouldn't,' he told her firmly. 'We're best as we are.'

But watching as he lifted Gareth on to his shoulders and grinned up at him, she knew just how much having a child of his own would have meant to him.

The baby was whimpering. Becky rocked the pram and saw her close her eyes. As Gareth came to sit beside her, Becky put a finger to her lips, whispering, 'She's lovely, isn't she, your little sister?' only to be surprised when he answered candidly, 'I don't like her very much.'

'Why is that?'

'Well, when my mama went to fetch her, she didn't come home.'

'Oh, but that wasn't the baby's fault, Gareth,' Becky told him. 'You had your mammy for six years, and Dilys never knew her at all, poor little soul.'

Becky knew that Gareth would be missing his mam far more than the orphaned baby but she wanted to enlist his sympathy for Dilys before the rift between them became any wider.

For a moment Gareth looked at her solemnly, his lashes glistening with tears, and her heart went out to him. Then he went across to Albert who was standing by Nellie's chair.

'Why don't you pick some daisies for Nana?' Nellie suggested. 'She'd like that, I'm sure.'

When he'd picked a bunch and given them to Nellie to mind he came to look down at Dilys again. As the baby stirred and opened her eyes he gently touched her hand. Becky, about to tell him to let her sleep, stilled her tongue as Gareth held out a finger for his sister to grip, echoing the words Becky had said to him as he bent over the pram, murmuring, 'Poor little baby, poor little soul.'

★ ★ ★

As the months passed Polly's concern for Sally mounted. The baby was due mid-September and the girl had no one in London to whom she could turn. When a letter came saying her mother-in-law had persuaded her to go to them to have the baby, Polly was very relieved.

Tommy and Josie had been married quietly at the beginning of August and as planned were living with her mam. They'd offered to put the wedding off but Polly had insisted they go ahead, having waited so long already. She missed Tommy's money but they

241

managed, for Roy was very good about giving her extra for the baby's milk and other expenses.

At the beginning of September Sally was with her in-laws at Tre-Mynydd and soon Polly was waiting anxiously for news of the birth, wishing she could be with the girl. But with two young children to care for and two men almost as dependent there was no way she could go. But she spent every free moment looking out for the telegraph boy and praying fervently that Sally would be all right.

The telegram came on 17 September. Polly turned it over and over in her hands, her heart beating fast. Bert had gone to fetch Gareth from school and she stared down at it, picking at the envelope, longing to know yet dreading its contents. When it was open and she drew out the slip of paper she willed herself to look down, her hands shaking so much the letters danced before her eyes. Finally she made out the words and her heart filled with joy as she read: SALLY HAD A LITTLE BOY STOP MOTHER AND BABY DOING WELL.

Now she couldn't wait for Bert to return and when he did she rushed to meet him, holding the telegram out for him to see, telling Gareth, 'You've got a little cousin, *cariad.* Youer Auntie Sally's had a baby boy.'

'Did God keep her when she went to fetch it?' he asked anxiously.

Polly shook her head and, putting her arms tightly about him, held him close.

'You'll be wanting to see them, Poll. Isn't there some way . . . ?' Bert began.

'Yes, I've got to see them somehow,' she replied. 'Sally'll be staying there a month. I'll think of a way.'

But it was Becky who provided the answer. 'We could easily have Gareth all day, and I suppose I could manage the baby too,' she added doubtfully.

'Oh, I can take the baby with me,' Polly told her gratefully. 'It would be too awkward to leave her, with her feeds and everything, and I can carry her Welsh fashion.'

And so on a late-September day, the chill of autumn in the air, she set off, a shawl about her shoulders with the child snugly wrapped inside. It was years since she'd been on a tram, even longer since she'd boarded a train, and Polly's eyes were bright with excitement at the thought of seeing Sally and the child.

As the train hissed into the station in a great cloud of steam she saw Peggy Thomas, waving to her. The next moment she was looking at Dilys and crying, 'There's bonny she's grown, Polly.' The baby slept on as they left the station and began to climb the hilly road. Peggy had taken the bag with the bottles and nappies and talcum powder and now she said, 'Shall I hold her for a while, *cariad*?'

'No, best not to disturb her,' Polly told her. 'How's Sal and the baby?'

'Blooming, both of them. Easy as shelling peas it was for Sal. Wants to get up, she does, but I told her, 'It's early days yet, my gul. Rue it you will if you get up too soon.' '

On arriving at the small terraced house, Polly was warmly welcomed, and after Peggy had admired the sleeping Dilys again and laid her in an armchair with a chair against it to keep her safe, Polly was led upstairs to the bedroom. Sally, looking much better than when her mother had seen her last, was resting against lace-edged pillows, wearing a pretty nightdress and bed-jacket, her arms outstretched to embrace her mam. Then Polly was bending over the cot where the baby lay asleep, crying, 'Bless his little heart, he's lovely! What are you going to call him, Sally?'

'No more Williams. Two's quite enough, thank you,' Peggy Thomas laughed. 'I must confess, when ouer Billy was small it caused a lot of confusion.'

'We're calling him Brynley,' Sally said

proudly. 'Where's little Dilys, Mam? Peggy says you've brought her with you.'

Dilys was brought to the bedroom and much admired, and when she'd had her bottle and been changed she went obligingly back to sleep.

'They're giving Bill a better round,' Sally told her excitedly when Polly was once more settled in the basket chair by her side. 'He'll have a van of his own too. There's a picture of a vacuum cleaner on the side of it,' she added ruefully, 'but we'll be able to go out in it sometimes, he says.'

A knock on the front door sent Peggy rushing downstairs, returning a few minutes later with two women she introduced as: 'Glad and Megan from next-door, and very good neighbours they are too. And this is Polly, Sally's mam.'

The introductions over, they made a bee line for the cot.

'Lovely 'e is an' no mistake,' Glad said, her chubby face one big smile. 'Got a look of Bill about 'im already he has, Peggy.'

Megan, the tall, thin one, was making clucking noises as she too bent over the cot, saying, 'Brought you a little present we 'ave, boyo.' And she put the brown paper parcel she'd been carrying on to the bed.

As Sally unwrapped it and drew out two

245

little matinee coats, one pale blue, one white, she cried, 'Oh, they're lovely! Did you crochet one each?'

'Only finished them last night we did, *cariad*. Made them on the big side, mind, to allow for him growing.'

Listening to their friendly lilting voices Polly wished that Sally and Bill were living here in Tre-Mynydd with his mam and dad instead of faraway London, but there was nothing much here in the way of work save the pit and as Peggy herself said: 'One son is enough, coming home from each shift as black as the hobs of hell!'

25

As autumn gave way to winter and Dilys thrived under Polly's loving care, the house was still steeped in grief. Despite her own heartbreak Polly wished the men would begin to take an interest in what went on around them; anything to lighten the atmosphere of gloom.

Rumours were rife that the new king was courting an American divorcee and when the story broke in the *Yorkshire Post* Roy's mother sent him a copy. But although the news was causing widespread speculation, Roy didn't even bother to read it through.

Soon everyone seemed to be talking about the situation, especially when it became clear that neither Parliament nor Queen Mary would ever agree to Wallis Simpson's becoming queen.

Bert did rouse himself to say, 'Well, so much for the promises he made the miners when he was Prince of Wales. Told you at the time he didn't mean a word he said.'

'I think he did mean it when he said it,' Polly told him, anxious to keep the conversation going.

'That's just it,' Bert replied. 'Got no staying power, that's his trouble. Pity he's the eldest son. The Duke of York would make a much better king.' + DID

'King George was a good man and he'll be difficult to follow,' Polly said, thankful to see Bert taking such an interest. 'What do you think, Roy?'

'I think it's time I got Gareth to bed, Mam,' he replied, steering his son towards their room.

This apathy isn't good for the children, she thought worriedly. Something will have to be done.

Soon speculation was rife. Would the king sacrifice the throne for the woman he loved?

Pictures of the Duke and Duchess of York and their daughters were on every front page, news of the two little princesses eagerly sought. When on 10 December Edward finally abdicated, most of his subjects gave a deep sigh of relief.

'What'll happen to all those souvenirs they've made?' Polly wondered aloud when Jessie came in for a cup of tea.

'Oh, they'll sell them easy enough,' was her opinion. 'Curios they'll be. They're saying that Wallis Simpson was divorcing her second husband in time to marry the king before his Coronation next May. There won't be no

Coronation now so she's going to be disappointed, isn't she?'

'They must love each other for him to give up his throne — ' Polly began when Bert cried angrily, 'Where's his sense of duty? Well rid of him we are, if you ask me.' *Yes. He was weak!!*

As Christmas approached Polly did her best to seem cheerful, for the children's sake, hanging the gaudy paper trimmings around the room and glittering baubles on the tree. Her heart was heavy when she remembered last Christmas and Laura putting up the very same decorations. Now, as Dilys bounced in her pram as far as the reins would allow, making excited little noises as she watched the baubles catch the light, Gareth went across to her. Pointing towards it, he said, 'Look, Dilys, pretty Christmas tree.' He was very attentive to his sister now and although Polly often wondered what had changed him, she was truly thankful for it.

There'd been a few awkward questions over the months, like the time he'd been playing with Dilys on the mat and, looking up suddenly, had asked in a puzzled voice, 'If my mama couldn't bring her, how did Dilys get here, Nana?'

She'd told him the well-worn lie that had served generations of children: 'The midwife brought her in her bag, *cariad*.'

Roy was looking gaunt and pale. She often heard him pacing his room when she got up in the night to see to Dilys, but he too put on a semblance of Christmas spirit, giving Polly money to fill the children's stockings and buy a big rag doll for Dilys, as well as what Gareth had asked Father Christmas for: some more rails and carriages for his train set plus a station and an extra tunnel.

Gradually Roy had begun to show a little interest in what went on in the outside world, particularly in a man called Hitler in Germany who had marched into the Rhineland in the spring against the advice of his generals and someone called Mussolini in Italy who'd invaded Abyssinia and captured the capital, Addis Ababa. In August, when thousands of people from all over the world had flocked to Berlin for the Olympic Games, pictures in the paper had shown the Germans enthusiastically waving their country's flag and generally demonstrating the power of the National Socialist government. Nazis

'They're building up for something, Bert,' Roy had remarked, passing him the paper.

'Britain would never be daft enough to go to war again,' his father-in-law told him.

At one time Roy would have aired his doubts but now he simply shrugged his shoulders and went back to his room.

A couple of weeks before Christmas Roy went to the kitchen to find Polly scrubbing the tiles. Watching her rising painfully from her swollen knees, he said, 'Give me the bucket, Mam. I can do that for you.'

'It's not man's work, Roy,' she told him, sinking to her knees again and scrubbing an arm's-reach patch.

He took the brush from her and helped her gently to her feet, saying, 'You go and sit in the middle room, I'll have this done in no time.'

Seeing he was determined, Polly heaved a sigh of relief, saying, 'The coconut matting's on the line. I'll go and give it a good beating.'

'I'll do that too,' he told her, steering her firmly into the passage.

I must have been blind all this time, he thought. Poor, good-hearted Polly, how could he have managed without her? Steeped in his own sorrow, he'd taken everything she did for granted: the clean starched shirts and snowy underwear, his rooms freshly polished and dusted, meals always ready on the table for him. She worked hard from morning till night and kept the children well fed and looked after. There were lots of jobs he could have done to ease her burden, Roy reflected as he scrubbed and dried the black and red tiles. Like cleaning windows . . . He remembered her saying the lace curtains needed a wash but it was a waste of time doing them until she could clean the windows too.

He thought of his own mother, always elegantly turned out with weekly appointments at the hairdresser's. He'd been agreeably surprised at her offer to take Gareth even though he'd no intention of parting with him. It was Polly who'd made it possible for them to stay together. Polly with her tired eyes and rheumatic knees, who never, ever complained.

I'll help her more, Roy promised himself, pleased that he'd found something constructive to do, something he knew would have pleased Laura.

As he beat the mats hanging over the line, the dust making him sneeze, he thought how easy his life had been in comparison. He'd been so deeply engrossed in his own grief he hadn't realised all Polly was doing for him and the children. Dilys was always handed to him freshly washed and changed. He'd seen the snowy white towelling squares blowing in the breeze or on the wooden clothes-horse around the kitchen range. Polly and Bert rarely saw the fire these days for all the drying and airing that had to be done.

'You can put the clothes-horse around the fire in our room from now on, Mam. I spend more time out here than in there anyway,' he told her over the cup of tea they were enjoying after the kitchen had been put to rights.

In his room later on he pondered over what special present he could get Polly for Christmas. A little while ago he'd been thinking along the lines of a warm scarf and gloves or perhaps a pair of cosy slippers. He'd seen some in a shop in Clifton Street, warm plaid cloth with bobbles on the front. It isn't enough, he told himself now. This year it must be something really special. But what? Polly was well off for dresses and best things she almost never wore for Auntie Vi still kept her supplied with clothes the mistress gave her. But Polly had had to give up serving tea at the socials in the Labour Hall and didn't dress up now, even though the last outfit had been black and quite suitable for mourning.

Roy sat gazing into the fire, his eyes misty as he thought of those wonderful days before Dilys was born with Polly quickly making friends with the other women who served the refreshments, enjoying their company and a bit of social life she hadn't had for years. But what could he buy her for Christmas? It must be something that reflected his gratitude for all she did.

The idea came to him in a flash. He'd have

to pay for it out of the savings he and Laura had put by ready for when they found a place of their own. They'd never need the money for that now, he reflected sadly, but he knew Laura would have approved.

Suddenly he was remembering last year and Laura wrapping presents at the table. How happy she'd been then, eagerly looking forward to Christmas and thrilled that a new baby was on the way. He could see her still in his mind's eye, her lovely face smiling with satisfaction as she tied on another label. When she'd finished she'd come across to him and sat on his knee, snuggling against him as he'd held her close. A lump came to Roy's throat at the memory. Dropping his head into his hands, he sobbed like a child.

26

It was Christmas morning and presents were being exchanged, but it was a subdued affair this year so soon after Laura's death. Knowing how much she needed them, Roy had decided to get the slippers for Polly after all, for the special present he'd ordered wouldn't arrive until later in the day.

'Ooh! They're lovely, Roy,' she cried, wriggling her toes in the warm fleecy lining and simultaneously picking up Dilys's rag doll for the umpteenth time. But the baby, chuckling and obviously enjoying the game, threw it from the pram yet again.

Sucking on his new pipe, Bert said, 'Thanks for this too, son. It draws a treat.'

Gareth was in the middle room setting out the extras for his train set. Asking Roy's advice, Becky had bought him a set comprising a couple of porters with luggage trolleys, a guard complete with green flag, and some passengers to stand about the station waiting for a train to arrive.

After lunch Sally, Bill and baby Brynley would be making the trip from Tre-Mynydd where they were spending Christmas. Watching from the parlour window, Polly saw the van pull into the kerb and hurried to open the door, hugging her daughter and little grandson then drawing them quickly indoors out of the bitter cold. Bill had gone to the back of the van, to fetch their things, she supposed. But then the kitchen door burst open and he and Roy came in carrying a long cardboard box and, after struggling to open it, drew out an upright vacuum cleaner.

'Going to give us a demonstration, are you, Bill?' Polly asked, thinking Christmas a strange day to choose, when Roy said, 'It's a present for you, Mam, from Laura and me. Goodness knows you've earned it with all the things you do for me and the kiddies, and I know she'd have wanted me to do it.'

At the mention of Laura's name Polly's eyes filled with tears. But swallowing hard she managed to say, 'But it must have cost you a fortune! You shouldn't have spent all that on me.'

'Cheaper than I expected,' he told her. 'Bill's refusing to take his commission.'

The tea she'd made was forgotten as the light bulb was removed and the cleaner plugged into the socket and switched on, making a loud purring noise that Dilys greeted with a howl of protest. This brought

Gareth's arms protectively about her as he murmured, 'It won't hurt you, Dilly love. Gareth's here.'

'Shall we try it on the carpet square in the parlour?' Roy suggested. 'There's not much room here, and as Bill says it will clean all sorts of things, curtains, floors . . . '

Sally's baby, now three months old, seemed used to the noise. He looked about him curiously before yawning widely, then closing his eyes and going to sleep.

Polly felt like pinching herself to make sure it was real. Fancy Roy buying her a luxury like one of them new-fangled vacuum cleaners! She was a little worried about him spending all that money, but thinking of all the back-breaking jobs it would soon be taking care of, she was filled with gratitude.

When Becky came over to see Sally she was surprised to find what seemed like a full spring cleaning in progress, and even more surprised when she saw Polly pushing around a gleaming new cleaner.

'Here, have a go, Becky,' she invited, propelling the machine towards her, and Becky was very impressed with the result when she'd glided it over the rug in front of the fire.

'Why don't we have one?' Albert said when

she found him alone in their room and told him about it.

'I think they cost a lot of money, love.'

'Well, what if they do? So long as it'll save you work,' he replied. 'Let's go to Polly's now while Sally's husband is still there, see if he can order one for us. We might just as well give him the trade.'

As the cleaner was started up once more, this time to demonstrate its virtues to Albert, Bert said, 'I'd better not stand still, Poll, or you'll be gliding it over me.' But he was really grateful to Roy, seeing how useful it was going to be, and only wished he could have bought it for her himself.

Bill was delighted with the new order and promised Becky and Albert it would be delivered from the firm's Cardiff branch just as soon as they got back to work after the holiday.

When they returned home and told Nellie what they'd done she tutted as they'd known she would, declaring them new-fangled things a sheer waste of money when all that was needed to keep a place clean was a bit of elbow grease.

Albert winked at Becky, saying as they went back to their room to take off their coats, 'Mam doesn't realise how hard it is doing the housework as well as a job, but with you at the shop all day that cleaner is going to be a boon.'

Dora, who was with them as usual for Christmas Day and keeping Nellie company, didn't say a word. She'd long ago made up her mind never to interfere. She got on well with her daughter's mother-in-law because of this, realising that if Nellie was sometimes cantankerous it was largely from frustration at not being able to do the jobs herself. Dora could imagine how she must feel, sitting in a chair for most of the day, able only to toddle painfully around and wash a few dishes, but not to lift her arms to take in the washing if it rained or even to dust properly.

Nellie had worked so hard to keep them when Albert was young, it must be difficult for her to come to terms with this enforced idleness.

Dora felt much more cheerful these days. Trade was improving a little and more bills were being paid up at the end of the week. But without Albert's generous help she knew she'd have been forced to close. He made jobs like lifting down and boning a side of bacon look like child's play, and would lift a heavy sack on to his shoulder and climb the cellar steps with no effort at all.

After Christmas, with the worst of the weather upon them and few trips out in her invalid chair, Nellie found more time to be critical, though she was always over-indulgent with Gareth when he scattered cake or biscuit crumbs around, for the little boy could do no wrong in her eyes. The days were long for her all alone in the house, but they were long and tiring for Becky too, and her work was by no means finished when the shop closed for the night. Drying the washing was a nightmare, with Nellie's thick interlock bloomers and woollen vests and Albert's long-johns. It was too risky to put them on the line with no one able to take them in if it rained. And that was all it seemed to do as January came to an end and an icy February came in, threatening snow.

Nellie didn't have a good word to say about the vacuum cleaner and often complained about the noise it made and what it had cost, so Becky was very surprised when without meaning to she overheard her mother-in-law's conversation with a neighbour. Becky had been on her way to work and was just about to close the front door behind her when Hetty Williams said, 'How's Nellie these days? I haven't seen 'er about for some time.'

'Would you like to go in and have a word?' Becky asked. 'She'll be alone now until I get back from the shop.'

'Well, just for five minutes then. I can't stay

long, our Alma's comin' round this after-noon.'

Becky pushed open the door and took Hetty to the kitchen. She was about to turn the corner and go into the shop when she realised she'd left her white shop overall over a chair in the middle room. Running back, she turned the key and had picked up the neatly folded apron when she heard voices plainly coming from the kitchen, the door of which stood partly open. She stood still to listen and swiftly realised what Nellie was talking about.

'Wonderful they are them vacuum clean-ers,' she boasted. 'Our Albert bought Becky one to save her 'cos working all day at the shop, she hasn't got time to beat the rugs on the line. You wouldn't believe the things they do, Hetty: walls, curtains. You just slide the attachment thing down them . . .'

'Cost a pretty penny though, don't they?'

'Yes, well, they're worth it, with the two of them out to work all day and me not able to lend a hand.'

Becky smiled to herself, wondering how she was to keep a straight face next time Nellie carried on about elbow grease being best!

As she turned her coat collar up against the biting wind Becky longed for the spring days to come when, with Albert pushing his mam in the chair, they could take Gareth and baby Dilys out to the park again. Gareth spent quite a lot of time with them at the house but quickly became bored. In the park there was plenty of space for him to run and play and Albert was good with him, pointing out birds and trees and flowers or throwing a ball to him. And Becky loved pushing Dilys in her pram, secretly hoping people might think she was hers. Then, remembering Laura, she'd be sad for her friend had wanted the baby so much and had never even held her in her arms.

27

As 12 May drew near, plans for the Wilfred Street party to celebrate the coronation of King George VI and Queen Elizabeth were well ahead. Gareth's excitement grew. Polly had bought him new black daps for running in the races and on the evening before the party he insisted on having them by his bed, ready to put on first thing in the morning.

As she kissed him goodnight his cheeks were flushed. All evening he had been running up and down the garden path, practising for the races, coming indoors to flop on the sofa with exhaustion in between. He must be tired out, Polly told herself. He'll soon be asleep. But as she was leaving the room he stirred restlessly, sitting up to ask, 'Will Dada see me racing, Nan?'

'Yes, he's got a day off. Now come on, Gareth. Settle down or you'll be too tired to run tomorrow.'

Next morning, the sun already streaming through the window promising a lovely day, Polly was stirring porridge at the stove when Gareth came down, still in his pyjamas and wearing his new plimsolls. Turning towards him, her smile froze at sight of his spotty face. She should know chicken-pox when she saw it, Polly thought sadly, turning his face this way and that.

'When will the party start, Nan?'

'I don't think you'll be going, son,' she told him gently, knowing how much he'd been looking forward to today. She lifted him to look in the mirror. He stared at himself then said, 'Victor Williams had spots. You know, the boy who sits by me in class. Miss Thomas sent 'im 'ome.'

'Oh, Gareth! Why didn't you tell me?' she cried. But what difference would it have made? He'd have caught it just the same. At least I would have tried to keep him away from Dilys, she told herself, and that wouldn't be easy these days for the baby was like his shadow, crawling after him whenever he was in the house.

When he realised that having chicken-pox meant no party for him, tears began streaming down Gareth's face. Taking him in her arms, Polly wondered what she could do to make up for the disappointment. When presently Roy came down and Bert came in from the garden, they were amazed to see his spotty little face awash with tears.

'He was all right last night, Mam. A bit restless but I thought it was all the excitement,' Roy said in bewilderment.

'It's a shame after all the practising he's been doing for those races.' Bert was wondering what he could do to make it up to the little chap.

There was no consoling Gareth especially now he knew he wouldn't be running any races in his new daps. After breakfast Roy, who'd been helping with the decorations the evening before, stringing red, white and blue bunting across the street from one bedroom window to another, went out to see if he could help with anything else.

Gareth huddled on the sofa, feeling a little out of sorts and very sorry for himself, and Polly racked her brains for something to cheer him up. In an attempt to keep them apart she'd wheeled Dily's pram to a shady part of the garden but the baby screamed and struggled against being buckled in until Polly, desperate by now to get the washing on the line, lifted her out and took her indoors where she wriggled free and crawled towards Gareth, pulling herself up for the very first time and staring in bewilderment at the red spots on her brother's tearful face.

'She might just as well catch it and be done with it, Poll,' Jessie said, having just come into the kitchen, and Polly sighed in agreement.

'Tell you what, Gareth,' Jessie went on,

'when your nan goes to Clifton Street tomorrow, I'll give 'er the money to get one of them Magic Painting books from the Penny Bazaar.'

★ ★ ★

Becky's mam's shop was closing at twelve and just after this she accompanied the errand boy who was wheeling his bike down the street delivering the groceries that had been ordered for the party, the basket on the front overflowing with loaves of bread, bottles of red and yellow pop glowing in the sunlight, slabs of fruit cake, tins of fruit, butter that had been kept cool in the shop by putting it in a basin of cold water. Some of the neighbours would have made jellies and blancmanges, setting them overnight in the mesh-fronted safes in the yards where they'd stay until they were needed.

When the goods had been delivered to the party organisers, Becky knocked on Polly's door.

'Where is he? Where's our little runner?' she cried when Polly opened it to her.

'He's got chicken-pox, Becky. Of all the times to get a thing like that! You'd better not come in, love.'

'I've had it,' Becky assured her, following

her to the kitchen. 'Poor little Gareth, he must be awfully disappointed.'

'He is,' Polly admitted. 'I wish I could think of something to cheer him up.'

'We can have a party of our own,' Becky told him, 'but I expect you're feeling poorly, love?'

'He doesn't seem too bad,' Polly assured her. 'It's probably a mild attack.'

'I'll get some calamine lotion from the shop, it's very soothing for spots,' Becky said, making for the door. 'We'll organise some fun for him, you'll see.'

When she got back and the lotion had been dabbed on, the street party was about to begin.

'We could watch it with Gareth from the front room,' Becky suggested. 'Help me get this table over to the window, Roy. Gareth can sit here where he'll see everything. I'm going outside a minute to have a word with Mrs Brown.'

Polly watched from the window as Becky talked to Enid. She'd never liked Enid Brown, too much of a gossip she was and spiteful with it, but Polly had a grudging admiration for the way she organised things: street parties like today's or a collection for a wreath when there'd been a bereavement.

Becky looks so pretty, Polly thought. She

was wearing a pale green crêpe-de-chine dress in the new longer length, a wide belt circling her slim waist, short auburn curls glinting red-gold in the sunlight. Becky and Laura had always been such good friends and she'd been wonderful with the children who both adored her.

When she came back carrying one of the brightly coloured paper tablecloths and some hats made out of paper Union Jacks, they sat around the table to watch the proceedings, Dily's eyes wide with wonder at what was going on. As soon as the children in the street were settled at the trestle tables, a neighbour seated at the shabby, out-of-tune piano that had been dragged into the street belted out the national anthem and Becky went back and forth, bringing Gareth and Dilys's share of the feast. He didn't have much of an appetite but the jelly shimmering invitingly on his plate soon disappeared as did his portion of ice-cream.

When the youngsters had finally finished their meal Gareth knelt at the window, wistfully watching everything that was going on as games were organised and party-pieces given. The day was getting hotter. Dilys fell asleep and was taken up to her cot. A whistle blew for the start of the races but Gareth's head had already drooped on to his hands.

Lifting him to carry him to the sofa in the kitchen, Becky smiled down at him indulgently, saying, 'Perhaps he's dreaming he's out there winning, Polly.'

Soon it was time for the adults to sit down for their tea. Bert and Roy decided to stay indoors while Polly and Becky went out to join the party. Later, when the tables were cleared and a barrel of beer had been hoisted on to the trestles, men came out to sup and talk and put the world to rights.

'Did you say youer mam was keeping Nellie company?' Polly asked when they'd gone back indoors in case either of the children should wake.

'Yes, they're at the Paul Street party. The shop being on the corner, we belong to both streets. I'd better be going, though. I expect they're back indoors by now.'

'Thanks for everything, *cariad*. It wasn't the same as if he'd been out there, but I know Gareth enjoyed himself thanks to you, Becky.'

Polly sat down at the table, staring before her, her chin cupped in her hands. Then, looking up she said, 'One year old our Dilys will be next month. We'll have to have a little tea, but I'm dreading it, Becky. I know it's unfair to the child but how are we to smile and be happy when it'll also be the anniversary of Laura's death?' She wiped away a tear.

'I've been thinking about it too,' Becky told her sadly. 'We could have her birthday tea at our house, if you like?'

'Oh, no!' Polly assured her. 'Dilys is our grandchild and we love her dearly. The children are all we have of Laura now, but you've been a very good friend and I'm grateful.'

As Becky and Polly were walking towards the front door the men came in, Bert waving an *Echo* at them.

'Special edition,' he said. 'Thought you'd like to see the picture on the front page.'

Polly took the paper, holding it out for Becky to see. It was a picture of the Royal Family waving from the balcony of Buckingham Palace after the ceremony. Queen Mary was in the centre, looking rather serious, her hand raised in salutation. The new king and queen stood on either side of her, wearing their crowns and smiling, as were the two little princesses.

'Don't they look nice? And such lovely little girls,' Polly said. Becky agreed.

Bert had gone to the kitchen and Roy to his room: Polly said he still sat for hours in there brooding. Over the years Becky had grown to love Albert dearly. It was a gentle love, nurtured by his tenderness and understanding. Yet a part of her still loved Roy as she had since their very first meeting. The old feeling had remained with her, and it seemed it always would.

28

Autumn 1938 and the pleasant days of hazy sunshine brought little pleasure when it was realised that Britain could soon be heading for war. Bert vented his fears in bursts of anger, railing against the government for allowing the country to get into such a position. 'My God! Wasn't there enough carnage last time? Look at them gas-masks we were given last week. What the hell are they expecting?' he yelled. 'When are they going to realise wars solve nothing? They only leave the losers with a festering grievance, spoiling for another scrap.'

'You can't let someone like Hitler ride roughshod through any country he fancies,' Roy told him. 'Neville Chamberlain has done his best to keep the peace. Twice he's been to Germany with no result. Hitler's already incorporated Austria into the German Reich. Soon it will be Czechoslovakia's turn and there are about three million Germans living there — '

Bert was getting agitated at all this talk of war and Polly quickly silenced Roy with a cautionary glance and a shake of her head.

But her husband broke out angrily, 'They took the best of the last generation for gun fodder. Now it seems likely to happen all over again. The thought of Tommy going through what our lads did, wallowing in mud in them trenches, waiting for a bullet to put a hole in them or to be gassed . . . ' He gave a sigh of despair.

'It won't be that sort of conflict next time,' Roy said with conviction. 'It'll be fought in the air as much as on the land. But as you said, Bert, it doesn't bear thinking about.'

The ever-increasing threat of war and Hitler's role in it had succeeded in bringing Roy out of his shell as nothing else could. He'd followed the man's swift rise to power, had even admired at first the work he'd done for the youth of Germany, but it had soon become only too apparent that his ambitions stretched much further afield.

At that moment Gareth ran into the kitchen, a rusty old colander turned upside down on his head, a toy rifle made of wood slung over his shoulder. Taking them off, he showed them proudly to Polly, saying, 'Look what Auntie Jessie just gave me, Nan.'

Bert lunged forward to take them, his expression furious, but Polly stopped him, saying, 'There's no harm in it, Bert. You don't want to upset Jessie, do you? It's only an old pop-gun of their Bobby's with the cork and string taken out. All the kids are playing soldiers, they don't know anything about war.'

Bert stamped off to the garden, puffing furiously on his pipe, and Gareth ran back to his friends.

You could hardly expect the child to understand his grandfather's fears, Polly told herself, and it was so good seeing him enjoy himself. Gareth was eight years old now and had made a lot of friends, especially since he'd been allowed to play out in the street.

Going into the front room, she pulled the lace curtain aside and looked out. Six little boys were marching up and down, toy guns slung over their shoulders. She watched Gareth fondly, smiling to herself as his rusty 'helmet' fell over one eye. Then as they turned sharply to march the other way, it fell off and rolled into the gutter but he marched on, his dark curly head held high, knees just visible between his new grey flannel shorts and his socks. He's a fine little chap, she thought proudly. If only Laura could see him now.

There were more neighbours than usual standing talking at their doors, no doubt about the possibility of war just as Bert and

Roy had been doing. As they'd said, it just didn't bear thinking about, and she knew how badly the prospect was upsetting Bert. Polly groaned when she thought of all the problems that could lie ahead, but the worst part of any war was all the young men being sent overseas to fight. Tommy and Roy would be the right age this time. It was only twenty years since the last war had ended and because of Bert's illness this family had suffered ever since.

★　★　★

Dora and Becky were having problems too on this late-September day. Remembering the shortages during and after the last war, people with a bit of money to spare were intent on buying up stocks of any commodity that would keep for a while, and there was no law against it. The trouble was that until more could be delivered to the shop, goods could become short for those able to buy only what they needed.

In the last half-hour there'd been two motor cars draw up outside the shop and people they'd never seen before had come in for large quantities of dry goods they thought might soon be rationed: sugar, flour, raisins, sultanas . . . anything that would keep a while. One smartly dressed woman had bought half a box of butter and half a whole cheese, but she must have had a large refrigerator or it would have been a waste of money.

'Thank goodness there's a delivery due tomorrow, Becky,' Dora said, adding, 'I'll have to refuse them from now on or it'll make us short.'

Enid Brown was coming into the shop as the woman and her partner were leaving, the driver of the car having been called in to carry the goods. As they passed Enid, she said to no one in particular, 'It's easy to see who's goin' to benefit from this war scare. Grocers must be making a pretty penny! Hope it'll all come to nothing I do then them rich buggers will have the stuff they've bought left on their hands.'

'We all wish that, Enid. No one wants a war, and Neville Chamberlain's doing his best to keep the peace. There's no shortage of food at the moment, it seemed silly not to serve them when we had some surplus stock, but from now on it's going to be regular customers first,' Dora assured her.

A few days later, on 28 September, the Prime Minister was addressing a worried House of Commons when a message was delivered from Hitler inviting him to fresh talks, this time in Munich, and once more there was hope.

Neville Chamberlain came back to Britain proudly waving a peace of paper which he said meant 'peace in our time', and a delighted nation signalled its approval then went about its business as though nothing had happened.

No one was happier than Polly at the news. Then on 1 October it was announced that German troops had begun the occupation of the Sudetenland. Roy said, 'I told you so. It's what Britain and France agreed to at Munich.'

'But it was the only way they could appease Hitler and get him to sign the pact,' Bert said. 'It is only the German-speaking parts of Bohemia he's taken over, and if that's the end of it, it could be worth it.'

Seeing Roy was about to explode, Polly gently nudged him from the room. Once in the passage she said, 'You promised not to upset him. After what happened to him in the last one, Bert can't bear to think there might be another war. Let's just be thankful Chamberlain signed that pact.'

'I'm sorry, Mam. I do get a bit carried away, but I can't help thinking we're not really out of the wood yet.'

Christmas came and went and as they

toasted in 1939 Polly thanked God for the continuing peace. It had been their third Christmas without Laura and it hadn't been any easier. Dilys was a constant reminder, if one were needed. She had her mother's colouring and often made Polly think of Laura as a baby. She had the same smooth dark brows, the same gentle grey eyes and creamy skin.

Now two and a half, the little girl was running everywhere. When Roy was at work and Gareth at school Polly sometimes found her quite a handful but she'd never regretted her decision to look after the children, and when little arms were flung around her neck or Gareth planted a kiss on her cheek, her eyes would fill with tears of gratitude.

Having made friends at school Gareth didn't go to Becky's nearly as often now, much to Nellie's disappointment, but Dilys loved to be taken there and made a fuss of, and in the spring when their trips to the park began again, maybe he'd want to go too.

★   ★   ★

One evening in March Tommy called in as he often did on his way home from work. He, like everyone else, was eager to talk about Hitler's latest outrage, for German troops had crossed the Czech frontier and occupied Bohemia and Moravia and the Czech Republic ceased to exist.

'Put that paper away, son, before youer dad sees it. We've had quite enough on that subject for today,' Polly told him, looking fondly at her son. Tommy was twenty-three now, tall and broad-shouldered, and doing very well at the bakery. Putting the paper away, he resigned himself to the fact that the main news he'd brought would have to wait. A few days ago, acting on impulse, he'd joined the Territorials. His ears were still burning from Josie's reaction and he wasn't looking forward to his dad's either. Wilfred Street wasn't much out of his way for although his round in Ely finished quite near home, he still had to come back to Roath every evening to stable the horse and pay in his takings.

'But it is happening, Mam,' he said in a low voice as they went towards the kitchen. 'You can't bury your head in the sand. Chamberlain's Peace Pact is falling apart.'

Gareth and Dilys looked up at him hopefully as he entered the room for he usually brought them some small treat. Tonight was no exception as he opened the paper bag he was carrying and gave them each a jam doughnut.

'How's Josie?' his father asked. 'We haven't seen her for a while.'

'Oh, she's fine, sends her love. Her mam hasn't been well and Josie's been tied to the house, but she's better now. Says to tell you she's finished the cardigans for Gareth and Dilys and will bring them out next week.'

Slipping a half-ounce of shag into Bert's hand and giving his mam the cakes that were left in the bag, Tommy kissed her cheek, saying, 'Well, I'd better be going. I've got to get two trams an' all.'

'Got time for a cup of tea? It's only to pour it out.'

'No thanks, Mam. I'll be on my way.'

Bert rose to accompany them to the door, his eyes warm with pride, and watching as Tommy put an arm about his father's shoulder, Polly was remembering the shaky start to their relationship when Bert had been invalided out of the army. Now there was genuine affection between them, an affection that had grown with the years, and she thanked God for it.

29

The sky over London was grey and overcast as Sally stood at the window, now bare of curtains, watching Bill load their few possessions into the van. Behind her the room, stripped now of everything but the shabby furniture, looked more dismal than ever.

They'd been living here for over three years and in the first few weeks had stripped off the peeling paint and redecorated. Sally had made floral covers to hide the grubby velvet settee and chairs, and with new rugs on the floor and the grate blackleaded until it shone, it had looked a different place. Then they'd started to save hard for the day they could rent a place of their own, though nothing had turned up until a few weeks ago when Bill had come home in high spirits, bursting to tell her the news.

'Arthur's moving, Sal,' he'd told her excitedly. 'You know, the rep who trained me. Getting a mortgage to buy a new house in the suburbs. He'll speak to the landlord for us if you'd like to take on their house?'

'Oh, Bill! Do you think he'd let us have it?'

Sally's eyes were bright. The house was unfurnished, but that's what they'd been scrimping and saving all this time for.

As though he could read her thoughts, Bill said, 'We'll be able to buy our own stuff, Sal. It will have to be just the basics to start with — '

She flung her arms tightly about him, stopping him in mid-sentence, but as soon as he could Bill continued breathlessly, 'Hang on, love. Best wait and see if we can have the place before we make any plans.'

The days passed in an agony of doubt and hope.

We're pretty sure to get it, Sally would tell herself. Arthur's a friend of the landlord. Then she'd think, But he may already have someone else in mind, and anyway we don't know Arthur and his wife very well, do we?

Then a couple of weeks later Bill came home to say they had an interview with the landlord that evening and Sally's heart leaped with hope even as she told him, 'I've just put Bryn to bed.'

'Isn't there anyone you can ask to baby-sit?'

Sally shook her head. She did occasionally chat to the woman who lived at the back of the house, but picturing her now, a cigarette always dangling from her lips as she talked, eyes screwed up against the smoke, Sally knew she couldn't leave Brynley with her.

'We'll take him with us,' she decided. 'I'll wrap him up well.'

Mr Burton the landlord and his plump little wife greeted them like old friends, making a great fuss of Bryn when he woke up and, staring about him, broke into an angelic smile.

They were taken to see the house where Arthur and his wife were busy packing up. Sally was delighted with everything. It was a terraced house built towards the end of the last century, the small porch bright with pretty mosaic tiles, the same tiles covering the forecourt which was surrounded by iron railings with a gate: a safe place for Bryn to play, she thought. There was a parlour, a middle room, and a narrow passage led to a kitchen and scullery where the gas cooker and boiler were to remain.

'Arthur thinks there'll be a war soon so we're getting out of London,' his wife explained.

Talk of war had been on everyone's lips since last year when, wheeling Bryn in the park, Sally had seen men digging trenches to act as emergency shelters. Since then they'd been issued with gas-masks and most people had Anderson shelters in their gardens, but then Mr Chamberlain had brought back his

Peace Pact and for a time the threat of war seemed to be over. But the euphoria hadn't lasted.

By March the Germans were renewing their harsh demands on Poland and the Poles had declared that any attempt by Germany to change the status of Danzig would mean war. A few days later France and Britain issued a joint declaration that they would guarantee the territorial integrity of Poland against any possible aggressors.

On the day Sally and Bill moved to their new home Chamberlain announced plans for conscription to the armed forces, the first call up to be in July. As the van weaved its way through the midday traffic Sally saw the news on a placard outside a newsagent's and could push her fears to the back of her mind no longer. If there was a war and Bill was called up, she'd be alone in a strange part of London with little Bryn. She'd never liked London even without this threat. She had no friends here, nobody spoke to you at the bus stops, no one smiled as you passed in the street. She pictured life in Tre-Mynydd where you couldn't take two steps outside your own gate without someone passing the time of day and making a fuss of the baby.

But thinking of their new home and the money they'd spent on furniture, she knew they must stick it out, war or no war.

Bill was drawing up outside the house. As she looked out of the window her heart filled with pride. It was such a dear little place, in a neat little street. They'd be happy here, she knew they would. Given half a chance. Pushing her fears to the back of her mind, Sally carried in Bryn's high-chair and settled him in it with a Farley's rusk before setting about helping Bill to unpack the van.

The furniture was being delivered that afternoon. They'd managed to pay for a dining suite and two easy chairs and for a double bed, but the bedroom suite they'd bought on credit and Sally promised herself they'd pay for it in full just as soon as they could.

When Bill had gone back to work with everything delivered and in place, she put Bryn in his push-chair and went in search of the shops. There seemed to be one on every corner, grocers mostly or general stores, and not wanting to go too far afield she went into one that looked promising and bought the few things she needed. She walked home in the evening sunshine for the grey clouds had dispersed and there were big patches of blue sky, promising a better day tomorrow.

The next morning they woke to a warm sunny day and as soon as breakfast was over and Bill off to work, Sally got on with the washing, anxious to get it on the line. As she was pegging it out she was hailed from the next garden with, ' 'Ello, love, I'm Megan. If there's anything I can do to 'elp . . . ' And Sally turned, amazed and delighted to hear the friendly valleys accent here in London.

A girl of about her own age stood the other side of the fence, round dark eyes in a plump rosy face smiling at her as Sally cried in amazement, 'You're from the valleys, aren't you? I'd know that accent anywhere.'

'From Tonypandy,' the girl agreed, 'and you're from Cardiff if I'm not mistaken. Bring youer little boy in and have a cuppa. Oh, I can't believe my luck!'

Megan's little girl Daisy was about a year older than Bryn. Her husband Peter, being in the reserves, was expecting to be called up shortly. Soon the two young women were wheeling their children to a nearby park every fine afternoon and Sally was overjoyed at finding such a good friend, especially as that friend came from Wales.

As the warm sunny days passed she felt more content than she had since she'd left home. One August day Megan took her to a street market and Sally saw a different side of London. The friendly banter and witty joking of the cockney traders warmed her heart as the crowds around her jostled good-naturedly, looking for bargains.

Perhaps I've never given Londoners a chance? Sally thought. Perhaps if I'd smiled at them and spoken first? Then she chuckled to herself, thinking of Dai the milk in Tre-Mynydd who delivered messages as well as dairy produce, and the ever helpful bus drivers who'd stop outside your door if it happened to be on their route — she was imagining the chaos if that happened here in London where everyone seemed to be in a hurry from morning to night!

The pleasant summer days were marred by gathering war clouds as the last week of August approached. When Megan's husband Peter had his papers, Bill seemed sure that something was in the wind.

'We'd planned to go home to Wales for a few days next week,' Megan told her tearfully.

'They're taking precautions, that's all,' Sally told her hopefully, but events were moving fast. When on the Friday she went to the draper's to buy some more black-out material for the windows, the placards outside the newsagent's screamed: HITLER INVADES POLAND, and Sally's heart sank. There was sure to be a war now. She hurried home to switch on the wireless.

Plans for the evacuation of mothers and

children from the danger areas were announced in the evening paper Bill brought home.

'You'll have to think about it, love,' he said worriedly.

'I'm not going to leave you in London by yourself, and Bryn's too young to go on his own,' Sally said stubbornly.

'If air raids start you'll have to go, for Bryn's sake,' he said emphatically. 'We'd better start thinking about it, Sal.'

The next morning a telegram came from Tre-Mynydd, which read: BRING BRYNLEY DOWN AND LEAVE HIM WITH US STOP MAM AND DAD.

Sally's relief was mixed with foreboding. 'If he's down there for long, he'll forget us,' she wailed.

'But you'll be with him, there's no need for you to stay here.'

'I'm staying,' she told him. 'Who's going to do the cooking and the washing, and who's going to keep the house clean?'

'I can manage. I'll take you home next weekend.'

'I'm staying,' she told him again. 'At least until you're called up. But what'll happen to the house then, and all the new furniture?'

'We'll have to lock it up and hope for the best,' Bill said with a cheerfulness he was far

288

from feeling. 'Anyway war hasn't been declared yet, has it? The government's just taking precautions.' But he knew there was more to it than that.

'They wouldn't be making all these plans for nothing, and we've signed that declaration to protect Poland. I can't see there's any way out,' Sally sighed.

At dawn on 1 September the Germans had invaded Poland and it was time for Great Britain and France to honour their pledge. An ultimatum was sent to Germany threatening war unless a withdrawal began immediately. It was timed to expire at 11 a.m. on Sunday, 3 September. At 11.15 Neville Chamberlain's sad, flat voice came over the air.

'I am speaking to you from the Cabinet Room at ten Downing Street,' he said. 'This morning the British Ambassador in Berlin handed the German government a final note, stating that unless we heard from them by eleven o'clock that they were prepared at once to withdraw their troops from Poland, a state of war would exist between us. I have to tell you now that no such reply has been received, and that consequently this country is at war with Germany.'

There was a stunned silence as they stared at each other in dismay.

'What'll happen now?' Sally wondered.

She didn't have to wonder very long for almost at once the wail of a siren broke the Sunday quiet, the dreadful sound growing louder and louder as Bill picked up a frightened Bryn and dashed with Sally to the shelter.

As they climbed down into the gloom of the Anderson the muddy floor sucked at their shoes. Inside it smelled fusty and damp. Taking the screaming Bryn in her arms, Sally sat down and cwtched him close until the screams became just a hiccup as, thumb in mouth, he rested his head on her shoulder.

'We'll have to make this place more comfortable, Bill,' she began. 'Bring some blankets down — '

But now there was a different sort of wail, far less frightening. The all clear? She'd read it was called that in one of the papers. As they opened the shelter door and looked out they could hear neighbours in their gardens on their way back indoors.

'Must have been a false alarm,' someone grumbled. Sighing with relief, they clambered out and went indoors to make a cup of tea.

30

'Bryn wants you to tell him a story tonight, Bill. I'll post this letter to your mam, shall I? I've told her we'll be arriving Saturday for the weekend and leaving Bryn with them,' Sally said reluctantly.

'I know nothing's happening at the moment, Sal, but it could at any time,' her husband told her on his way upstairs.

Sally closed the door to the house behind her. The night was as black as pitch, the moon lost behind thick, scudding clouds, and there wasn't a star in sight, not a chink of light anywhere as she fumbled with the gate. She opened it and clung to the railings as slowly she made her way along the street, counting the houses for the post-box was about six down. It was the first time she'd been out in the black-out and she hadn't expected it to be as total as this. At the sixth gate she stepped gingerly into the middle of the pavement and strained to see the post-box but there was nothing there. Instead she found herself tripping over the kerb but managed to keep her balance and a moment later walked straight into the box. She fumbled for the opening and dropped the letter inside.

Footsteps were coming towards her and, trying to regain the railings, Sally's heart beat fast.

'Is that you, Sal?' Bill's anxious voice came to her and she fell into his arms, weak with relief.

'I'd forgotten about the black-out until I looked out of the window,' he told her as, clinging to each other, they made their way back to the house.

'It's going to be dangerous going out at night,' he went on when they'd closed the door behind them, pulled the curtain over and switched on the light. 'Why don't you stay at Mam's?'

'We'll take Bryn on Saturday, like we've promised, but I'm coming back with you,' she told him firmly.

'I think we'd better go by train,' Bill said thoughtfully. 'Apart from saving the petrol it wouldn't be easy driving back in the black-out. We can still take Bryn's push-chair and clothes.'

But when on Saturday morning they reached Paddington, they found the platform taken over by young evacuees herded together in large groups, all of them wearing labels with their names, gas-masks slung over their shoulders, and gripping small cardboard cases or carrier bags with their possessions. Sally was moved almost to tears by their sad, uncertain little faces.

Thank God Bryn is going to his nan, she thought, giving him an extra big hug.

One trainload had long since departed and another train stood at the platform, filling up. More children arrived and were being shepherded towards it by their minders. Children's faces pressed against the windows, anxiously scanning the platform as doors were slammed. Further along a woman in a navy hat and coat, accompanied by a girl of about ten, was peering anxiously into every doorway while the girl yelled 'Alfie!' over and over again at the top of her voice. Then a small boy came from the direction of the toilets and, seeing the almost deserted platform, began to howl.

'Alfie!' He turned in the direction of the voice and they were quickly united before the two children were hurried towards the waiting train. He'd looked so vulnerable, the little lad, his thin bony legs struggling to keep up with the minder's long stride, that Sally's heart went out to him.

When Bill went to enquire about the train that, according to the timetable, was due in for South Wales, he came back to tell Sally in a disappointed voice: 'It's no use, love, they've had to cancel it because of the evacuees. There's one for sure this evening or we can hang about in the hope they'll put one on.' Reluctantly they decided to go home.

When they returned that evening the platform was full of hopeful travellers but it was almost an hour before the train steamed in at last. Since it was long past his bedtime Bryn was fast asleep and by the time they'd reached Reading it was dark, the blinds had been drawn and a pin point of blue light was the only illumination as the train rushed on through the night. It was a long journey, with many stops and passengers constantly coming and going from platforms shrouded in darkness. When they at last reached Cardiff General that too was quickly deserted as people fumbled their way down the dimly lit steps to street level.

'There won't be a train to Tre-Mynydd tonight,' Bill said resignedly, leading Sally towards the blacked out waiting room and closing the door before switching on the shrouded light. She stared around her at the cheerless room, dead ashes in a grate that badly needed clearing out, benches all around the walls. As she sank thankfully on to one of these, Bryn stirred and began to whimper.

'You stay here,' Bill told her. 'I'll see if I can

find out the time of the first train.' He was already making for the door, adding, 'I'll have to switch off the light to open the door but I won't be long.'

Not wanting to disturb Bryn who had gone back to sleep, Sally sat in the darkness, dreading the long night ahead, picturing Bill's mam and dad waiting up for them, disappointed and probably worried when they realised they weren't coming. They'd have been expecting them all day for Bill hadn't been able to let them know about the cancelled train.

The thermos flask was empty, the sandwiches long gone, but she did have a bottle of milk and a few rusks for Bryn if he should wake.

The door was being pushed open and she watched anxiously. Supposing it wasn't Bill? A moment later, when the light went on, she heaved a sigh of relief. She scanned her husband's face anxiously but he was shaking his head, saying, 'There's nothing until six o'clock. We'd better try and get some sleep.'

As the night wore on it grew colder and Sally pulled the Welsh flannel shawl tighter about her shoulders, wrapping it about Bryn as she had when he'd been a little baby and cwtching him close.

They must have dozed fitfully. Finally, Bill

glanced at his watch and saw it was almost half-past five. Time to go out on to the platform. Putting off the light, he opened the door to a pre-dawn full of lowering clouds and shivered, hoping they were right about the time of the train. He woke Sally and they stayed in the waiting room with the light switched off and the black-out pulled back a little to watch and listen for the train, rising swiftly when they heard its first rumblings in the distance and hurrying out to the platform to join the half-a-dozen other passengers waiting to get on board.

Climbing stiffly into a carriage, Sally settled herself into a corner seat, thankful that at last they were on their way.

When the train reached Tre-Mynydd Bill's dad was on the platform, anxiously scanning the carriages before hurrying forward with a wide smile of welcome when he saw them. Despite the warm smile Sally noticed how tired he looked and felt a pang of conscience for being the unwitting cause. Her father-in-law's first words confirmed her fears.

'Come down to meet the train last night, I did, but I soon realised you'd missed it. The trains are all over the place at the moment. Everyone's grumbling.'

'We had to stay in the waiting room at

Cardiff,' Bill told him. 'There was no way of letting you know.'

'If it had been daytime you could have phoned Bessie Roberts at the post office. Good about handing on messages she is, soon as she sees someone who lives nearby. Give you 'er phone number Mam will before you go back.'

They left the station and began to climb the hill. Bryn, refreshed by his long sleep, insisted on walking between his dad and granddad, clinging tightly to their hands. Watching his plump little legs going twice as fast as theirs, a lump came into Sally's throat. He would be three years old next week and his nan would be having a birthday party and watching as he blew out the candles — and Sally wouldn't be there to see it.

You could be there if you liked, she told herself. They all wanted her to stay at Tre-Mynydd, but she couldn't tear herself away from Bill, especially as he might be called up very soon. And anyway, despite what he'd said, he couldn't look after himself properly, not when he was out at work all day.

Peggy was waiting with open arms and the first one to go into them was Bryn. There was a delicious aroma of bacon cooking and the table was laid ready for the meal. Sally hadn't realised how hungry she was until the plate of bacon, eggs, tomatoes and fried bread was set before her together with a steaming cup of tea.

All the disappointment of the long wait was forgotten as the conversation flowed. Brynley had just finished dipping toast soldiers into his boiled egg when the kitchen door opened and Mostyn came in, eyes and teeth gleaming in his coal-blackened face. For a moment Bryn stared at his uncle open-mouthed then let out a yell of dismay.

'He's got to know me, mun,' Mostyn protested.

'I expect he's forgotten since last time,' Sally told him.

Grinning, her brother-in-law made for the scullery with his empty tommy box and could be heard splashing vigorously. He came back pink of face at least and Bryn gave him a watery smile.

Watching them, Bill laughed and said, 'He'll get used to it. He'll have to, won't he? Seeing your ugly mug every day, brother.'

Giving him a playful swipe, Mostyn finished the tea his mam had poured and made for the yard to bring in the tin bath and set it in the scullery, while Peggy went to put more bacon in the pan.

The time seemed to fly. They had to leave again at five and Sally was dreading the parting from Bryn. She was worried too because she hadn't let her mam know of their visit. There'd have been no hope of visiting her in such a short time and Bill had said that if she knew they were there, Polly might make the journey to Tre-Mynydd and have to return in the black-out — and after their own experience the other night, they wouldn't want that to happen. Sally would write and explain tomorrow how short their visit to the valleys had turned out to be.

31

After they'd returned to London Sally went through all the motions of normal living — cooking, cleaning, washing, shopping — but her heart was heavy with longing for little Bryn. As the days grew shorter it became very cold and wet and the Anderson shelter sunk deep in the garden was once more waterlogged. Sally thanked God the expected air raids hadn't yet materialised.

As the weeks went by nothing much seemed to happen on the home front, except for queueing for foods in short supply and barrage balloons floundering about in the sky. Coping with the black-out became a lot easier when the government allowed hand torches, providing the light was covered with two thicknesses of tissue paper, was aimed at the ground, and turned off during a raid. Bill was truly thankful when civilian drivers were also allowed to fit headlight covers, showing a thin beam of light through a horizontal strip.

As one cold, wet, uneventful day followed another, Sally began to question the need for Bryn to stay in Wales but Bill was adamant, saying they daren't take any risks. Then in

October the battleship *Royal Oak* was sunk at Scapa Flow by a U-boat, and in December the German pocket battleship *Graf-Spee* was scuttled off Montevideo. But at home more and more people were leaving their gas-masks behind, cinemas and other places of entertainment that had closed down at the outbreak of war had reopened, and Sally bided her time to try again.

'Bryn won't know us, Bill,' she ventured one day.

'He's safe with his nan and granddad who love him dearly, and you can go and stay with him whenever you like,' was the reply.

'I will when you're called up. Oh, Bill! How are we to pay the rent on this place when you're in the forces and I'm home in Wales?'

Bill sighed. He'd been worrying a lot about this and giving it some thought.

'I think we'd better give up the house,' he said reluctantly. 'When I'm called up we'd better put the furniture in store. With nobody living here it'll be cheaper than paying the rent, and no one knows how long the war will last.'

Just before Christmas they made the journey to Tre-Mynydd again, taking the presents. Although Sally's maternal feelings were a little dented, she was relieved to see the ease with which Bryn had settled down.

He ran to her and Bill as soon as they arrived but it was his nan's arms he sought when he fell kicking a ball with Mostyn and Bill. His cheeks rosy from all the fresh air, wrapped up well in coat, scarf and bobble-hat, he watched anxiously as Peggy bathed and bandaged his knee even though it was only a very small graze. Sally had to swallow her keen disappointment that he hadn't run to her.

He looks so well and happy I should be very grateful, she told herself, and at least this time when we leave there'll be no tears and tantrums.

They'd managed a few hours in Cardiff and Sally could hardly believe how both Gareth and little Dilys had grown. At nine he was tall for his age and a real help to his nana, and Dilys, whom Polly hoped would be starting school at Easter, was so like Laura as a child that it pulled at Sally's heart strings.

When the holiday was over they returned home. The weather was bitterly cold, threatening snow. As they baled out the damp fusty-smelling shelter once more, Sally thanked God again that they could still remain indoors. On 8 January sugar, butter, ham and bacon were rationed, and wherever you turned there were warning posters exhorting you to 'Be Like Dad: Keep Mum!' or telling you 'Careless Talk Costs Lives'.

In April the war seemed suddenly to gather momentum as Germany occupied Denmark and invaded Norway, and it was a blow to morale when the British and French attempt to land and maintain an expeditionary force in Norway ended in disaster.

In May, on the day Churchill succeeded Neville Chamberlain as Prime Minister, Germany attacked Belgium and Holland, and on that day too Bill got his call up papers. He and Sally regretfully set about packing up their furniture and belongings and made arrangements for them to go into store. On their way to the station they returned the key to the landlord. There was no one else to say goodbye to for, with her husband already called up, Megan had gone home to Wales.

At the station, as they hugged and kissed each other goodbye, Sally fought to hold back the tears, dreading the moment when Bill would have to dash for a carriage. They'd lost the home they'd worked so hard to build together and most of their possessions were in store. Then her heart lifted as she thought: I'll have Bryn back with me tomorrow. She'd go to her mam's tonight then tomorrow she'd make the short journey to Tre-Mynydd to fetch Brynley back to Cardiff; she'd already written to Peggy about it.

He won't want to come, she warned herself, not after all this time. But he'd get over it, wouldn't he? And at Mama's he'd have Gareth and Dilys to play with, that should help him to settle down.

The guard was lifting his flag. Bill dashed for the nearest carriage and leaned out of the door towards her. The whistle blew shrilly. As the train got underway, steaming slowly out of the station, they waved to each other until it gathered speed and was quickly out of sight.

Eyes misted with tears, Sally went in search of the train that would take her home to South Wales. There were men in uniform everywhere, and a few women too. When at last the train came in everyone surged forward, pushing her into a compartment. She was lucky enough to get a corner seat. As the train left Paddington she stared out of the window at the cheerless scene and wondered if they'd ever come back here to live? Would they be able to find another house to rent when they needed it? Would Bill's job still be there on his return?

At home she was to have Tommy's old bedroom. Roy had the two middle rooms but she'd have to share the kitchen with her mam and dad. Roy was expecting to be called up soon then the sole responsibility for looking after Gareth and Dilys would fall on her mam. Sally was glad she'd be there to help.

★ ★ ★

It was tea-time when she got off the tram in Newport Road and made her way to Broadway. Turning into Wilfred Street, hurrying past the familiar narrow, grey-stone houses, she was greeted by one of their old neighbours.

'Your mam will be pleased to have you home, Sally love,' she told her. 'On the go from morning 'til night she is. Fagged out she looks these days.'

'See you again, Mrs Green,' she said, hurrying on her way.

Just before she reached the house Polly opened the door and next moment Sally was in her mother's arms.

When she hugged her father, she thought he too looked pale and withdrawn.

'Worried about Tommy he is, love,' her mother confided when Sally followed her to the wash-house. 'Over in France he is, as you know, and with the Germans attacking Belgium and Holland . . . '

She broke off as Roy came in. Seeing Sally, he welcomed her with a hug then turned to Polly to ask, 'Anything I can do, Mam?'

'Sally will help me here. You get the children washed and to the table,' she told him.

'All youer dada talks about is the war,' Polly confided to her daughter, 'and things are looking bad. Though fair dos — Roy plays it down when he's talking to Bert.'

Looking at her mam, Sally knew it wasn't hard work making her look peaky. She was used to that. Polly was worrying about her only son. Bill had said only this morning that the Germans were advancing rapidly on the Western Front and at the rate they were going, would soon be in France. There were vast numbers of British troops in northern France and their Tommy was one of them.

32

On the second day of their march towards Dunkirk, cold, hungry, bleary-eyed from lack of sleep, their uniforms splattered and torn from diving into ditches or under hedges whenever the swarming Stukas came hurtling overhead, for the umpteenth time Tommy patted the pocket where Josie's letter was secured and allowed himself to wonder if he'd ever see her again.

The tiff they'd had on his last leave weighed heavily on his mind. Josie had begged for a chance to have a child but he'd been stubborn about taking the usual precautions. After all, he'd been on embarkation leave and hadn't known when or if he'd ever get back. Josie would be left to bring up a baby alone, and on the pittance of a pension she'd get if anything happened to him, that could mean a lifetime of struggle.

When they'd got married and gone to live with her mam, he and Josie had decided they'd wait for a family until they'd saved enough for a place of their own, but the uncertainties of war and him being abroad had brought it home to his wife that to wait now might be to wait for ever. She wanted his baby now . . .

'Christ Almighty, Tommo!'

A sharp push in the back sent him face down into the ditch as more Stukas went screaming overhead, peppering the road with bullets. DIVE BOMBERS

A few minutes later, as they struggled to their feet, he muttered, 'Ta, Don.'

'Where the 'ell were you, mate? Thinking of that wife of yours, I suppose.'

Nearer the beach, the roads were clogged with refugees and vehicles of all kinds: horsedrawn wagons, army trucks, motor-bikes, bicycles. When they finally reached their goal and sank exhausted to the sand, Tommy stared about him in disbelief. There were boats in the Channel as far as the eye could see. He could pick out a destroyer, paddle steamers, yachts, a cabin cruiser, fishing boats. Two rowing boats were plying to and fro and long queues of men, still carrying their rifles, stretched along the beach and into the water, some already wading in up to their necks. The sea was calm, the sky overcast from smoke drifting on the still air, and all around them was the constant scream of planes flying low.

Fumbling in his pocket, Don brought out a crumpled packet of Woodbines, examined the three squashed cigarettes it contained and handed one to Tommy. Lighting his cigarette, he watched a small boat, so heavily laden that it lay low in the water, men clinging to its sides. Suddenly there was a Stuka screaming above them, diving low, and Tommy flung himself flat on the sand beside Don, his heart beating fast as the beach around them was sprayed with bullets.

Almost at once there was a dreadful choking noise and he turned to see his friend's face contorted with pain. The choking noise went on. Before Tommy could scramble to his feet, with a final convulsion Don lay still, the expression on his face set in a rictus of pure agony.

Tommy crouched over him, listening, but there was no sound from his heart, no breath on his hand when he held it close to Don's mouth. Then he saw the gaping wound in his friend's back from which blood was still oozing.

They'd been together from the beginning, him and Don, and his friend had come back from his last leave proudly showing around photos of his new baby son. Vera, Don's wife, would have only that baby to comfort her now.

Eyes misted and a painful lump in his throat, Tommy beat the sand with his fists, muttering, 'Damn them to Hell! German bastards!'

If only he'd given Josie some hope of having a child. If he died out here there'd be nothing to show he'd existed, no one to bear his name. Pressing his head down once more as bullets raked the beach and picturing Don's wife opening the telegram that must come, he thought sadly, Poor woman. Poor, poor woman. It was strange but he felt he knew Vera although they'd never met. 'Bloody war,' he muttered angrily. 'Bloody, bloody war!'

Much later, with the light fading, he watched anxiously as a Spitfire and a Messerschmitt fought it out over the water, cheering when the Messerschmitt eventually burst into flames and spiralled into the water in a plume of smoke. As darkness fell and fires lit the desolate scene, Tommy took Don's papers from his pocket and the precious photo of his baby son and walked the few yards to the rest of his unit. Handing over the papers, he decided to keep the photo and return it to Don's wife when he wrote.

Light-headed with hunger and the trauma of seeing his best mate die, Tommy lay there with his sombre thoughts. Don was only one of the many casualties that littered the beach and who knew who'd cop it next?

His thoughts went to his father and the way he'd been invalided out of the last war. If only Tommy had been more understanding when he was young. He could remember plainly even now the shock of their first meeting, and his disbelief that the pale, thin man with staring eyes they'd brought into the house on a stretcher could possibly be his handsome soldier dad whose photo stood by his bed. He knew now that part of the trouble had been the jealousy he'd felt at the amount of time his mam so willingly gave the invalid, when once Tommy himself had been her pride and joy.

He'd been just four years old when his father came home, but as the years went by he should have been more understanding. God forgive him for ever being ashamed of his dad. Now at last he understood what Bert had suffered in the flea-ridden filth of the trenches where he too had lost a best friend.

'If ever I get out of this lot alive, I'll make it up to him,' Tommy vowed fervently.

Something wet and cold was nuzzling his hand. He sat up to see a lanky dog of indeterminate breed, its eyes pleading in the light from a nearby fire. But he was as hungry as the animal itself. Leaning forward, he stroked the dog's bony back and a tongue came out to lick his hand, but as the roar of a plane drew nearer it sprang away and was lost in the shadows.

The plane passed over. Was it one of ours? Tommy must have dozed for when he woke, stiff and with cramp in his legs, it was to the half light of dawn and a sea of bodies lying inert on the sand. It was only when they began to stir and move that you knew who were the living and who the dead.

The long queue of men still stretched into the water. Had they been there all night?

It was two more days before Tommy was dragged aboard a boat bound for home, days in which he had grown weaker as he scavenged for food, often to no avail. Then they were on the move towards the shoreline and gradually, as the day advanced, getting nearer and nearer the sea until they too were in it and wading waist-deep towards a small boat that would ferry them out to a Campbell's paddle steamer. Was it the *Waverley* or perhaps the *Westward Ho!* or maybe the *Glen Gower?* Tommy was remembering taking Josie on a trip to Minehead on the *Wesward Ho!* Just after they'd first met it was. It seemed a lifetime away now.

Certainly these pleasure steamers could never have had a stranger cargo or a more appreciative one. The decks were crammed with dishevelled, exhausted servicemen, those who could no longer stand lying on the deck with the wounded. As they slowly edged their way out into the Channel, Tommy, jammed tight against the rail that was supporting him, watched plumes of smoke rising from the beach and thought of those they'd left behind who would never make it back. He felt sick at heart.

When ten minutes later he once more looked back towards the devastation, it was to the sickening sight of a ship going down stern first, the water around swarming with servicemen and crew, struggling to keep afloat. Already a few small boats were making their way towards the fast-disappearing ship. Tommy's empty stomach retched painfully as he bent over the rail.

By the time the cliffs of Dover came into sight he'd sunk to his knees from sheer exhaustion. He struggled to his feet as the men began slowly filing off and somehow managed to stay on them as, carrying rifles and any equipment they still had, they dragged themselves along the quayside. They even managed a smile for the cheering crowds, haggard, dirty, unshaven, but thankful, so very thankful, to be going home.

Once on the train they were handed

much-needed cups of tea, biscuits, cakes, chocolate and cigarettes by motherly volunteers. The train moved out to cheers and good wishes. Tommy closed his eyes and thought longingly of Josie and his parents before falling into a troubled sleep.

★　★　★

Josie had sent the message with the baker, Old Fred, who'd taken on Tommy's round. He had brought the note when he came to Roath to get his horse and van. A telegram might have been quicker but Josie, remembering her own dread when she'd opened the one that had come, the indecision and fear that had gripped her heart as she'd stared at the envelope, terrified of the news it might contain, didn't want Polly and Bert to be upset.

'Your Tommy's comin' 'ome then,' Fred had told Polly with a wide grin, unable to keep the joyous news to himself.

Her fingers clumsy with excitement, she'd torn the envelope and fumbled with the single piece of paper it contained, the words leaping up at her.

'Wonderful news, Mam and Dad! Tommy expected home tonight or early tomorrow.'

'Good news, innit?' The old man's eyes

were bright with pleasure at the glad tidings he'd brought.

'Thank you, Fred. Would you like a cup of tea?' Polly asked, though she couldn't wait to show the note to Bert.

'No, love. Got to get on. Wish the lad all the best from me.'

Polly sighed with relief, glad for once that her offer hadn't been taken up, and hurried to the kitchen, anxious to put Bert's mind at rest, knowing that like her he'd been worried sick as he'd followed news of the retreat of the BEF and of the evacuation from Dunkirk.

Watching his joy as he read the note, seeing the burden of worry lift from his shoulders, she went across and put her arms about him.

'Get a cab we will tomorrow, Poll,' he told her. 'Even if Tommy does get back tonight, it may be very late and he'll be exhausted after all he's been through. Thank God he's on his way home!'

'Yes, thank God,' she echoed with feeling. 'I hope he's all right.'

'How can anyone go through what those lads have been through and be all right?' Bert said bitterly. 'Still, we're lucky he's coming back to us, *cariad*, very lucky.'

'He can't be badly injured,' Polly told him thankfully, 'or he'd be in hospital.'

Bert didn't answer. He knew better than

315

most the effect that seeing your mates dying around you could have on your mind. But Polly was already wondering what little treat she could take with her tomorrow, reviewing just what was left in the pantry and cupboard until next week's rations were due.

They were alone in the house, for the day after Sally had arrived home Roy had received his papers. He was now training to be a rear gunner with the RAF but thankfully wouldn't be operational for a while. Gareth and Dilys were at school, and Sally and little Bryn were spending a few days at Tre-Mynydd with Peggy. Already the customary photograph had arrived showing Roy, handsome and smiling, in uniform. It stood on the small table between the children's beds, just as Bert's had stood by Tommy's all those years ago.

Many times during the long day Polly wondered how she was to get through it, and Bert was equally restless, going from room to room or pacing up and down the garden path. Hoping to see someone to share the good news with, Polly thought with a smile. But she'd seen Jessie going off with her daughter early that morning and the neighbours the other side were away.

Soon it was time for Dilys to be fetched from school. Watching Bert going up the street, stopping whenever he saw anyone to talk to, she hoped he'd arrive on time. But Dilys had been told she must always wait and Gareth would be looking out for her anyway.

Who would collect Dilys and give the children their dinner tomorrow? Polly thought. But when, a little later, she went to the corner shop, eager to tell them her news, Becky offered as she'd done so many times before. Only I don't like taking her for granted, Polly told herself.

Next day, waiting for the cab to arrive, she could barely contain her impatience.

'You'd better be prepared, love, the boy's been through a lot,' Bert cautioned. As they arrived at the house and he was paying the driver, Josie opened the door.

'Tommy's having a bath in the kitchen, he hasn't been home very long,' she told them. Then, seeing the anxious expression on Polly's face, she added with a smile, 'Don't worry, Mam, he's all in one piece, thank God.'

They sat in the front room while Josie and her mam brought tea and biscuits and Polly listened anxiously for her son's footsteps. When the door opened and he came into the room she was shocked by how pale he was and the exhausted look in his eyes. As she went into his arms, Josie and her mam took the trays to the kitchen. 'Oh, son!' was all Polly could think of to say.

Over Tommy's shoulder Polly could see tears of thankfulness in Bert's eyes, then he too was embraced and Tommy was saying in a broken voice, 'Sorry, Dad. I'm so sorry . . . I never really understood 'til now.'

And Bert replied, his voice vibrant with emotion, 'Nothing to be sorry about, son. Thank God you're home. I've been with you all the way these last few days, believe me.'

Both men had tears in their eyes now and Polly slipped quietly out of the room, her heart full. It had taken a war to bring these two together, and that war, far from being over, was only just beginning.

33

'Couldn't you spare me a bit more sugar, Becky?' Enid Brown put on her friendliest smile and waited hopefully.

'Sorry, Enid,' Becky told her. 'We can't treat one different from another. We wouldn't have enough for the rations if we did.'

The smile vanished as Enid huffily swept a loaf of bread from the counter and left the shop.

Becky sighed. It was a question that was often asked: 'Can you spare me a bit extra, love?' Keeping a corner shop, customers were also your neighbours and as such some expected favours. But Dora had made it clear from the beginning: 'No favours for anyone. It's the only way not to offend.'

But I have offended Enid Brown, Becky told herself, remembering the woman's stony look when she'd refused her and what a spiteful gossip the woman had always been.

Meat had been rationed in March, but thankfully that only affected them personally. Now, in July, tea had been put on ration, and with all the worry over the Germans being just across the Channel since Dunkirk, and all the scares about an invasion, people seemed to be drinking more of it than ever.

Albert had been down in the dumps ever since he'd failed his medical because of poor eyesight. He'd started to wear glasses for work a while back but hadn't realised they were that bad. Secretly Becky had been very relieved, though a little ashamed of her feelings when so many around them were having to part with their loved ones. Albert was her strength; his tolerance and common sense had helped her through many a situation. As her love had grown, so had her respect and admiration and if he had been called up, Becky wondered just how they would have managed. At the shop they still relied on him to carry anything from the cellar they couldn't handle, and since rationing began he'd shown them how to deal with all the paperwork. Besides, Nellie's legs were getting worse and he practically carried her to the shelter when there was a warning, though nothing much had happened until 19 July when a lone bomber had swooped suddenly over the docks, scoring a direct hit on a ship where seven men were killed. The hero of that raid had been a man called Tim O'Brian who, heedless of his own safety, went down into the hold three times to rescue the injured, though nobody knew whether or not it was filled with gas.

Now, with only the Channel between them, everyone was on edge, bracing themselves for the expected invasion. Many a tale was told in the shop which Becky would repeat for Nellie's entertainment.

'Mrs Bowden said today someone told her they saw German parachutists landing on the tide fields, Nellie, and someone else saw lights bobbing about.'

Dilys was painting a picture at the table, tongue between her teeth in concentration. Now she looked up, her wide grey eyes intent, a puzzled expression on her face as Nellie said scornfully, 'The only Jerries they'll ever see are the ones they keep under their beds!' for all that was kept under Dilys's was her china po with the pink roses on it, same as on the jug and bowl on the wash-stand.

Becky wanted to hug the little mite. Dilys would be going away in a few days' time and she knew just how much they were all going to miss her. Peggy had written several times since the air raids had begun, asking Sally to bring little Bryn and come to stay with them at Tre-Mynydd, and she'd also invited Polly to send Gareth and Dilys.

'It'll be too much for you, Peggy,' Polly had written back, 'but I do appreciate your offer. Anyway, you wouldn't have room.'

A reply had come by return post. Better a bit of overcrowding than the children being in danger, Peggy insisted. And there'd be Sally to help out, and Mostyn when he wasn't down the pit. She'd be expecting them — and their ration books — on Thursday.

★ ★ ★

When the warning siren wailed, Becky waited behind the front door for Dora to come and share their shelter. It would be lonely being on her own. But her mother was a long time coming. When at last Becky opened the door to look along the street, it was to find incendiaries already falling, little firebombs dropping from the sky and weaving their way to the ground, bathing everything in a ghastly light. Where was her mam? Was she still at the shop?

Becky opened the door again just as Dora breathlessly arrived and a worried Albert came into the house to look for them both. Now the sky was stained red with the reflection of fires started by the incendiaries.

They ran to the shelter with Dora apologising all the way. But as they tumbled down into it, hearts in their mouths as bombers droned overhead, Becky had already decided. Next time she'd go to the shelter in her mother's garden and Albert could stay with Nellie. She had a key to the side door so no one would have to wait for her.

The throbbing of the planes was fading but now there was the whistling sound of bombs falling and then muffled explosions. Listening intently, they made out the all clear five minutes later. It sent Becky and Albert scrambling to their feet to ease Nellie from the bench and lift her up the shelter steps.

Over a cup of tea Albert and Dora began to argue against Becky's decision to go to the shop when there was a raid, but support came from an unexpected quarter as Nellie said, 'Becky's quite right, you know. She's much quicker on her pins than you are, Dora, and that way nobody'll have to wait about.'

The next time there was a raid Becky was at the corner and turning the key in the side door before the siren had ceased its wailing. She and her mother were down in the shelter with the door shut before the throb of approaching planes could be heard.

'I wish you'd stayed put, love,' Dora told her, but a welcoming smile belied her words. She'd brought down sandwiches and a flask of tea. Before either of them could take a bite there was a faint throbbing which quickly grew louder, then the whistle of bombs falling and the rat-a-tat of anti-aircraft fire. When at last they heard the welcome sound of the all clear Becky hurried home. As she was letting herself in one of their neighbours, an air-raid warden, got off his bike to tell her: 'The docks area took the brunt of it tonight, Becky. One killed and nineteen injured, poor souls.'

'Albert's gone to meet you,' Nellie told her when she opened the kitchen door. 'Must 'ave missed you in the black-out, I suppose.'

Nellie had been very quiet since Dilys had gone away and Becky knew how much she was missing the little girl whom she'd treated like the grandchild she'd never had. Watching her now, Becky felt a pang of conscience that she hadn't been able to provide Albert's mam with the one thing she craved for most.

The children had been at Tre-Mynydd for over a month and Polly had told Becky that Roy was sending a generous allowance for their keep. 'He's good to me too,' she had added. 'You couldn't wish for a better son-in-law. He didn't deserve to lose Laura like that.'

There were tears in her eyes and in Becky's too as they remembered, but Becky didn't need Polly to tell her how wonderful Roy was. She'd long ago decided her own feelings for him were a sort of hero worship, much the same as she'd felt for Rudolph Valentino the film star during her adolescent years, only she'd soon grown out of that. How else could she explain the love she also had for Albert, something that had started from nothing and grown into a deep and fulfilling emotion with the years.

34

On a cold December night as the banshee
wail of the siren rent the frosty air, Polly and
Bert scuttled along the garden path and
scrambled down into the shelter to sit
opposite each other in the dim light of the
hurricane lamp. Sitting there in its sickly
glow, Polly looked anxiously at her husband.

Before the children had left for Tre-
Mynydd he'd always seemed calm during a
raid, if a little overprotective of Dilys and
Gareth. Now, with German planes based just
across the Channel, the constant fear of
invasion and air raids ever more frequent, he
would sit in the shelter lost in his own dark
thoughts. As ack-ack guns kept up their
constant racket and shrapnel rained down on
the shelter, he seemed to become more and
more withdrawn, his jaw clenched tightly,
eyes closed. She knew he was reliving the
past, imagining himself crouched with his
mates in some flea-ridden trench under
constant bombardment.

'Bert,' she called softly. Then, when he
didn't answer, 'Bert!'

Startled, he opened his eyes and stared at

her. He looked panic-stricken. Seeing her sitting there so calmly, her hand on his arm, he seemed to give himself a little mental shake, saying with a deep sigh, 'Sorry, Polly, I was far away.'

The nightmares had started again recently, not every night but often after a raid, and he worried constantly about the situation the country was in.

'I can't understand why they don't invade,' he'd frequently remark. And if the Germans did invade, Polly thought worriedly, what would happen to them? Then gave herself the answer: God help us all!

There were rumours that an invasion had been attempted. Some people said that bodies had been found in the sea, but they were only rumours and the atmosphere was ripe for these, with beaches barricaded with barbed wire and everyone on the alert.

Tommy was back at camp awaiting orders and would be worrying about Josie who, to their delight, was six months pregnant. Where would he be sent this time? Polly wondered anxiously. Roy had completed his training as a rear gunner and was now airborne. Polly and Bert were worried sick for even Roy couldn't downplay the dangers of the job he was doing. When recently he'd come home on leave he'd stayed for only one night, spending the rest of it by Peggy's invitation at Tre-Mynydd with the children, sleeping next-door in Glad and Megan's spare bedroom and probably being spoiled rotten, for it wasn't every day Peggy's spinster neighbours had a handsome young airman to stay.

Becky had seemed upset that she hadn't seen Roy while he was home. Probably thought he'd bring the children to Cardiff for the day, Polly told herself, for Becky was always telling her how much they all missed them. Not half as much as I do, she thought with a sigh. She'd gone to see them once a week at first but now in winter, with darkness falling just after four o'clock and the air raids getting earlier and earlier, she daren't take the risk.

The Christmas presents had been wrapped up and sent with Roy, but the thought of Christmas Day without any of the family, just her and Bert sitting either side of the fire, filled Polly with dismay. When they were alone her thoughts would often turn to Laura. 'Poor little love,' she'd whisper to herself, throat aching with unshed tears. Laura's life had been so short, her death so sudden, and she'd been looking forward to the new baby so much.

Something else troubled Polly too. Being

away all this time, would Gareth and Dilys forget her? And Sally ... it had been wonderful having her and Bryn at home but now she'd probably stay with her mother-in-law for the duration.

Polly was remembering the last time she'd visited Tre-Mynydd. The house was bursting at the seams but Peggy had never seemed happier. While Dilys 'helped', Gareth had quickly become Mostyn's shadow, following his burly uncle around and constantly waiting to be taken on long walks over the mountain or for them to kick a ball about on the grass patch at the top of the street.

In the last letter she'd had from Sally, her daughter said she was starting work at the Royal Ordnance Factory at Llanishen on the following Monday. She'd said it had been that or the Land Army, and at least working in the munitions factory on the outskirts of Cardiff, she'd be home with little Bryn between shifts. Although she was working in the same town she wasn't able to pay them even a flying visit for a factory bus picked the workers up at Ararat Chapel at Tre-Mynydd and returned them there at the end of the shift.

★　★　★

On that cold December night Sally and half-a-dozen others were waiting in the porch of the chapel for the bus to arrive. It was bitterly cold, an icy wind keeping coat collars up and gloved hands plunged deep into pockets. Her new friend Brenda, who lived with her family a few doors from Peggy, was talking to another girl and as Sally stared out into the gloomy night the whole village seemed to be in darkness. She was thinking of Peggy tucking Bryn into his bed with a hug and a kiss, then telling him a bedtime story. She wondered if after all she'd been wise to volunteer to work at the ordnance factory before she really had to.

'It's one way of saving towards setting up home again when the war's over, *cariad*,' her mother-in-law told her. 'I can manage Bryn and the other two, don't you worry about that.'

Nearly everyone was doing something for the war effort and Sally thought she owed it to Bill. Besides, if she waited until they conscripted people she might be drafted into some other service that required her going away from home. Peggy said she didn't think that would happen, not with Sally having a young child, but made no secret of the fact that she was more than willing to look after her grandson, come what may.

330

At last the dimmed headlights of the bus were coming towards them. As it drew into the kerb everyone clambered quickly aboard, anxious to get inside out of the cold. Sitting in the darkened interior, listening to Brenda's chatter, Sally's thoughts were still with her little son. At least living with Peggy in Tre-Mynydd he was tucked up warmly in bed, not shivering down a damp shelter as he would have been had they stayed in Cardiff. She worried a lot about her mam and dad. Several girls at the factory who lived nearby told worrying tales of scary, sleepless nights that were getting more and more frequent, vowing they'd rather be at work then for at least they could sleep peacefully during the day.

As Sally and Brenda entered 'A' shop, the catchy tune *Run, Rabbit, Run* was blaring from the loudspeakers and the strong smell of hot lubricating oil and burning swarf met them. Tying a snood about her hair, Sally made her way to the large machine holding a gun barrel, the one on which she'd been working ever since she'd finished her training. She smoothed Roselex into her hands and called a greeting to Ernie, the middle-aged tool setter who'd been keeping an eye on her for the first few weeks.

Starting up the machine and delicately

adjusting the cutting tool, Sally brought it into contact with the gun barrel and as the hot swarf curled and rose above the machine, an old man who'd been sitting patiently, waiting, rose and lifted his long-handled hook to pull away the scalding metal.

There was no time for thinking now as the noise of the various machines competed with the music from the tannoy. Sally was all concentration as she stopped the machine and slid the calipers in place, measuring carefully.

There were smears of oil on her face and boiler suit when the time came to go to the canteen for supper. In the cloakroom she washed her face and combed her hair. She put the snood in her coat pocket and slung it about her shoulders for the short walk to the canteen, beginning to run with the others when she saw searchlights sweeping the sky and heard the distant sound of anti-aircraft fire. I'll never get used to eating at night, she told herself, the smell of oxtail soup wafting towards them as they went in.

It was the early hours of the morning but the long room was buzzing with chatter and laughter and already a long queue had formed at the counter. Unable to face the soup, fish and chips, or other cooked meals on offer, she took a plate of Spam sandwiches and sat down. Just as Brenda joined her at the table the curtains swished aside on a stage in front of them and a stout lady began to play a medley of tunes while a thin one with a plunging neckline sang in a high reedy voice.

'You'll be starving before the shift's over,' Brenda warned, tucking into a meat and vegetable pie, a large helping of apple pie and custard ready by the side. Sally shook her head. At this hour of the morning she couldn't face a big cooked meal and it was the same with sleep when she finally got to bed after spending a little time with Bryn. At first, tired as she was, she'd toss and turn, listening anxiously for the second post, always hoping for a letter from Bill who was now in the Middle East. Then she'd toss and hear the baker's van arrive and his friendly chatter as Peggy took her pick from the big cane basket. Children would come running home from school, neighbours would talk at their doors. When it was almost time for the alarm bell to ring, she'd finally drop off into an exhausted sleep, only to wake feeling sick with tiredness and a little bewildered when the alarm shrilled.

The musical medley had come to an end and when the clapping petered out and the curtains swished across a young man announced that a hypnotist was about to entertain them and would require absolute quiet. A few minutes later the curtains swung back to reveal a row of chairs and a tall man in black braided trousers and a frilly silk shirt, dangling what looked like a large pocket watch on the end of a chain. Sally stopped eating and listened intently as he began.

'I'd like to invite any one of you up to the stage to take the trip of a lifetime. Come along and wish yourself anywhere you'd like to go. Your dreams will come true.'

'Anywhere I'd like to go?' Sally breathed softly. Oh, if only she could be with Bill just for a few blissful minutes. Even if it was only in the imagination, it would feel real under hypnosis, wouldn't it?

Several girls were making their way to the stage, giggling self-consciously. Sally half rose but Brenda pulled her back to her seat, whispering, 'Don't do it, Sal. Let them up there make fools of themselves. And they will, you'll see.'

Perhaps Brenda's right, Sally thought, watching them seat themselves on the row of chairs. After all, the hypnotist wanted to control them. And if he did, they might do all sorts of daft things. Yet for a moment as she saw his subjects nod off a feeling of regret came over her.

She might have been with Bill again, if only

in her mind. But common sense told her, watching the women now falling foolishly about, that she too would have acted stupidly, perhaps kissing and hugging a non-existent Bill and making herself a real laughing stock. Giving Brenda a grateful smile, she settled down to watch the antics on the stage.

35

With Christmas over Becky found herself glad to get back to the bustle of the shop. Albert, still depressed at not having been called up to serve in the armed forces, had said as they'd sat down to supper last night, 'I feel awful being the only man working at the shop, and I know customers are talking about me.'

'But it's not your fault, love,' she assured him for the umpteenth time. 'You're doing a useful job, especially now they've made you manager.'

'Well, I only got that because Richard was called up. It's as though I'm benefiting from the war while everyone else is making sacrifices.'

'Why can't you just be thankful?' his mother told him impatiently. 'I can't even get to the shelter on my own. If you were away it would all fall on poor Becky, and these days I'm far too heavy for her to pull up and down.'

'I know all that, Mam.' Albert gave a deep sigh. 'But how would you feel with customers talking about husbands and sons who were at

Dunkirk being sent abroad again? What must they think of me? I can't go about with a notice around my neck saying I've failed my medical, can I?'

'You're too sensitive, Albert, that's your trouble,' his mother told him. 'Just think of all the useful jobs you do for Dora and Becky.'

'I feel I should be doing my bit,' he told her stubbornly. 'You don't seem to understand at all.'

Albert's getting paranoid about it, Becky thought worriedly, but who could blame him? Because of Nellie's almost total reliance on him whenever there was a raid, he hadn't even been able to volunteer for any of the local services either, like the Civil Defence perhaps. *Why*

Dora had come as usual for Christmas Day but there'd been little to talk about except the war, and with the children away at Tre-Mynydd there hadn't been even the customary visit with their presents to look forward too. The gifts had been posted to them long before. Becky did make a flying visit to Polly's after tea but apart from a few precious apples in a fruit bowl on the table, and the slice of Christmas cake and glass of home-made wine she'd felt bound to partake of, it had been like any other day, with Bert reading by the fire and Polly knitting warm socks in airforce blue.

'I've already sent two pairs of khaki to Tommy,' Polly told her, 'but I don't expect he'll be needing them out there in the Middle East.'

At the mention of Tommy's name Bert looked up and Becky had the impression he hadn't really been reading at all. 'He'll be glad of anything that comes from home, Poll,' he told her with feeling. 'I used to read your letters over and over again.'

They'd seen the New Year in just as quietly, with a glass of Nellie's port, optimistically wishing each other a Happy New Year, but they hadn't stayed up until midnight for as Nellie said, you had to snatch a good night's sleep when you could.

Next day Becky was in the Maypole just before closing time when the young woman Albert was serving suddenly remarked in a loud voice, 'I'm surprised to see an able-bodied man like you still in civvies.' Snatching the bacon ration he'd wrapped, she rushed from the shop before Albert could say a word in his own defence.

Ten minutes later, as they walked home together in the black-out, Becky could sense his deep unhappiness. Stretching up to kiss him she told him, 'Don't let it upset you, love. We know the truth, and I'm very thankful you're still at home.'

'She's right, Becky, and it hurts,' he said sadly. 'I'm living a normal life here while others are away fighting for their country.'

'But it isn't your fault, and you're doing a useful job. I couldn't bear it if anything happened to you.'

'Oh, Becky.' Albert, suddenly lost for words, hugged her gratefully.

Now with darkness falling so early her mother closed the shop at five o'clock, hoping to have finished their evening meal before any air raid began. On 2 January there was a full moon and it was freezing. Becky had just washed the dishes and put them back on the dresser when at about six-thirty the siren began to wail. As Albert quickly got Nellie into her warm coat, Becky, troubled as usual at leaving him to cope with his mother, grabbed hers from the hall-stand and rushed into the street where sky and buildings were already lit by the crazy light of falling incendiaries, bathing everything in their sickly greenish glow.

Searchlights were sweeping the sky and before she'd reached the corner the thunder of anti-aircraft guns began. Above their barrage the heavy drone of bombers was audible, faint at first but growing louder by the second.

Suddenly the key to the side door flew from her fingers and, with a sob of despair, Becky crouched down to look for it, but despite the full moon and the light from the little firebombs that were doing their work so well there was no sign of the key. She had just knelt on the pavement, her heart racing with fear, fingers desperately exploring inch by inch, when her name was called in an urgent tone. She'd never been so thankful to hear her mother's voice, but as they rushed through the house and out into the garden, she knew the dreadful risk her mam was taking.

They almost fell into the shelter. Dora slammed the door and, white and trembling, collapsed on to the bench just as a loud explosion rocked the ground beneath them, extinguishing the hurricane lamp that swung overhead and shaking the shelter to its very foundations. I know about that.

'For God's sake, where did that fall?' Dora asked, searching with her fingers for the matches. With the lamp lit again, she took the thermos flask and poured two hot beakers of tea, forcing one into Becky's ice-cold hands.

In the lamp's sickly glow the girl looked ghastly. I probably do too, Dora thought, her hands stiff with tension as she screwed the top back on to the flask.

'Mam,' Becky said in a small voice, 'that

explosion was near by. I hope Albert and Nellie are all right. I wish I could go and see . . . '

'Oh, I don't think it was that near, love,' Dora told her comfortingly. 'And they'll be thinking the same about you. But like you, they'll have the sense to stay put. Anyway, it should be over soon.'

But the explosions seemed to be coming at shorter and shorter intervals and the barrage from the guns was deafening.

'What time is it, Mam?' Becky asked a little while later. Dora glanced at her watch. 'It's ten to nine,' she said. 'Surely it can't go on much longer?'

But it did. Instead of the usual few hours, wave after wave of bombers kept up their onslaught through the night, and with each explosion that seemed near Becky worried more about Albert and Nellie.

'They'll be worrying about you just the same,' her mother told her. 'As I've said before, love, there's no need for you to come here to be with me. Especially after that scare tonight with you losing the key.'

'Oh, Mam! Then I'd only be worrying about you.' And Becky managed a weary smile.

There was no let up as the night wore on. Becky found herself thinking of Roy. Was he at this very moment flying over some town in Germany in a Lancaster bomber? Crouched in his little space as rear gunner, the throb of the engines striking terror to the people below. She could only imagine what it was like for him, she'd no real idea. Closing her eyes, Becky said a little prayer for his safety. For the children's sake, she told herself.

Cold, tired and hungry, the sandwiches having been eaten many hours before, they sat side by side, longing for the all clear to sound, dozing occasionally from sheer exhaustion despite the racket overhead.

It was ten to five the next morning before the all clear was given. As they climbed stiffly from the shelter, Dora said, 'I'll make us a cup of tea.'

But Becky told her anxiously, 'No, Mam, I just want to get home.'

The stench of oily smoke was everywhere but after the stuffiness of the shelter the frosty air felt clean and fresh. They hurried down the path to the house, as fast as their cramped legs would carry them. Switching on the light, Dora said, 'You look all in, *cariad*. Are you sure you're all right?'

'It's just a headache, Mam,' Becky told her, adding with a weary smile, 'You don't look so good yourself.'

'Nothing a good night's sleep won't cure,'

Dora told her, adding ruefully, 'There's very little of this night left, though. Come on then, Becky. I'll stand on the corner until you reach the house.'

Dora opened the side door, her foot kicking something metallic as she stepped into the street. As she bent down to pick up the key Becky was turning the corner. The cry she gave sent her mother running to her side. There she stared open-mouthed, taking in the scene of devastation. Becky raced towards the smouldering ruins that had been her home, now reduced almost to rubble. To either side the roofless bedrooms of neighbouring houses were exposed and hanging at crazy angles. Amidst the smoke and dust and stench of fire, men in tin hats tore at the rubble. By the amount they'd already moved, they had been working for some time.

Becky had thrown herself to the ground and was tearing at broken bricks with her bare hands, sobbing, 'Albert — Albert! Nellie!'

Strong arms lifted her away despite her protests and one of the men said, 'We found them, missus, in the shelter at the back. It's 'is wife we're looking for now . . .'

As someone informed them, 'She's 'is wife,' Becky cried, 'The shelter? Are they still there? Can I go to them?'

'Took a direct hit it did. In the mortuary they are now, love, but you wouldn't recognise them. Had to get over the back walls to get to them — '

Becky would have sunk to the ground if Dora's arms hadn't been about her. Someone rushed to their home on the other side of the street to get a chair while one of the ARP men supported her gently and would have carried her across to it until Dora said, 'She'd be better off at home, the shop's only just along the street.'

When an unconscious Becky was settled on the sofa he rubbed his red-rimmed eyes wearily with the back of his hand, saying, 'It's a bad business, poor girl, but I'm glad she wasn't under that rubble too.'

'She was here, thank God! Keeping me company. But she'll be breaking her heart when she does wake up.' Fetching the smelling salts from the bathroom cupboard, Dora's eyes swam with tears.

36

For as long as she lived Becky would never forget that desolate scene. It was with her every waking moment and became part of her nightmares when, from utter exhaustion, she fell asleep. She got up on the second morning, her heart heavy with grief, shocking Dora by announcing, 'I'm going to serve behind the counter today, Mam.'

'I can manage, Becky,' Dora told her gently. 'You get back to bed. I'll have to open, they'll be wanting to collect their rations, especially after me closing all day yesterday.'

'I'd rather serve in the shop.'

Seeing the frozen expression on her daughter's face, the eyes mirroring her sorrow, Dora told herself: It's the shock. Poor girl, she's hardly in her right mind. She'll crack up if she goes on like this. A good cry might alleviate some of the pain.

She felt ill with shock herself but must remain strong for Becky's sake. She'd been very fond of her son-in-law and had got to know Nellie quite well since the young couple had married. It was hard to believe Albert would never come into the shop again, crying cheerfully, 'Anything you want done today, Mam?'

'I'll unbolt the door,' Becky was saying, and following her into the shop, Dora felt pity well up in her again. Every customer that came in was sure to voice their condolences. Would Becky be able to stand it over and over again?

The funeral arrangments had been made yesterday and they'd been told there was to be a civic funeral at the cemetery for the many victims of the night's raid. News had been coming into the shop of other casualties of the heavy raid, and of the businesses that had suffered. Bristow Wadley's in Mill Lane set on fire, Noah Rees's warehouse in Working Street, Peacock's Bazaar in Queen Street, Cavendish Furniture warehouse, all burnt out . . . The list seemed endless.

Still stony-faced, constantly murmuring thanks for all the messages of sympathy, Becky was about to serve old Letty Roberts who'd just come into the shop. Putting her gnarled hand on Becky's arm, the old lady said, 'So sorry to hear the dreadful news, love. If there's anything I can do?' The same message with almost the same choice of words had been given by customers all day, but now Letty, a devout churchgoer, added,

346

'A lovely young man your husband was, but it's God's will and we can't fight it. He always takes the best.'

Suddenly the colour was back in Becky's cheeks as she cried, 'That's rubbish, Mrs Roberts. God doesn't start wars. It's the Germans who took Albert's life, not God.' The words ended on a sob and tears were streaming down her face as she dashed for the kitchen, leaving a startled old lady apologising to Dora.

'I'm sorry, Mrs Morgan, I only meant to comfort the poor soul.'

'It's the best thing that could happen,' Dora assured her with a gentle pat on the hand. The floodgates were open now. They could hear Becky's abandoned sobbing even in the shop, and though her mother longed to go and comfort her, it was perhaps best she was left alone.

In the kitchen, her sobbing bout over, Becky lay back against the sofa cushions, dabbing her puffy eyes. She'd needed to work today because she hadn't wanted time to think. She'd done enough of that last night, staring up at the ceiling unable to sleep, remembering that she hadn't even kissed Albert goodbye before dashing out of the house. Then, the main priority had been to get to the shelter — and a lot of good that had done him and Nellie. Direct hit, they'd said.

She was remembering the early days of their marriage, how he would watch her hopefully, month after month. He'd wanted a child so much, but when at last he'd realised it wasn't going to happen, he'd never mentioned it again. Unlike Nellie who would never let the subject drop, never let Becky forget.

If only they'd been able to live in the rooms they'd furnished over the shop, Albert might still be with them. But his mother and her sister Ruth would have been in the shelter in Paul Street then, and knowing how conscientious Albert had always been, especially where his mother was concerned, he'd probably have been over there too.

'I'll make us a cup of tea, Becky.' She hadn't heard Dora come into the room. 'We'll have to do some more shopping for you soon, love,' her mam went on. 'I got you that underwear at Goldberg's but you need to try on dresses. I'll put a notice on the door tomorrow, if you like? We shouldn't be more than a couple of hours and the customers will understand.'

It had been some time after the shock of finding her home demolished that Becky had realised she had nothing but the clothes she stood up in.

The volunteer who'd carried her home had brought her some things they'd rescued from the rubble: Nellie's handbag and her own, both charred and filthy but the purses and their contents undamaged. Becky had put Nellie's away. She'd give it to Ruth who was sure to be at the funeral. Becky hadn't seen Albert's aunt since her wedding day. His watch, the glass smashed, and the contents of his pockets still lay on the kitchen table, bringing a fresh lump to Becky's throat. She didn't want to go out, didn't want to listen to any more condolences, but with the funeral only four days away she'd have to get something to wear.

* * *

The next morning they got up early so as to be in town as soon as the shops opened. Hurrying along Wilfred Street passing children dawdling on their way to school and people on their way to work, Becky marvelled that everything seemed so normal when her own world had been turned upside down. In Broadway, a woman sweeping her front had left the door ajar and the strains of Vera Lynn singing *We'll Meet Again* came to them, bringing tears to Becky's eyes once more.

Once in town they made straight for David Morgan's and the fashion department where there was a section for mourning wear. The assistant they'd approached soon had her arms laden with black dresses and coats. Her eyes sympathetic, she led them to the dressing room and Becky was suddenly surprised to find she was looking forward to trying on the garments, and immediately felt guilty at the thought.

Well, they'll have to last a very long time, she told herself. It's no good buying any old thing. But when the first dress she slipped over her head fitted her slim figure to perfection, the unrelieved black showing up the unaccustomed pallor of her face and warm colouring of her curly auburn hair, that pang of guilt persisted.

They hurried home with their purchases to find a little queue waiting outside the shop. But they all waited patiently, nodding their understanding when Dora apologised and reminded them that the shop would be closed again for the afternoon on the day of the funeral.

When Ruth arrived and was given Nellie's handbag, she burst into tears, saying, 'I promised to stay with our Nellie when Albert got married and she was so disappointed and upset when I had to go home. I feel I let her down.'

'It wasn't your fault your other sister was taken ill,' Becky consoled her, thinking, It's funny the way we all feel guilty over things we haven't done as soon as a loved one dies.

Ruth proved a tower of strength: serving in the shop, helping with the arrangements for the funeral, and, when the day arrived, working in the kitchen with Polly Evans until everything was ready and waiting for the mourners' return.

It was surprising how many men, either too young or too old to be in the forces, came to walk to the cemetery. As the funeral procession making its way along Paul Street neared the gap where their house had been, Becky looked away, her lips trembling. Dora glanced at her anxiously. Dr Powell had said she'd have to be patient, for Becky had suffered a severe shock that would affect her for a long time to come. She herself had been shocked to the core. How much worse it must be for her daughter.

It was a bitterly cold day, a biting easterly wind tearing at hats and scarves as they stood around while the service was intoned. The civic dignitaries were there, including the Lord Mayor, but it was the little groups of relatives that Becky's heart went out to in her own suffering. Sad-eyed, supporting each other in their grief, their faces mirrored the loss that had come on them so suddenly on that dreadful night.

As the weeks passed Becky dreaded the sound of the siren's wail. Stomach churning, heart beating fast, she'd sit by Dora's side in the shelter, eyes wide with fear, hands nervously clasping and unclasping each other, the shock and horror of that night early in January still filling her mind.

Life should have been easier with nothing much to do after the shop closed except sit by the fire reading or listening to the wireless. It was certainly a far cry from the nights in Paul Street with so many jobs to catch up with and Nellie to be settled for the night. But whenever Becky turned on the wireless there'd be someone singing sentimental songs like *There's A Lovely Day Tomorrow* or *There's A Boy Coming Home On Leave*. Although theirs had never been a passionate love affair, she had loved Albert with all her heart and the sound of Vera Lynn, Gracie Fields and other favourites assuring her everything would be all right tomorrow, when her world had just been wiped out, was more than she could bear.

37

'Anything else you need brought up from the cellar, Mrs Morgan?'

'No, Bob, and thanks again. We're very grateful.'

'Well, you've only got to ask.'

Dora had hardly recognised the man who'd carried Becky home that awful night when a few days after the funeral he'd called to offer his help.

'Mam says you may be needing sacks brought up,' he'd explained. 'It was such a tragedy, your daughter losing her husband and mother-in-law like that. I can't get it out of my mind. I see enough of it every time I'm on duty but I'll never get used to the suffering.'

He's a nice young man, Dora thought, remembering that awful night and his soot-blackened face streaked with sweat. Wearing his tin helmet, he'd looked much older. She'd been surprised to learn that this sturdily built man with dark curly hair was still the right side of forty and had a wife and young children.

Until then they'd been bringing things up

to the shop in small quantities, making frequent journeys and constantly running out of stock.

As the weeks went by Becky remained stony-faced, taking little interest in anything that went on. Frozen with shock was how Dora thought of her. She knew the girl now dreaded the long, dark nights, listening for the siren's shriek.

When spring came and the evenings grew lighter, the raids began later. Becky couldn't concentrate on anything as she waited for the unearthly sound which now brought panic as well as fear to her heart. New rationing in May meant even more paperwork, and with so many disturbed nights it was difficult to keep up to date with all the book-keeping that had to be done. Often in the early hours they'd climb wearily from the shelter, fit only to fall into bed.

When in March a delighted Polly came to tell them that Josie had had a baby girl, Becky expressed her delight. If only she and Albert had had a child, what a comfort it would be now in her grief.

By the summer Bob was still helping them regularly, though Dora often wondered how he could spare the time what with his shifts at the ordnance factory and duties with the ARP. But by now she didn't know how they'd manage without him effortlessly carrying heavy sacks from the cellar and keeping them informed of all that went on.

She at any rate was grateful for his cheerful chatter, though becoming more and more alarmed by her daughter's lack of interest in what went on around her. If only Laura's children were here, she thought, knowing how fond of them Becky had always been.

She voiced her concern to Polly one day when they were alone in the shop. 'Roy's got a weekend pass, Dora,' Polly cried eagerly. 'He'll be going to Tre-Mynydd Saturday morning. Perhaps Becky could go with him, just for the day? He'll be staying there until Monday but he'd see her on to the train and she'd be home long before it got dark.' Then, putting her hand to her mouth, she added, 'I'm sorry, Dora. I didn't think — Saturday's a busy day for you.'

'Don't worry, I'll manage,' Dora said gratefully. 'It's just what she needs, to get outside these four walls. How are Josie and the baby?'

'Fine. I went to see them last weekend. I can't expect her to come out very often, it's two tram rides and at three months little Marion's quite a weight to carry.'

At first Becky was adamant, saying regretfully, 'I can't go, Mam, much as I'd love to see Gareth and Dilys. It's too soon, isn't it?'

'Of course it's not,' Dora told her, 'and it's time you came out of mourning too. Albert would be the last one to want you to stay in black. You could go to town tomorrow and buy a couple of summer dresses.'

'Supposing Roy doesn't want me to go with him?'

'Oh, but he will, *cariad*. Polly was saying he'll be glad to take you. You and Albert helped him so much when Laura died, he hasn't forgotten that.'

On Saturday morning, as she slipped one of the pretty floral dresses she'd bought over her head, Becky couldn't help feeling a stirring of excitement. She'd hardly been outside the house since that awful night and felt a little guilty at the pleasure she was feeling now at the prospect of a day out with Roy and the children. Though would they even remember her? she wondered. Gareth will, she thought, but what about little Dilys?

She hadn't seen Roy since he'd come to offer his sympathy back in January, apologising that he hadn't been able to attend the funeral.

Now as she answered the side door and he followed her into the kitchen, so handsome in his smart blue uniform, her heart quickened and she was glad she'd taken her mother's advice and bought a pretty new dress.

Smiling down at her, Roy said, 'The children will be excited when they see you, Becky. It's been a long time.'

'Won't they wonder about Albert? He and Gareth got on so well.'

'I have explained to them, told them he's gone to Heaven just like their mam. I haven't told them about the air raid, and since Laura went so suddenly they seemed to accept it, although the news was sad. I know just how you feel, Becky. I felt the same too until I went into the RAF.' He gave a wry smile as he went on, 'You can't afford to think of anything but the job in hand when you're flying over Hamburg or Bremen or any other German city, with their fighters on your tail. But when I'm back at base I never stop thinking of Laura and longing for the past.'

★   ★   ★

As the train steamed into the station Peggy and the children rushed towards their carriage and a moment later, as Becky hung back, both children were in their father's arms.

Hugging her warmly, Peggy said, 'We're so glad you could come, *cariad*, and so very sorry over what happenened.'

Then Gareth and Dilys were rushing headlong towards her. With Dilys hugging her about the waist, Becky looked down at the child's wide grey eyes and smooth dark brows and hair and felt a familiar tug at her heart, for she was Laura over again.

The steep climb up the hill was punctuated by friends shaking hands and being introduced and the children pulling at Roy impatiently. Then, when they finally arrived at the house, Glad and Megan from next-door brought Brynley back, and Becky would never have recognised Sally's little boy, he'd grown so much.

Mostyn was on day shift at the pit and Sally at work at the ROF yet even when Peggy's friendly neighbours had departed with a cheery wave, the kitchen was full to overflowing. Becky had brought a tin of corned beef, butter, sugar, and sweets for the children. You didn't descend on people these days without bringing your welcome. A delicious smell had greeted them as they'd entered the kitchen. Now, as Peggy lifted the savoury pie from the oven and Roy opened doors and windows to cool down the room, she confided ruefully, 'There's not a lot of meat in it, Becky, but there's plenty of veg, and a couple of Oxos and a spoonful of

Marmite makes all the difference.'

The pie tasted as wonderful as it looked and Becky ate as she hadn't done for a very long time. There was rice pudding and mouth-watering Welsh cakes to follow. After the washing up was done and they'd had a little rest while they drank their tea, Roy suggested a walk with the children over the mountain to the next village. Becky felt joyful anticipation at the thought of the hours ahead.

The higher they climbed, the fresher the breeze. With the warm sun on her face, and Roy and the children's company, the gloom of the last months seemed to melt away. Anyway you couldn't be miserable with Dilys swinging on your hand and Gareth racing in front in case the shop that sold glasses of herb-beer was shut.

They reached the village with time to spare and settled gratefully on the worn wooden bench outside the shop. Their fizzing drinks tasted like nectar after the long walk on this warm summer day.

Although he'd been told many times, Gareth wanted to hear again all about the plane his daddy flew in. Dilys snuggled into Becky as though they'd never been parted. Becky wanted the day to go on for ever, but mindful that she had a train to catch and must be home long before dark, Roy got them reluctantly to their feet again, hoisting his sleepy daugher on to his shoulders as they started back to Tre-Mynydd.

The lovely day was over and Roy was taking Becky to the station when he said, 'I ought to see you back to Cardiff but staying here is the only way I can be with Gareth and Dilys. I'm really grateful to Peggy and Will for having them, it's a big load off my mind.'

'But it's only a tram ride once I get to Cardiff, Roy, and I've had a wonderful day,' she told him.

'I enjoyed it too and there'll be other times.' A note of caution crept into his voice as he went on, 'I may as well tell you, Becky, though I haven't mentioned anything to Polly yet — I've met someone, a girl from the camp. Her name's Shirley. No one can ever take Laura's place, but it's been a long time and life has to go on. Besides the children will need a mother when they come back home. It's getting too much for Polly and Bert, they aren't getting any younger.'

He hadn't noticed the colour drain from Becky's cheeks. Now, despite the warmth of the summer evening, she shivered, her heart plummeting, all the newfound happiness of a few moments before shattered. She'd been picturing happy days like today whenever Roy had leave, sharing Laura's children as she had in the past. When the war was over and they came home, she'd have helped Polly with them all she could. Becky hadn't consciously thought beyond this for she'd been sure Roy would never marry again. Well, not for a very long time anyway. Laura had been his world. She knew too that despite her sadness at losing Albert, Roy could still pull at her heartstrings. Now, if he married Shirley, he'd go out of her life for ever. They were bound to move away and take the children with them.

The train steaming noisily into the station drowned her murmured reply, giving her the excuse to cover her confusion by diving for a carriage. Somehow she managed to smile as she leaned from the window to thank him again. As the train drew away from the platform and gathered speed she waved until he was out of sight then sank into a corner seat, thankful to have the carriage to herself. Shocked and disappointed by Roy's news, and troubled about her own feelings, she felt the hot tears roll slowly down her cheeks.

Becky hardly noticed when pit-wheels and slag-heaps gave way to gentler countryside as the train rushed on towards Cardiff. She had been looking forward to telling her mam about her day; now she was dreading her questions, wondering how she could hide her own shock and disappointment.

The trauma of the dreadful thing that had happened to Albert and Nellie was still with her and would be for a very long time to come. She'd have valued Roy's sympathy and friendship, and occasional trips to Tre-Mynydd to see the children. But once Polly had been told, it would be Shirley he'd take with him — perhaps those lovely neighbours of Peggy's would even put her up. It would be Shirley the children would run to then and one day call Mam. Tears trembled on Becky's lashes again at the thought but she forced them back, telling herself she had no right to feel this way. Roy must be very fond of Shirley or he wouldn't be considering marrying her. And if it was a mother for his children he was looking for, she hoped the unknown girl would make a good one.

38

As Becky let herself in and hurried along the narrow passage to open the kitchen door there were no eager questions. Dora lay back in the armchair, her face ashen, forehead beaded with perspiration. But she managed a smile as she asked, 'Had a good time, love? It's been a lovely day.'

'Oh, Mam! What's wrong?' Becky crouched by her side. Taking Dora's hand in hers she said, 'I'd better fetch Dr Powell.'

'There's no need, *cariad*. I had one of my turns, but I'm feeling a lot better now. A cup of tea will do the trick.'

'Well, you don't look it. I should never have left you to cope . . . I'll make a pot of tea, see how you feel then. Have you taken one of those tablets the doctor gave you?'

'Yes, ages ago. They're on the table, it's time I took another.'

Becky was worried as she put the kettle on the stove. It was all her fault, going off to enjoy herself and leaving her mother on her own. I should send for Dr Powell right away, she told herself, but knew that if she went against Dora's wishes, her mother would get very upset and become even worse.

The tea made and poured, Becky tipped a tablet into her mother's hand and placed the cup of tea on the little table at her side.

When she'd swallowed the pill and lay back against the cushions once more, Dora asked again, 'Did you have a good day, love? You didn't say?'

'Lovely,' Becky told her. 'I really enjoyed it. But I should never have left you to manage on your own like this.'

'Don't be silly, Becky. It probably won't happen again.'

Rinsing the cups at the brown-stone sink, Becky thought, If only we could give up the shop. Although she'd seemed better lately, Mama's heart wasn't strong and she badly needed a rest. But it was their livelihood, they couldn't manage without it. Especially now, with Albert gone, for apart from their small savings, which she had hoped to leave in the bank, Becky was nearly as dependent on it as her mam.

After she'd taken the second tablet Dora slept fitfully, refusing to go to bed in case there was a raid. The evening was a busy one for Becky. Feeling unwell, her mother had closed the shop early and for a while there was a constant stream of customers at the side door, but at last everything in the shop was covered and fresh sawdust sprinkled on the floor.

As the hours went by and there was no warning Becky heaved a sigh of relief for her mam was in no fit state to go down the shelter. When in the early hours they decided at last to go to bed, her normal colour had returned to her mother's cheeks and she said, 'The pain's gone now, Becky, there'll be no need to send for the doctor.' Sighing with relief, Becky hoped she was right.

As they went up the stairs she said, 'If there should be a warning, put your warm dressing gown on, mind.' And Dora nodded, promising to put it on the bed ready.

Thankfully nothing happened and although she listened anxiously for a while, Becky's mind eventually turned to thoughts of Roy and the disappointment she'd felt when he'd told her he was taking out a young woman from the base. It shouldn't be any surprise, she told herself. It has been a long time.

But if it wasn't unexpected, why had she been so upset? He had always treated her just as Laura's friend. Had she hoped, deep in her heart, that one day she and Roy would come together? The answer she gave herself was yes. But not in the near future, Becky assured herself guiltily. Anyway it wasn't going to happen, was it? Not now he'd met Shirley.

365

Tossing and turning, remembering the children's joy at seeing her again and the love she'd always felt for them, her heart was heavy with disappointment. Just as a rosy dawn lightened the edges of the blind, she fell into a troubled sleep.

★　★　★

When Polly received the letter from Roy she too was upset. He was home for a night last week, she thought, why couldn't he have told us then? Was it serious? Well, he'd asked to bring this Shirley home next time they could both get leave. How would it affect the children? That was what mattered. They wouldn't take easily to some stranger, would they? But Shirley wouldn't be a stranger if he took her regularly to Tre-Mynydd, as he said in the letter.

'The boy has to get on with his life, Polly,' Bert told her. 'He's said he's met a young lady — he hasn't said he's necessarily going to marry her.'

'It's the children I'm worried about, Bert. I've been longing for them to come home. But if he's serious about this girl and she's not from Cardiff, they could go and live away and then we'll never see them. It'll be a big upheaval for them too, especially after being sent away because of the raids.'

'They're having the time of their lives with Peggy. It's getting them settled down here when they come home that'll be the trouble,' he told her. 'Don't worry, Poll. I'm sure this Shirley must be nice or Roy wouldn't have taken up with her.'

'He says he's bringing her home to meet us as soon as they can both get leave. I can put her in Sally's room, it's only for one night, then they're off to Peggy's. Those neighbours of hers are going to put her up. Perhaps it's all for the best as you said, Bert,' she told him doubtfully, folding the letter and putting it behind the clock on the mantelpiece.

But Becky's going to be disappointed, Polly thought. She'd been so excited about seeing the children again and said she'd really enjoyed the day. But it would be Shirley Roy would be taking from now on.

At the end of April, when a lone bomber got rid of his lethal load over a small village in the Rhondda, killing twenty people, Polly had wanted to bring the children home right away, but Peggy and Bert between them persuaded her that it had been a one off and nowhere near Tre-Mynydd, whereas raids on Cardiff were still fairly regular.

It was October before Roy managed to bring Shirley home and Polly was pleasantly

(often happened

surprised. Looking at the girl as they shook hands, she saw a pretty rosy-cheeked young woman with a ready smile. After tea and cakes, it was Shirley who piled the dishes on to the tray and followed a protesting Polly to the wash-house eager to help. As Polly washed and she wiped, Shirley said she was the eldest of a large family.

She's no stranger to looking after children then, Polly told herself, feeling easier in her mind.

Shirley seemed genuinely appreciative of everything, exclaiming with pleasure at the bright airy bedroom Polly had slaved over for more than a week. The curtains had been so faded she'd washed them then dipped them in the dolly-tub until they were sunshine yellow. Now, freshly ironed and hung, they fluttered in the breeze. Vacuuming the rugs to either side of the bed and the expanse of shabby oil-cloth before polishing it, she'd thought how much easier the tasks were now with the cleaner Roy had bought. The old-fashioned heavy oak furniture had been polished until her arms ached, pervading the room with the scent of lavender; the small iron grate had been blackleaded until it shone. The snowy white sheets and frilly embroidered pillow case made the bed look very inviting, prompting Shirley to confess,

'At home we've got to sleep three to a bed. This room looks a real treat, Mrs Evans.'

At least she's not la-di-dah, Polly told herself thankfully. She's used to hard work and looking after children. It could be worse, I suppose. And if they do move away, I'll still have little Bryn and Tommy's baby Marion to visit. But would Sally and Bill go back to London after the war? His job was there after all.

Shirley got on well with Peggy too. Peggy had thought Roy must be interested in that lovely girl who'd come for the day but had soon realised Becky was just an old friend to him. Roy's children obviously loved her, they must know her well, but of course it would have been much too soon for a widow to be thinking of anyone else.

Peggy liked the way Shirley quickly made herself at home and very soon endeared herself to everyone, including Glad and Megan.

The children had a lovely day out with Roy and Shirley and that first evening, with their neighbours baby-sitting, they'd all gone down to the Collier's Arms where there was sure to be a bit of a sing-song if old Gwynfor Jenkins was there to play the piano. It was very old and badly out of tune, but with everyone singing lustily it really didn't matter.

At first they sang songs like *Bless 'em All* and *The Quarter Master's Stores*, but as the beers and shandies flowed, the songs grew more and more sentimental. *A Nightingale Sang in Berkeley Square* was clapped with enthusiasm, as was *There's A Boy Coming Home On Leave*. Finally they sang Vera Lynn's tear-jerking *We'll Meet Again*, and when at the end of it time was called, they sang it again softly all the way back to the cottage.

As they reached the gate, Shirley said, 'Thank you, Peggy and Will, for a wonderful day. I'll never forget it.'

39

It was late in October 1942 and there hadn't
been a letter from Tommy for weeks. Polly,
feeling as worried as Bert looked, watched
him with sad eyes when at post-times he'd
walk restlessly to the front door to peer
anxiously along the street for any sign of the
postman.

'It won't come any quicker, love,' she'd told
him a few minutes ago when he'd come back
from one of his trips and slumped disappoint-
edly into his chair.

'It's not knowing what's happening, Poll.'
Bert clasped and unclasped his hands in the
way he did when he was agitated. The rattling
of the letter-box sent Polly dashing along the
passage but it was only a notice about a
meeting to be held at the Labour Hall. Her
heart heavy with disappointment, she picked
it up and took it back to the kitchen where
Bert was waiting, hand outstretched.

'Sorry, love,' she said, watching his
expression of hopefulness fade.

Bert listened to every news bulletin on the
wireless and perused the *Echo* for any word
of the war.

'He's been moved to the front somewhere, Polly, I know it,' he told her in a worried voice. 'If only we knew where.'

'No news is good news,' she said, with an optimism she was far from feeling.

Roy was expected home on sick leave at the end of next week and would be on crutches, his flying days probably over. When she'd heard, despite his injuries Polly had heaved a sigh of relief. The accident had happened about six weeks ago on a routine practice parachute jump. Roy had fallen awkwardly, breaking a leg and fracturing his ankle badly. She hoped fervently they'd find him something to do on the ground when he'd recovered.

This was his first time home since it had happened but he and Shirley wouldn't be going to Tre-Mynydd this time apparently.

'I don't know if I could manage that steep hill on these things. I'm longing to see the children but I wouldn't be able to take them out. Even if I made it we'd be under Peggy's feet all day, and God knows the kitchen's crowded enough as it is,' he'd written.

When they arrived Polly wondered had she imagined it or was Shirley relieved at not going to the valleys? They hadn't been home an hour when the girl suggested they go to the pictures. 'Only the local cinema, Roy,' she pleaded. 'I know you can't get very far.'

'Suppose there's a raid?' Polly asked. 'They always put a notice on the screen but Roy couldn't get home, could he?'

'We'd stay put, Polly. Lots of people stay in the cinema.'

Watching their slow progress along the street, Polly hoped everything would stay quiet. Shirley was a nice girl but she did seem to like her own way . . .

When they came home again Bert and Roy discussed the war situation at length, both of the same mind — that Tommy had probably been sent to North Africa where Monty was launching an offensive at El-Alamein.

On Monday, when Shirley had to go back, Roy soon became restless, taking himself off to the garden to practise with his crutches, promising to be expert enough to go to Tre-Mynydd very soon. But he knew he couldn't manage it without Shirley, and she'd said she was getting bored just going for walks with the children, and that she'd really enjoyed that night at the cinema on Splott Bridge when they'd seen Laurence Olivier and Joan Fontaine in *Rebecca*.

'It's so romantic, Roy,' she'd said when, with tears in her eyes, she'd snuggled up to him in the back row. 'And it's lovely to have you all to myself.'

He'd been going to ask her about getting engaged at Christmas but now, with his future in the RAF uncertain and doubts about his job in civvy street still being there when the war finally ended, he wondered if it was wise. Besides it had dawned on him long since that despite the war Shirley was intent on having a good time — and who could blame her for wanting to enjoy herself? She was young, ten years younger than him, and as eldest child of her family had worked hard all her life.

'I've never had it so good, Roy,' she'd confided one day. 'I'm glad I volunteered before they pushed me into a munitions factory or I'd still have been slaving at home.'

He was really fond of her, Roy told himself, but he knew he could never love anyone the way he'd loved Laura. And Shirley was so full of life . . . Was he being fair to her? What had he to offer except the constant chores of looking after a ready-made family?

The war seemed to be extending around the globe and no one now predicted that it would soon be over. The towns were full of American servicemen with money in their pockets, but everyone felt relieved when they were in at last. There was fighting in the Middle East, the Far East, North Africa, Russia and many other places. Tiny Malta was suffering devastating air attacks; London and other big cities under almost constant bombardment; the cities and towns of Germany were getting their share too. A few weeks later came the news of Rommel's retreat from El-Alamein, and Bert and Roy, who would still be home for some weeks, sat up until the small hours discussing the situation, both convinced by this time that Tommy was there.

As the days went by Polly, herself sick with anxiety, watched the worry lines deepen on her husband's face, knowing nothing could calm his fears but a letter from their son telling them he was alive and well. When at last several letters arrived at once she heaved a deep sigh of relief.

★ ★ ★

On the day Roy and Shirley went to see *Rebecca*, Becky watched their slow progress along Paul Street from an upstairs window. She'd been changing into a fresh white coat, having got butter across the front of the one she'd been wearing, when, hearing the rhythmic tap of crutches, she'd pulled the curtain aside to see Roy with a girl who must be Shirley beside him making painful progress along the street.

Feeling a quick stab of jealousy, she hadn't been able to take her eyes from the pair who were fast beginning to fade into the gloom of the murky October twilight. Becky wished with all her heart that she was the one at Roy's side.

She too had heaved a sigh of relief when Polly had told her he was grounded. So many nights she'd listened as planes went over on their missions, wondering if Roy was up there far above the clouds, and if he was, praying he'd come back safely. She knew now that she'd always love him and the children, and that his indifference to her feelings would just have to be borne.

She was heartily tired of working in the shop. The points system had been extended in January to cover dried fruit, tapioca and pulses, and again in February to include canned fruit, tomatoes and peas. In April it was the turn of condensed milk and breakfast cereals; in July treacle and syrup; in August biscuits. There seemed no end to all the extra work. By now white bread had disappeared, being replaced by the National Wheatmeal Loaf, which although nutritious was highly unpopular.

Everyone said it was hard work at the ordnance factory but there she would have had the chance of making friends of her own age, for although she was surrounded by people for most of the day, Becky was deeply lonely. She and her mother never went out at night for fear of an air raid, for these days even the sound of the siren would send her into a panic, her mouth dry, heart beating fast. If they did go to the cinema, it had to be on a Wednesday afternoon. The evenings were taken up with all the additional paperwork that must be done.

When, late in November, Polly came into the shop with the wonderful news that they'd had letters from Tommy at last, telling them he was safe and well, she also told them Roy's injuries had been slow to mend and that he was upset at the prospect of spending the rest of the war behind a desk.

'Hobbling about with a stick he is,' Polly said. 'Got leave for Christmas he has, but he'll be spending it with the children at Tre-Mynydd. I'll be glad when they're back home with me. And they will be as soon as the raids are finished.'

'They're not so regular now, Polly,' Dora said thankfully.

Becky wanted to ask if Shirley would be with Roy but a waiting customer, tut-tutting impatiently, sent her hurrying to serve. She was dreading Christmas again this year. It would be the second Christmas without

Albert and Nellie and it didn't get any easier. They'd been dead for almost two years. Tears welled up at the thought. This year, like the last, there would be just the two of them, and the memories. They'd listen to the radio, there'd be nothing else to do — though life was brightened sometimes when Lord Haw-Haw was broadcasting and they had a good laugh at his affected voice and ridiculous predictions.

There was plenty of real humour too if you had time to listen, with millions tuning in to Tommy Handley's *ITMA* which was full of hilarious characters all with wonderful catch-phrases. For the gifted, fast-talking Handley it was, 'It's that man again.' Mrs Mopp would ask: 'Can I do you now, sir?' Then the broker's men, Cecil and Claude, with their oh-so-polite, 'After you, Cecil.' 'No, after you, Claude.'

There was plenty of humour on the wireless these days but the highlight of every day was the nine o'clock news when work would be pushed aside as Becky and Dora and countless millions of other people tuned in. Because of the war announcers had to identify themselves and everyone was familiar with the words, 'This is the BBC Home Service. Here is the news and this is Alvar Liddell reading it.' Yes

Sometimes Becky would think of the future, which always made her sad. She could never envisage their being able to sell the shop, which was their living, and could see herself growing older and older, stuck behind the counter. When her mother became too old to work, she would be there alone. There'd be few real friends for she wouldn't be able to go out and meet people; she'd be just another war widow, pitied at first but soon forgotten.

If only I could have gone to a factory or a draper's to work, she thought, then I'd have got to know other girls and made friends. Even in wartime a lot went on beyond the confines of the shop but she knew little of it.

Hearing her mother call, Becky sighed deeply and went to serve the waiting customers.

40

It was Christmas 1942 and Shirley and Roy were once more on their way to Tre-Mynydd but this time, although Shirley was being as kind and helpful as ever, Roy could sense her growing frustration at his slow progress. Still hobbling on a stick, he could no longer give her the good time she craved so much.

Peggy was as welcoming as ever if a little harassed, and very appreciative of everything they'd brought. She looks tired, Roy thought. Taking care of three young children is no picnic. Polly had looked after his two for years until the raids got too bad, and hadn't wanted to part with them even then. She had looked tired too, and she wasn't getting any younger. He'd made up his mind to settle things with Shirley very soon. That was until he'd broken his leg. Now, though, he wasn't so sure.

A delicious smell of cooking had wafted towards them as Peggy had opened the door and hugged them warmly. She led them to the kitchen where she'd just removed mince pies from the oven and there was some ham cooking in a saucepan on the range. When a few minutes later it was drained and put on a plate to cool, the piece looked pitifully small and she explained apologetically that it was to be augmented by some corned beef and Spam.

Mostyn arrived home from his shift, coal dust black and glistening on his face, only his eyes and lips showing any colour. Giving them a cheerful grin, he drank a mug of tea thirstily before going to the yard to fetch the bath from its hook. Peggy rolled up the rag rug from in front of the range then ushered Roy and Shirley into the parlour, returning to the kitchen to scrub her son's back.

A few minutes later when Will returned he and Gareth were carrying a Christmas tree, their cheeks rosy from all the mountain air. The children flung themselves into Roy's open arms with squeals of delight. When Peggy called to them, 'Mostyn's finished now,' they all trooped out to the kitchen which was smelling strongly of carbolic soap.

'There's a social at the Working Men's Club tonight,' Mostyn was saying. 'Would you two like to come?' Dragging his shirt over his head, muscles rippling, he went on, 'Got a band, they have. There'll be dancing, a couple of turns and refreshments of sorts.'

'Dancing with this leg?' laughed Roy. 'I think my stick might get in the way, don't you? You go, Shirley. I'll stay and help Peggy with the kids, I'm sure she could do with a hand.'

'I expect Mostyn's already taking a girl?' Shirley looked up at him hopefully.

Mostyn shook his head, saying, 'I'll be glad to take you, *cariad*. The girl I was going out with joined the ATS.'

Shirley sang under her breath as she fiddled with her hair then went up to Peggy's room to put on her precious pair of silk stockings and a pretty dress. Out of uniform she looked younger than ever and Roy asked himself again if he was right to think of asking her to marry him and tying her down with a ready-made family?

As soon as tea was over Mostyn, towering over her in his best suit and Melton overcoat, smiled down at Shirley as he took her arm and led her out into the black-out.

Three overexcited children tried every trick in the book to put off going to bed until Peggy told them: 'If you're not up there when Daddy Christmas comes, he'll think you don't live here and he won't leave any presents.' It sent Dilys and Gareth hurtling for the stairs. Carrying Brynley on his shoulders, Roy followed them up.

Will had gone to the Collier's Arms and Sally was spending the day with Polly and

Bert, so for once the little house wasn't crowded. The children settled, Roy and Peggy went back to the kitchen where she poured him a generous whisky and herself a port and lemon. They settled into the armchairs to either side of the range.

'Best part of the day, Roy,' sighed Peggy thankfully.

'You work much too hard,' he told her with a pang of conscience that his own two were an added burden. 'I just wish the raids would end, then Gareth and Dilys would be off your hands.'

'Oh, but they're no trouble,' she assured him, 'and Sally helps out whenever she's home from the factory. She should be back soon.'

After a few moments' silence Peggy said, 'Look, Roy, I know it's none of my business and perhaps I shouldn't ask this, but are you and Shirley serious about each other?'

Surprised by the question, he said, 'Well, I was going to ask her to get engaged this Christmas — until this happened.' He glanced down at his leg.

'You shouldn't let that stop you, son, not if she loves you and is fond enough of the children to want to look after them.'

Something in Peggy's voice made him look up as she went on, 'I've no right to put doubts in youer mind but Shirley reminds me a lot of myself when I married Will. I was the eldest of six and as a child I never went out without a baby in my arms and a toddler holding on to my skirt.

'When Will started taking me out, I couldn't get enough of the cinema or the chapel hops. I thought marriage would be the answer to my prayers — until nine months and a fortnight to the day we were married young Bill was born, and just over a twelve-month later ouer Mostyn.'

'But you love your family, Peggy, anyone can see that.'

'Of course I love them. They're mine, aren't they? If I felt any resentment at being tied down again so soon, the love I had for them soon melted it away.'

'But you think Shirley might feel resentment at being tied down with someone else's children?'

'I don't know, Roy. All I'm saying is, don't rush things. Give her a good time first then maybe she'll be ready to settle down. She'll grow to love the children, I'm sure.'

Now it was his turn to be silent. Was he expecting too much of Shirley? Was it after all just a mother for Dilys and Gareth he was seeking?

Seeing the sadness in his eyes, Peggy

384

wondered if she'd gone too far. When the silence continued, she said, 'I'm sorry, Roy. I shouldn't have interfered.'

'I'm glad you spoke, Peggy,' he told her. 'You've only confirmed my own fears. Shirley's a lovely girl but she's so young and restless. She's not ready to settle down, especially with a ready-made family.'

Pouring two more drinks, Peggy said, 'Polly adores those children, you know. She'll be happy to carry on for a while.'

At the sound of the front door slamming, Peggy gave a sigh of relief, saying, 'That'll be Sally, thank goodness. I always worry when she's out in the black-out.'

'Why didn't you say? I'd have gone to meet her.'

'And you could easily have broken that leg again. It's pitch black and these are unfamiliar streets.'

'Hello, Roy. Where's Shirley?' his sister-in-law asked him.

'Gone to the hop with ouer Mostyn,' Peggy told her. 'Do you want a drink, love?'

'Not unless it's a cup of tea. I'm absolutely whacked.'

When ten minutes later Sally climbed the stairs, silence fell again on the kitchen and Roy saw that Peggy had fallen into an exhausted sleep. But soon there was singing outside the door and a key turning in the lock and Peggy woke with a start just as Shirley and Mostyn came into the room. Seeing Shirley's happy face, Roy was glad that she'd gone out.

It was late, and realising they were keeping Glad and Megan up, Roy made ready to leave. He could smell gin on Shirley's breath as outside the front door she put her arms about his neck and kissed him. He'd had a couple of glasses of whisky himself. It was Christmas after all.

Suddenly, standing there between the two cottages, the blackness so deep you had to feel your way along the railings, Shirley clung to him, her lips pressed hard against his. As his arms came about her, she whispered, 'Why don't we get engaged, Roy?' And holding her close, he felt all his recent resolutions crumbling away.

'Would you like us to get married, Shirl?' He felt her body stiffen and the question seemed to have the effect of sobering her up for after a short silence she said in a normal voice, 'I only said engaged. Before we talk about marriage, what about the children? Will Polly still look after them for a while when they can go back to Cardiff?'

Sighing with relief that the subject was at last being discussed, he said, 'She can't be expected to look after them if we're married. It's too much for her anyway.'

'It would be too much for me, Roy. I've only just begun to have a life of my own. Perhaps if we got engaged, in time I might — '

'I haven't been fair to you, Shirl, I can see that now. You'd be much better off with someone your own age. Let's just stay friends, shall we? Then you can have all the good times you want.'

'We'll talk about it in the morning, Roy. I really am fond of you, you know. I had a lovely time tonight — only Mostyn's friends kept buying me gin and limes. I had the sense not to drink them all, though!'

But in the morning, with presents being exchanged and everyone laughing and talking at once, no mention was made of last night's little heart to heart. Only Sally looked a little sad, wondering how many more Christmases must pass before Bill would be home to share them with her and Brynley. She'd done her best to keep the memory of his daddy alive for the little boy, but it wasn't easy. Daddy was a photograph in a wooden frame by his bed. Uncle Mostyn was the substitute he followed everywhere, squealing with delight as he was picked up and swung into the air. Mostyn was his hero, someone who could magic sweets from his pocket and was always ready to get down on all fours and give him a ride.

When Gareth and Dilys were given Becky's presents, a compendium of games and a china-headed baby doll with a stuffed body covered with black-out material — the only kind of doll freely available — Dilys asked, 'Why doesn't Auntie Becky come to see us any more?'

Roy answered gently, 'I think she's kept busy with the shop.'

'Well, she came before. Won't she never come any more?' Dilys lovingly cradled the baby doll in her arms as she waited for his reply.

41

January 1943 was bitterly cold with leaden skies threatening snow and an easterly wind cutting through anything but the stoutest of clothing, making the shop a haven for anyone venturing out for food. Customers would arrive, stamping their feet in the sawdust and chafing hands numb with the cold to restore some feeling. The awnings over the shop windows groaned constantly as the strong wind shook the heavy canvas up and down.

The main subjects under discussion were the weather and the war, both inextricably bound, for although the air raids weren't so frequent, when they did occur the freezing nights made the journey to the shelter hazardous for all but the fittest.

Just after lunch Polly came into the shop, the warm coat Roy's Aunt Vi had given her all those years ago wrapped tightly about her.

'Roy's home for the day again,' she told Becky. 'Discussing the war they are, him and Bert. They never seem to talk about anything else.'

But with that one subject they found plenty to discuss. Bert listened to every bulletin and made little notes in an exercise book he'd bought for the purpose. It gave him something to think about and was beginning to make more cheerful reading, for on New Year's Day the Japanese had begun to evacuate Guadalcanal. On 3 January the British had sunk an Italian light cruiser in Palermo harbour. On that day also the Red Army recaptured Mozdok in the Caucasus. On 5 January they'd taken the main airfield used by the Luftwaffe to supply Stalingrad, and only yesterday had come the news that the Russians had taken back the last German airfield within the Stalingrad pocket. Meanwhile, in Libya, Allied forces were attacking Buerat, starting a drive for Tripoli.

The heavy black-out curtains had been drawn for some time when Becky locked the double doors and began to tidy up, leaving a dim light on in the shop when at last she went through to the kitchen, for Bob would call in at the end of his shift to bring anything they needed up from the cellar.

Bob had come and gone and Dora was poring over the books at the table when there was a knock on the side door. Putting down her sewing with a sigh, Becky went to open it.

'Roy!' She couldn't keep the surprise from her voice as he stepped into the passage and she closed the door behind him.

'Polly forgot the eggs,' he explained. 'She didn't realise until she'd started baking. Says there's some due to her. She wanted to come herself but it's pitch black out there.'

'And freezing too. You go through to the kitchen and have a word with Mam while I get the eggs.'

'I won't stay long, Becky. Polly's waiting for me to come back.'

Wishing he wasn't in such a hurry, she put the eggs into a bag and followed Roy to the kitchen where he and Dora were discussing the awful weather. But as soon as the bag containing the three eggs was in his hand, he limped towards the door, saying, 'I'd better get back.' Then, as Becky followed him, 'I almost forgot — the children loved their presents. I think they sent you little notes? Dilys has named the doll after you, Becky.'

'I'm making some clothes for it, Roy. I couldn't finish them in time for Christmas but I'll let Polly have them as soon as I do. It only has a baby gown and I know Dilys will want to dress it up.'

'Why don't you give them to her yourself? I'll be going to see them just for the day next week, then I'll be spending the night at home before going back to base. I could meet you at the station, Becky, when I change platforms for the valleys.'

'I can't, Roy,' she told him reluctantly. 'My mam was taken ill last time I left her alone. I daren't risk it again.' What about Shirley? she wondered. Perhaps she couldn't always get leave? But Roy was already stepping out into the street. Pulling the door behind her, she watched him limp away into the darkness. Swallowing her disappointment, Becky went back to the kitchen.

★　★　★

It was almost time to close for lunch when Polly came in next day. Going straight up to Becky she said, 'Roy told me about asking you to go to see the children. You can go, *cariad*. I can come to the shop and spend the day with youer mam, then she can come home with me until you and Roy get back so you'll have no worries that way.'

Dora, coming into the shop and getting the gist of what Polly was saying, said, 'What's all this about then?' And when Becky explained, she told them, 'Well, that's all right with me. Of course you can go, love. I'll be grateful for Polly's help, we'll manage just fine.'

Whenever she thought of the coming trip to Tre-Mynydd Becky wondered if after all Shirley would be there. Roy hadn't said but probably hadn't known at that time if she could come.

The day arrived at last and the weather had taken a turn for the better, bright sunshine belying the bitter wind. When Becky reached the platform Roy was already there — and alone. Glancing first towards the paper stall then around the platform Becky saw no sign of Shirley and Roy didn't mention her as the train steamed in and they got into a carriage.

'I've brought the doll's clothes,' Becky told him, trying to overcome the shyness she felt. Had Roy really wanted her to come or had he just felt sorry for her?

'I've got a book for Gareth,' she went on, 'an adventure story. He likes those, doesn't he?'

'You don't have to bring them presents, Becky.'

'I've missed them since they've been away. Nellie and Albert loved them both.'

Peggy was waiting with Dilys at the station. Gareth was at school but the little girl had been allowed to stay home and now ran up to fling her arms about them both.

The doll's clothes were a great success and Becky was glad she'd taken so much trouble, making dainty little dresses and petticoats and pants, and knitting a little bonnet. When she looked up to find Roy's eyes fixed on her, his expression soft, the colour rose warmly in her cheeks and she bent her head to cover her confusion. The old attraction was still there. She kept her eyes on the doll, embarrassed at the colour in her face.

Becky had brought a few things for Peggy too. It couldn't be easy these days with three hungry children, and Mostyn and his father to feed. The time flew as, chatting easily, she helped Peggy prepare the meal then went with Roy and Dilys to meet Gareth from school. The February afternoon was short and with the winter sun gone was freezing once again. Soon the black-out curtains were being drawn and after a tea consisting of thick slices of grey-looking bread toasted in front of the fire then spread with margarine and delicious home-made blackberry jam, and a generous helping of rice pudding, they sat round the table and played some of Gareth's games. Then it was time to leave for the station. Mostyn had gone with his father to the Collier's Arms and Roy wouldn't allow Peggy to come even as far as the gate.

'It'll be freezing out there,' he told her, 'we'll say goodbye in here.' He kissed the children and Gareth was instantly ready to go back to his new book, but Dilys clung to him tearfully.

'She'll be fine as soon as you're gone,'

Peggy assured him. 'She always is.'

As they stepped out into the darkness Roy shone the dimmed torch at the pavement with one hand and took Becky's arm with the other, saying, 'I know this road well, you cling to me.' And she did, enjoying every minute.

Getting to the station with time to spare, their breath steaming before them, they found a bench and sat down to wait. It was only a small halt, with no waiting room or refreshment hall, and as the minutes passed, then a quarter of an hour, with an icy wind cutting along the open platform, Becky shivered.

Taking her arm, helping her to rise stiffly from the seat, Roy said, 'Let's walk briskly up and down.' But although they did this for some time, stamping their feet and beating their arms about, it didn't seem to generate much warmth. Looking impatiently at his watch, he said, 'It's already more than half an hour late.'

There was no one to ask, the door to the station office remaining firmly closed. It was clear by this time that the train had been taken off and a timetable at which Roy shone his torch informed them the next was at a quarter to nine.

Mama will be worrying, Becky thought anxiously. Thank goodness she'll be waiting with Polly and Bert.

'They'll soon realise what's happened,' Roy assured her. 'I don't suppose there's a cafe open anywhere . . . ' But the street was deserted, the black-outs drawn and the few shops shuttered, so they continued to walk up and down. It was too late to go back to the cottage now.

Presently other people, obviously more knowledgeable about the vagaries of the local railway than they were, began to arrive and at twenty to nine the office door was unlocked, but it wasn't until the train was steaming towards the station that someone came out with a flag and a whistle and stood waiting for the few passengers to alight and them to get on.

Sharing the carriage with a young soldier and his fiancée, the journey passed quickly, especially when he told them he'd been born and brought up in Tre-Mynydd and had known Peggy and her family all his life. He was on leave and going to spend a few days with his fiancée's parents in Cardiff. They'd just got engaged. The girl showed off her ring, a pretty cluster of diamonds, holding her hand almost under their noses so that they could see it in the thin pencil of blue light that dimly illuminated the carriage.

'Dad's meeting us with his van,' the girl

told them as they got off the train and raced off down the platform.

Pulling the torch from his pocket, Roy took Becky's arm in his and guided her towards St Mary's Street where they hoped to get a tram. An icy wind whipped their scarves about their faces and Becky held on to her tam with her free hand as they turned the corner. There were few people about and no one waiting at the tram stop as they listened for the familiar rattle of one approaching. When, some five minutes later, the raucous wail of the siren rent the air, Becky shivered at the sound, her legs turning to jelly.

Searchlights swept the sky even before the terrible sound died away. With the throb of planes growing louder by the second, incendiaries hung like drifting fairy lights against the velvet black sky. Roy was pulling her arm urgently, forcing her to run with him towards the nearest shelter. Suddenly, with a whooshing sound, a bomb exploded some-where nearby and the booming of ack-ack guns seemed to be directly overhead, lending wings to Becky's feet. The shelter being still some distance away, Roy dragged her into the deep doorway of a large department store where he gently put his arms about her shivering body, holding her close to try to calm her fears. No wonder she's frightened, he thought, with Albert and his mother dying in that awful raid.

Gradually the shivering stopped, and feeling Roy's arms so comfortingly about her and his breath warm on her cheek, Becky was filled with wonder. The raid was almost forgotten. She wanted to pinch herself, to make sure this was real. Outside the barrage of noise was receding. The square of sky they could see was an angry red but she didn't move from his arms, wanting this moment to go on for ever. Then a thought crossed her mind and reluctantly she drew away. 'If you're worrying about Shirley,' Roy told her, 'we aren't seeing each other any more.' Becky gave a deep sigh of contentment.

When she looked up to the pale blur of his face above hers, their lips met in a long, tender kiss. Finally she broke away to draw breath and it was Roy whose lips sought hers again. As he kissed her, over and over, he was saying in a puzzled voice, 'I must have been blind all this time, Becky. But perhaps it's too soon after — '

Her answer was to bring his head down to hers and kiss him with all the feeling that had been pent up for so long. He was quick to respond. How could she tell him she'd always loved him, from the moment all those years ago when she'd mistaken him for her date?

And that she'd never stopped loving him even though she'd grown to love Albert too? But there seemed no need for words.

The all clear had sounded and there were people running past. As they broke away and went out into the smoke-filled street and saw distant flames licking the sky, a bemused Becky quickened her steps, saying anxiously, 'Mama will be sick with worry, Roy.'

There was no sign of trams running or of traffic of any kind. Everyone seemed to be legging it along St Mary's Street in the same direction. Down a side road from which smoke was pouring, they caught a glimpse of tin-hatted men digging in a pile of rubble, but they hurried on, Roy's arm protectively about Becky. Yet despite the rush, they were unable to resist stopping now and then to hug and kiss and bless their own good fortune.

42

Dora had been agreeably surprised at the way Polly coped with the shop, but then she hadn't been a customer all these years without getting to know where everything was kept, and being a keen shopper knew most of the prices. They'd got on like a house on fire and when the shop was closed and they'd tidied up and Dora had gone home with her, Bert had been quite chatty. They'd played cards after tea and it wasn't until about half-past eight, when she'd expected Becky and Roy to return, that Dora began to worry. After that none of them had been able to concentrate on the game so Bert had shuffled the cards together while Polly made more tea.

By the time the siren sounded the three of them were worried sick, and when Bert hurriedly shepherded them to the shelter they sat there, staring at each other in dismay.

'Whatever could have happened?' Polly voiced their mutual fears. 'Getting a train about seven o'clock they were.'

Trying to push his own fears aside, Bert said comfortingly, 'The train was probably taken off, nothing's certain these days.'

'Becky's terrified of air raids since Albert went,' Dora told them worriedly.

'Roy will take care of her — ' The rest of Polly's words were drowned in the deafening boom of ack-ack fire and above that the throbbing of enemy planes. Bert gripped his hands together tightly until the nails bit into his palms, determined Dora shouldn't see his fear.

When the all clear sounded and they climbed stiffly out and went in for more tea, stewed now with being on the range so long, they listened intently for Roy's key in the lock, turning anxious faces when at last it was heard and footsteps headed for the kitchen. Polly hurried to open the door and there, framed in the doorway, were two glowing faces. Expecting to find Becky distraught, Dora looked in wonder from one to the other of them. When a little while later Roy saw them home, she wasn't surprised that they lingered in the passage after she'd gone through to the kitchen, but she was mystified, for what had happened to that young girl Shirley that Roy had been bringing home?

★　★　★

Becky couldn't sleep for excitement, but tossing and turning in the early hours doubts began to trouble her. It had all come about because she'd been terrified of the air raid. It had seemed the most natural thing to be comforted in Roy's arms. She remembered clinging to him, half out of her mind with fear. Would he regret what had happened in the cold light of day? But I didn't imagine his kisses, she comforted herself.

Next morning, yawning with tiredness, she went into the shop and unbolted the door to find Roy waiting there, his kit-bag by his side. With a grin he closed the door behind him and turned the key, opening his arms wide. Thankful that her mother was busy washing the breakfast things, Becky went into them.

An impatient knocking on the door tore them apart. Trying to compose herself, she quickly unlocked it.

'Usually open by this time you are,' Enid Brown grumbled. 'I 'aven't got a bit of marge to give the kids their breakfast. 'Ave Polly run out of something too?' She glanced curiously at Roy.

The coupon was clipped from her ration book, the small amount added to her bill, but still Enid lingered. Feeling sick with apprehension when she saw Roy glancing at his watch, Becky willed her to go. The moment Enid was out of the shop he closed the door and drew Becky into his arms again, saying,

'Write to me. I'll try to get home again soon.'

She stood outside, oblivious of the freezing cold, watching him go down the street. He still limped a little, probably always would, but it was hardly noticeable now. Roy had told her regretfully there was no chance of his flying again, and despite his obvious disappointment she was very thankful.

As the weeks passed the letters flew between them, each one more loving than the last, and Becky was happier than she could ever remember. Then in the spring, when Roy asked her to get engaged, the doubts began. Was she being fair? Should she tell him she believed she might be barren? And something else was worrying her. When they married and she had a husband and two children to look after, how was she to manage working full-time at the shop?

I did it with Albert, she told herself. It hadn't been much of a life, though, going home each night to start work all over again. Anyway it would be different with children to care for; she'd have to be there for them. But Mama can't manage on her own, Becky thought worriedly. Look what had happened the first time she'd gone to Tre-Mynydd, when she'd come home to find Dora ill from the strain.

In April, to Becky's delight, Roy was

discharged and able to go back to his old office job, and as the raids had been few and far between he was talking about bringing the children home very soon. Then on a sunny May morning a jubilant Britain woke to the news that 617 squadron, led by Wing Commander Guy Gibson, had destroyed vital dams in the Ruhr Valley, causing floods that would rip the heart out of industrial Germany. *The Dam Busters*

As Bert gleefully wrote the details in his little book, Polly said, 'There's a piece in the paper about that Wing Commander Gibson. I've just been reading it. Says his wife's from Penarth, not very far from here.'

No one saw the significance, or guessed the dreadful consequences, even when at 2.36 next morning the sirens began to wail. It was a bright moonlit night and almost immediately low-flying Dornier 217s and Junkers 88s throbbed overhead, bringing terror and destruction to the city below. Sick with fear, Becky shivered as she sat gripping Dora's hand, praying with all her heart that Roy would be safe.

Forty-five minutes later they were able to climb stiffly from the shelter. It wasn't until daylight that the rumours began. The raid that had killed 45 people and injured 128, damaging over 4,000 houses and bringing terror to people's hearts, was retaliation for the Dam Busters' exploits.

The children stayed where they were but as the summer advanced and there were no more bombs the question of their future was raised again. At Peggy's suggestion they would remain at Tre-Mynydd until school broke up at the end of July. Polly as well as Roy and Becky was a frequent visitor there, and Polly also managed weekly visits to Josie and little Marion as well, telling Tommy in her letters how pretty and bonny his little daughter had become.

At last the children came home and at first things didn't run smoothly. Dilys frequently protested, 'Auntie Peggy let me stay up later than this, Nana.' Or, 'I don't like cabbage now, I didn't have to eat it when I lived there.' But with a little give and take on Polly's part, she soon settled down.

Gareth had only one more year to go before he left school. Roy had always regretted the fact that the upheaval in his education when he'd gone to live with Peggy had meant he hadn't sat the scholarship exam, but he'd done very well at school and now settled easily back into his class at Stanley Road.

'Makes me feel like an old man, having a son of thirteen,' Roy said with a smile.

When he suggested they marry just before Christmas, Becky knew she must tell him her fears. The first he dismissed with, 'It's you I want, Becky. It would be wonderful if we had a baby, of course, but I'm perfectly happy to settle for you.'

The second problem couldn't so easily be solved and Roy confessed that he'd wondered about it himself.

'How would it be if we could rent a house big enough for Dora to come too?' he asked hopefully.

'She won't give up the shop, Roy. Can't afford to yet, it's her living, and she can't manage on her own,' Becky said worriedly.

There seemed to be no solution to the problem but he was determined they'd get married as soon as they found a suitable place. Getting a home together wasn't going to be easy either. Shortages were biting harder and harder; even the most mundane things were in short supply. Tea-sets and dinner plates were now only available in plain white, and with this year's new stock, to save material, the cups were without handles. There was little choice of other household equipment, there being only one quality of sheets, blankets, pots and pans, kettles, carpets and linoleum. Utility furniture was practical if not exciting and available only to those who qualified, which Becky did, having lost everything in that awful raid.

Roy had decided to leave the furniture in his two rooms for Sally and Bill for their own furniture, which they'd saved so hard for and had put in store, had been destroyed in the blitz. Sally didn't want to return to London when the war was over where they now had neither furniture nor accommodation. Bill had promised that when he was demobbed he'd ask for a transfer back to South Wales.

When through a friend Roy managed to get the key to a house in Richards Terrace, he and Becky were both overjoyed. It was a tall grey-stone house with ample room for Dora if she ever wanted to come and live there. Becky gave a gasp of delight when, walking into the spacious middle room, they opened the door to the garden to find a conservatory attached with a white-stone sink with running water and a shabby gas cooker that could easily be replaced. Her mother had always treasured her independence. Here she could still have that, and their company too.

'You don't have to worry about me, *cariad*,' Dora had said when she'd realised what was on Becky's mind. 'Get someone in to work part-time, I will, as soon as you and Roy are married.' But Becky knew how much she disliked the idea of a stranger working with her after all this time, and part-time wouldn't be enough anyway.

When Roy said, 'What do you think, Becky? It's a lovely house, the rent's quite reasonable and the school's just around the corner,' she answered, 'It's got everything we want, but what am I to do about the shop?'

'Polly worked there for a day,' he told her. 'They got on well, didn't they? And they still do.'

'Polly wouldn't want to be tied like that, Roy. Besides, she's got Bert and the house to look after.'

'She's a glutton for work, Becky. Remember when Laura and I took her to a social at the Labour Club and she ended up serving the teas?'

'Yes, Laura told me. And Polly was very disappointed when she had to give it up.'

'Well? What do you think?'

'We could ask her,' Becky said dubiously. 'But how will she manage with all she has to do at home?'

'Well, Sally's only waiting for me to move out of the rooms then she's bringing Brynley home. She's already asked to be released from the factory to look after him. She can't go back on the machines since she cut her hand with the swarf. It's healed all right, but her finger's still a bit stiff.'

408

Polly didn't need any persuasion when, at Roy's suggestion, Dora asked for her help, and Dora was equally delighted at having an old friend to work with her instead of a total stranger. So the plans for the wedding went ahead. The house was got ready, the linoleum laid and the curtains hung. Soon the new utility furniture was delivered and in place and Becky carried the white tea and dinner service around, together with all the other things she'd bought. By now it wanted just a fortnight to their wedding day, and for her and Roy it couldn't come quickly enough.

43

'You look lovely, Becky,' Polly told her admiringly. It was mid-December and their wedding day. Becky knew Polly must be thinking about the day Laura and Roy were wed, which was why they'd chosen a register office. St Margaret's would have held too many poignant memories. Dora, Roy's mother Celia and her sister Vi, Polly, Dilys, Gareth, and Jessie's son and daughter, who were to be their witnesses, would accompany them. Jessie, good neighbour that she was, stayed behind to put the finishing touches to the wedding breakfast, ready for their return.

Becky had chosen a pale green suit and a little velvet hat in the same shade which set off her copper-gold hair to perfection. All eyes turned to Dilys as she came into the room, looking very pretty in a dress of pale rose crêpe-de-chine edged with rosebud trimming. Gareth gazed admiringly down at his new long trousers then looked up suddenly to ask, 'What shall I call you now you're marrying Dad? Is it still Auntie Becky?'

'Call me Becky if you like, Gareth.' After all, he would soon be leaving school and considered himself grown-up.

'Well, I'm going to call you Mama,' Dilys decided, "cos all my friends have got one 'cept me.' *ah!*

Putting her arms lovingly about the little girl, Becky saw that Polly's eyes were moist with tears.

The ceremony over, they returned to find Sally and Josie had arrived minus children. Bert was minding Brynley and Marion was left with Josie's mam. The long table in the dining room, rarely used, was beautifully laid and waiting for them. As the conversation flowed Becky looked around with deep satisfaction. Being an only child with few living relatives, she'd always longed for a family like this. The happy talk went on through the afternoon, and after tea and sandwiches, when everyone except Polly and Jessie who were helping with the clearing up got up to go, Becky and Roy said their heartfelt thanks and goodbyes.

Dora promised she'd go to Polly's if ever she felt lonely of an evening. The children were to stay a few days more with Polly and Bert to give the young couple time to settle into their new home, for neither had wanted a honeymoon.

'We'll have a nice family holiday when the war's over,' Becky promised, but when that would be few now ventured to predict. There was an acute shortage of men for industry and the coal pits, and early in December Ernest Bevin, the Minister of Labour, announced in the House of Commons that by April, 30,000 men of under twenty-five would be chosen from those called up and directed into the mines. Becky was thankful Gareth was not yet fourteen.

As Roy laughingly carried Becky over the threshold of their new home, a smell of fresh paint pervaded the air. They hardly noticed it, too eager to fling off their coats and be in each other's arms. A cheerful fire that he had lit earlier burned brightly in the living-room grate. As Becky unpacked Laura's photographs and placed one in each of the children's rooms he watched her lovingly, sure that if it had been Shirley he'd married they would have been shut in a drawer out of sight.

By this time, despite the bitter cold, the windows had been flung open in the hope of dispelling the strong odour and they went into the cosy kitchen to make a pot of tea. Becky's heart sang as she looked around her at the spacious room with its cream-painted walls and cupboards and diamond-patterned oil-cloth on the floor; at all the new pots and pans and brand new gas cooker. But as their eyes met she knew that Roy was the real reason for her happiness. Soon the last packing case was empty and, a little self-consciously, they went up to bed.

★ ★ ★

It was early in June of the following year and the last six months had been the happiest of Becky's life. Dilys and Gareth had settled down well and Becky was hugging a secret that she hardly dared hope was true. Walking towards Dr Powell's surgery she steeled herself for any coming disappointment. Half an hour later, her hopes confirmed, she felt she was walking on air.

Outside the newsagent's on the corner of Richards Terrace the placards proclaimed:

MONTGOMERY LEADS BRITISH,
US CANADIAN FORCE
WE WIN BEACH-HEADS
4,000 Ships, 11,000 Planes
in Assault on France
'All Going To Plan' — Premier

The second front, talked about for so long, had begun.

Roy wouldn't be home until tea-time so she waited in a fever of impatience to tell him her

413

news. She remembered Albert and Nellie's bitter disappointment that she hadn't been able to give him a child and was glad he hadn't known he was the reason. These days Becky often found herself thinking of Albert and his generous nature, sure that his example had taught her a fortitude that had helped her through those turbulent years.

As soon as she heard Roy opening the door Becky rushed to meet him. Drawing his head down to hers, she kissed him warmly. Sensing her excitement, he held her close, asking gently, 'What is it, Becky? What's happened?'

'We're going to have a baby, Roy! I can hardly believe it but Dr Powell confirmed it today.'

'What?' His voice was high with delight. 'Oh, but that's wonderful!' Holding her close, he cradled her in his arms then went suddenly quiet, the colour draining from his face. She knew he was thinking of what had happened to Laura.

'There's lots of babies born every day, love, and everything fine,' she told him, as much to convince herself as Roy.

'I know, Becky, but I've never got over the shock of that day, and you've become so precious to me. We'll book you into a good maternity home as soon as possible.' Then, winding one of her curls around his finger, he smiled down at her, saying, 'I hope it'll have a lovely coppernob like yours.'

She'd tell her mother this weekend, Becky thought happily. A few weeks after the wedding the middle room with its spacious conservatory had been furnished with spare pieces from the rooms above the shop. Roy had painted the walls and laid a new floor covering, and Becky's single bed had been delivered to make it into a bed-sitting room for the time being. Now Dora spent every Saturday evening and Sunday with them.

There was no sign of her wanting to give up the shop. Polly had proved a quick learner and they got on well together and with the customers, most of whom loved to chat and have a laugh whenever there was time.

Despite the continuing hardships of war the shop would often ring with laughter, for as one customer put it: if you didn't laugh you'd cry, and it was better to see the funny side.

Only that morning her daughter had gone out to queue for face powder she'd heard was in a shop in town. She'd drawn the usual seam along the back of her legs with eye-brow pencil but it was an unknown make, and as soon as she got out in the rain it began to run in long streaks. She'd been unaware of it until a lady pointed it out to her. Then, after queueing for ages, when she dabbed on the face powder, also an unknown make, that too went in streaks all over her face.

'Well, you had a good laugh anyway, Phoebe,' Polly said, wiping her eyes. 'When our Sally worked in the ordnance factory she got a ration of Coty and makes like that, and she hardly uses any. I'll see if she's got some to spare. I'm that thankful she's back home with me now those awful doodle-bugs are falling on London.' 'ghastly

'Dreadful things they are.' Mavis Coleman had just come into the shop. 'You don't know where they're going to land until the engine cuts out, then there's a whoosh! of air and an explosion. I got a friend in London and she wrote and told me all about them.'

The mood in the shop was solemn now, pity for all the long-suffering Londoners stilling the laughter of a few minutes before.

There was encouraging news from the second front but everyone was weary of the increasing shortages; queueing for fruit and vegetables whenever they came into the shops was now a way of life. Even the most mundane things, like combs and hair-grips, razor blades and batteries, had disappeared under the counter. But despite all this, as the summer passed and autumn turned slowly to winter there was a new feeling of hope that the men would soon be home.

With no raids over Cardiff since May 1943, regular letters from Tommy, and little Brynley following his Grampy around like a shadow, Bert was now a different man. And with a little money in her purse for a change, and the new interest she'd found serving in the shop, Polly was happy too.

By the time Christmas was over Becky was feeling tired and cumbersome and longed for the baby to be born. Dr Powell had given her a date early in January but on New Year's Eve, late in the afternoon, the pains began. Dora had told Becky what to expect and when they grew stronger and more regular, Roy, his face white with anxiety, dashed to the phone to call a cab. Gareth was at a friend's house and Dilys in bed but Dora, who was to have seen the New Year in with them, had just arrived.

As Becky was taken to the room they'd reserved in a nursing home, she left Roy pacing up and down. Knowing how worried he was, she wished she could comfort him. But soon she could think of nothing but the pain which was coming in waves of increasing intensity. It must be soon, she thought, gripping the midwife's hand as another bout of pain came stronger than before. The doctor came back and this time he stayed.

The baby, a little girl, was born at about

three o'clock. Washed and wrapped in a shawl, she was laid gently in her mother's outstretched arms. Then Roy was by her side, beaming from ear to ear. Sighing with relief, he bent to kiss Becky. 'I've got my wish, love. She's a coppernob, just like you.'

'We'll call her Laura, shall we, Roy? You don't think Polly will mind?'

He shook his head and kissed her again. A nurse soon came to tell him he must go, and as he turned and waved and the baby was taken from her, Becky gave a sigh of contentment before drifting into an exhausted sleep.

Back home Dilys couldn't wait to wheel her baby sister in the smart second-hand pram they'd managed to buy, but only up and down the hall for it was bitterly cold outside. Gareth bought her a pretty rattle with pocket money from his meagre pay as an apprentice electrician. Dora and Polly, who'd been knitting furiously for many months before Laura was born, now bought soft pink wool with the rest of their precious coupons and started on larger sizes.

Soon spring was in the air and it was lovely to have the light nights without fear of an air raid. A small patch at the bottom of the garden that hadn't been dug up for vegetables glowed with the bright yellow of nodding daffodils, and soon tulips, planted like the daffodils by some previous owner, were pushing their way through the damp, black earth.

Little Laura, plump and bonny, had inherited Becky's warm colouring and copper-gold curls and had big, warm brown eyes, the combination making heads turn as Becky proudly pushed her in the pram. On 1 May when she wheeled her into her mother's shop to get groceries, there was such a hubbub going on it was some minutes before even Polly noticed she was there. Customers crowded round the pram then, making a fuss until the frightened baby looked as though she would burst into tears, but the subject they'd been discussing was far too important to let drop.

'Did you know that Hitler and that Eva Braun committed suicide yesterday in a bunker in Berlin?' Jessie asked. Becky looked at her in disbelief which quickly turned to joy.

'He'd only just married her,' someone else volunteered.

'The end of the war can't be long now,' Polly said hopefully.

Customers were drifting back to the pram and when Enid Brown poked her fingers into the baby's mouth to see if there was any sign of teeth, causing little Laura to scream, Dora rescued Becky with, 'Go through and make yourself a cup of tea, love. I expect you can do with one.'

The flap in the counter was raised and the pram wheeled through, and in the quiet of the kitchen the baby soon calmed down and gave a watery smile.

Although people were on tenterhooks for news it wasn't until 8 May that Churchill declared the war officially over. It was three o'clock in the afternoon when Becky settled into one of the comfortable armchairs in the sitting room to listen to his broadcast. As the clock stopped chiming the gravelly voice came over the air.

'The German war is at an end. Advance Britannia! Long live the cause of freedom! God save the king!'

Tommy and Bill will soon be home, she thought joyfully. Many would have to wait for the war with Japan to be over for the hope of seeing their own loved ones. Becky prayed that would be soon.

Tonight bunting would be strung across the streets and the celebrations would begin but in this quiet moment, with Dilys still at school and baby Laura asleep in her cot, she looked around the comfortable room and counted her blessings. Remembering the lean years of her childhood, the sadness at losing her best friend, and the traumatic years of the war itself, especially that awful night when Albert and Nellie were killed, she knew that however long she lived she would never forget the way things were.

THE END

We do hope that you have enjoyed reading this large print book.

Did you know that all of our titles are available for purchase?

We publish a wide range of high quality large print books including:
Romances, Mysteries, Classics
General Fiction
Non Fiction and Westerns

Special interest titles available in large print are:
The Little Oxford Dictionary
Music Book
Song Book
Hymn Book
Service Book

Also available from us courtesy of Oxford University Press:
Young Readers' Dictionary
(large print edition)
Young Readers' Thesaurus
(large print edition)

For further information or a free brochure, please contact us at:
Ulverscroft Large Print Books Ltd.,
The Green, Bradgate Road, Anstey,
Leicester, LE7 7FU, England.
Tel: (00 44) 0116 236 4325
Fax: (00 44) 0116 234 0205